CRUEL PRINCES

PRINCES OF DEVIL'S CREEK BOOK ONE

JILLIAN FROST

CRUEL PRINCES

PRINCES OF DEVIL'S CREEK BOOK ONE

JILLIAN FROST

Also by Jillian Frost

Princes of Devil's Creek

Cruel Princes

Vicious Queen

Savage Knights

Battle King

Boardwalk Mafia

Boardwalk Kings

Boardwalk Queen

Boardwalk Reign

Devil's Creek Standalone Novels

The Darkest Prince

Wicked Union

For a complete list of books, visit JillianFrost.com.

CRUEL PRINCES

PRINCES OF DEVIL'S CREEK BOOK ONE

JILLIAN FROST

Chapter One

ALEX

My cell phone beeped with a text message. I swerved and almost hit a parked car as I read my brother's words.

All the Devils are here.

Fear trickled down my spine.

Gripping the leather steering wheel, I floored the gas pedal and didn't bother to text back. I blew through several red lights in a row. No matter how hard I pushed it, the car didn't seem to go fast enough.

There was too much traffic.

Too many damn people living in this city.

I shared an apartment with my twin brother in Williamsburg, a neighborhood in Brooklyn. The Salvatores owned one of the tallest buildings in Manhattan. They controlled just about everything in the city and my life. It was a horrible feeling to know I would never escape them.

I made it five years without them interfering with my life. They had kept their distance while I attended art school and began my art career. But now, it was time to pay for my freedom.

I pulled into the garage on Berry Street and parked in my

reserved space. Still dressed in my café uniform, a short black skirt and a red tank top, I rode the elevator to the top floor. My clothes smelled like coffee and paint, both occupational hazards.

I worked at the coffee shop around the corner for extra cash, so I wouldn't have to spend any money from the Wellington trust. Asking my grandfather for money came with too many strings attached. So I sucked it up and waited tables, fixed drinks, anything to keep us afloat.

As the elevator doors opened, nerves stirred in my belly, twisting my stomach into knots. I strolled down the hall and walked through the open door of my apartment.

A wall of muscle blocked my path. All four of the Salvatore brothers—Luca, Marcello, Bastian, and Damian—stood in my living room, looking intimidating as fuck, dressed in black Brioni suits.

Luca and Marcello were biological brothers with the same black hair and pretty blue eyes. Except Luca always had a sinister look, like he was seconds from snapping someone's neck. Marcello usually looked as if he were in constant mourning.

The other two weren't Arlo's sons by blood, but he treated them as if they were his flesh. Damian was a psychopath. He would have been happy to paint the town red with my blood. As for Bastian, he was still such a mystery to me. I knew he had sick kinks like his brother, but he hid them well.

Something had always drawn me to Bastian… and that made him curious about me.

Bastian stepped toward me, a wicked smirk on his full lips. He cupped my cheek with his big hand and studied my face. "I've been waiting for you, Cherry. Did you miss me?"

"No, get your hands off me." I pushed his hand away from my face, teeth gritted. "I'm not your Cherry." Attempting to move around them, I yelled, "Aiden."

Damian laughed.

So did Luca.

Bastian scratched his jaw while Marcello just stared at me. He was quiet, most of the time stuck inside his head.

"What the fuck are you assholes doing in my apartment? And where the fuck is my brother?"

"Your brother is safe." Bastian smirked. "For now."

I slammed my palms into his chest and tried to rush past him. But Damian was on my ass, reaching out to wrap his fingers around my wrist.

He yanked me back into his chest and breathed against my earlobe. "Haven't you learned your lesson, Pet?"

I laughed in his face. "I'm not your pet, you sick fuck."

Damian was gorgeous, with alabaster skin that was so perfect and smooth I wanted to touch it. But despite his good looks, a monster hid beneath his tailored clothes.

Like his brothers, he was the devil in disguise. I feared him most of all because he was so unpredictable. With Luca, I expected rage and chaos. Marcello was the most level-headed of the group.

Bastian was still somewhat of a wild card. I could never figure him out, but I knew he was hiding something. A secret. I liked secrets and wanted to uncover his.

Damian's fingers closed over my throat. "You're whatever I want you to be, Pet. Get out of line this time, and your brother will pay the price."

I dug my fingernails into his forearm to loosen his hold. "Let me go, psycho."

"Now, now, Pet." He stroked the side of my face gently like he was petting a kitten. "It's not nice to call your owner names." My eyes widened at his comment, and he gave me a creepy smile that sent a shiver down my arms. "You know why we're here. Now be a good girl and go pack your shit."

"It's time to choose, Drea." Luca was the only person who ever called me that. He moved beside Damian, glaring at me with the usual hatred in his dark blue eyes. "We let you off your leash long enough. You're coming back with us to Devil's Creek."

Damian held me tighter, his breath ghosting over my cheek. "This time, we're keeping you."

I gasped. "I'm not yours to keep."

"When you sign a contract with the devil," Bastian said as he stroked his fingers roughly through my hair, "your soul belongs to him."

I raised my hand to slap him, but he caught my arm midair. "Don't test me, Cherry. I'll bend you over my knee and spank your ass until it's black and blue."

I rolled my eyes and flicked my long ponytail over my shoulder. "Your threats don't scare me."

Damian inspected me with fascination. I knew my anger and hatred toward him turned him on, yet I always poked the demon.

When I turned to walk away, he grabbed me from behind. He lifted me in his arms and dropped me onto the living room couch as if I weighed nothing.

"I see you're going to be a pain in my ass, Pet." Damian shoved my face into the cushion and held me down as he hiked my skirt up my thighs. He tugged on the string of my thong so it slapped my skin. "Such a dirty little whore. That skirt barely covers your ass."

Bastian sat on the couch cushion beside my head, and his long fingers wove through my hair. At first, he was gentle, but he got rougher and more forceful as he continued to touch me. "We're not sharing you with the world, Cherry." His hand slid down my back and over my ass. "This," he said as he grabbed my ass cheek, "is ours. And you better remember that the next time you leave the house dressed like a slut."

"I'm not dressed like a slut." I turned my head to the side to look up at him. "Fuck you."

"You want to go first?" Bastian asked Damian with a crazed look in his eyes.

4

I thrashed and kicked my legs at Damian, who held me down with the weight of his body. "Get off me!"

"Not until you take your punishment."

"Punishment for what?"

"For talking back," Damian growled right before his palm crashed down on my backside.

My eyes slammed shut from the sting of his skin slapping mine. But my pride and dignity hurt much worse. Luca and Marcello stood behind them and watched without speaking a word. They were used to their father handing out punishments. It surprised me Luca wasn't the one holding me down, spanking me like a spoiled child.

After the third whack, Damian and Bastian switched places. They enjoyed torturing me so much that they turned it into a sport. Who could make me scream the loudest? Which of them could make me cry first? I wasn't the same scared girl anymore.

Bastian spanked my ass three times, the same as his brother. Then he reached between my thighs to feel what he'd done to me. I was so wet his hand slid right down the soaked fabric. Every time he touched me, I had the same reaction.

I couldn't control how my body responded to his cruelty. There was something about him I craved. Somewhere deep down inside, I was just as sick as him. That was what scared me most about the Salvatore brothers.

They lived to torture me.

But I could handle their abuse and would play their sick games. My real fear came from not understanding why I liked it so much, why I needed them to hurt me.

"Always so wet for men you hate," Bastian taunted. He dipped his head down and whispered in my ear, "Did you save yourself for me, Cherry?"

"She's not yours, Bash," Luca growled.

Bastian glanced over at his brother. "Right, she's *ours*."

He pulled me up from the couch and helped me to my

feet. I couldn't even look at them as the shame heated my cheeks.

I walked out of the living room and down the hallway toward the back of the apartment. "Aiden, where are you?"

Four sets of footsteps pounded the hardwood floor behind me. The cruelest men I had ever met caged me in, and I wasn't getting out of there without doing what they wanted. My brother was the only leverage they had over me. They would do awful things to him and make me watch so I would comply.

I heard a muffled moan and raced into the dining room, where they tied my brother to a wooden dining chair with his hands behind his back and a bandana covering his mouth. Red-hot anger flooded my veins, burning me from the inside out.

I moved behind him and worked on untying the knots, but I couldn't get them to budge, no matter how hard I pulled. As I studied the intricate knots, I realized it was no use. Bastian had tied them. He was into bondage and other sick shit and had perfected his craft.

"Untie him," I yelled as I glared at Bastian.

A cocky smirk graced his lips. "Say the magic words, Cherry."

He didn't want me to beg. I knew what he wanted, and it killed me to accept my fate.

But what choice did I have?

We were out-manned and outmatched. I couldn't even untie the restraints, let alone defeat all four of them.

"I'm yours," I whispered.

Bastian inched toward me, a sly grin in place. "I didn't hear you, Cherry. Say it again."

I pressed my lips together, then glanced down at Aiden. He shook his head, screaming for me to stop. Aiden didn't care what they did to him—anything to keep me from marrying into this sick and twisted family.

"I'm yours, Bash."

"Answer my question from earlier." His fingers burrowed into my hip as he pulled me closer.

"I'm still a virgin."

"Good girl." He rolled his thumb across my lips. "It's time to take you home."

Home.

To Devil's Creek.

Chapter Two

ALEX

After Bastian untied my brother, Aiden shot up from the chair and got in his face. They were around the same height, over six feet tall, facing off.

"Do it," Bastian challenged, hands balled into fists at his side, ready for a fight. "I'll bury you."

Aiden bumped his forehead against Bastian's. "I'd like to see you try."

"I'll go with you." I moved between them to break up their staring contest. "Leave my brother alone."

"Lexie, you don't have to do this," Aiden groaned. "You don't owe them shit."

"Maybe you should worry about your responsibilities to your family," Luca snapped. "After your sister becomes a Salvatore, you will become a Knight."

"Never gonna happen," Aiden shot back. "I'm not joining your secret society of criminals."

Our grandfather was a high-ranking member of The Founders Society, the parent society that oversaw The Devil's Knights. The Founders required every man in our family to become a Knight. It was the only way to rise within the ranks, ensuring our family's legacy.

The Salvatores were currently in charge of the Knights, but to ascend to The Founders Society, one of Arlo's boys had to marry a Wellington. They were among the founders of Devil's Creek but not related to one of the United States Founding Fathers. And since I was the only living female of marrying age from a Founding Family, they needed me.

And my family owed them.

My grandfather still hadn't confessed why he owed Arlo a favor. But whatever it was, Arlo held it over his head. Pops had given Aiden and me an escape from our crazy parents.

So I felt like I owed him.

When we were eighteen, Carl Wellington III gave us his last name, money, and opportunity. We attended the best art school in the country on his dime. The Rhode Island School of Design didn't take just anyone. But doors opened for us between the Salvatores and their art connections and my last name.

I glanced up at my twin, who had dark circles around his eyes. We both knew they would eventually come for me. It was only a matter of time before Arlo Salvatore retired as the CEO of Salvatore Global. And that meant one of his sons would take over for him and become the head of the family.

I slipped my fingers between Aiden's and led him to my bedroom. Once inside, I tore apart my closet for suitcases and stuffed whatever would fit into the bags.

"It's not too late to run, Lexie." Aiden sat on my bed, leaning forward with his hands on his knees. "Pops made the deal. You don't have to honor it."

"Aiden, there's no point in running from them. We both know it's a waste of time."

His already flushed face got even redder. "Do you want to marry one of those psychos? You deserve so much more."

"I wouldn't have an art career if it wasn't for them," I pointed out. "Luca has pulled a lot of strings to help me. He's a jerk, but he has his moments."

"They're going to ruin you. Hurt you. I don't think you understand what you're getting yourself into."

"I can handle them," I assured him, though my words lacked certainty. "Maybe you should take Pops up on his offer. Then you could come with me."

He shook his head, not the least entertained by the idea. "I don't want or need anything from him. I would rather starve."

"Pops gave us a new life, Aid. We would probably be dead in a ditch right now if it weren't for him."

Until now, we'd never spent more than a few hours apart. Some nights, I had terrible nightmares from my childhood, reminders of the parents we left behind. But Aiden was always there for me. He was my rock, my person. Pops wasn't a shoulder I could cry on, but he'd given us advantages. It helped me to heal from my trauma.

My grandfather was there when we needed him most, and I would not let him down. An arranged marriage wasn't that big of a deal. Plenty of people married without knowing each other. My grandparents had the same agreement, their marriage nothing more than a merger of two powerful families.

Before Aiden could talk me out of leaving Brooklyn, I stepped into the hallway to grab toiletries from the bathroom. I found a large bag and stuffed it with deodorant, makeup, and the usual things.

Luca watched me from the doorway.

I advanced on him, but he didn't move. "Get out of my way."

He clutched my chin and slammed my back into the door. "Stop talking back, baby girl. I've had enough of your princess act."

"I'm no princess. If I were, you would be a prince, and this would be a fairytale. Instead, I have to live in a castle with the villains, held captive against my will."

His eyebrows lifted. "Who said you're a prisoner?"

"You're not letting me go. Not until you take my virginity."

He laughed in my face, his minty breath sliding across my lips. "You will beg me for the privilege of coming on my cock."

"The privilege?" I snorted with laughter. "In your dreams, asshole."

Luca's hand dipped beneath my short skirt and skimmed my panties. He brushed my pussy with his long fingers over the top of the fabric. I bit my lip to stifle the moan about to escape.

"Look at how easily you give in to me." He pressed his hand to the door above my head, caging me with his muscular body. "It's no fun. Fight me."

I stood painfully still as he touched me. "So you like the fight? That's nothing new." He pinned my arms above my head, his hard cock grazing my stomach. "Do you want me to smack you around and pull your hair? What turns you on, Luca?"

Shoes tapped the hardwood floor. Damian strolled down the hall toward us with a cocky smirk in place. He had the highest cheekbones I'd ever seen on a man and full lips that looked blood-red against his pale skin.

A beautiful nightmare.

Nothing about his personality matched his handsome features. His insides were as black as tar. I didn't think he had a heart. How could he when he treated everyone as if they were disposable? But he was different from his brothers, Bastian especially.

They were childhood friends before their parents died in a horrific plane crash. But Damian Townsend and Bastian Kincaid were not always Salvatores. Not until they were nine years old and parentless. They had made the headlines back then because they were the youngest billionaires in history.

They became the sole owners of Atlantic Airlines and the heirs to a massive fortune overnight.

I understood their pasts shaped the men they had become. It also didn't help that Arlo Salvatore had raised them. That alone probably enhanced their psychotic tendencies. Plenty of people lost their parents at a young age and didn't turn into monsters. I could only sympathize so much with the Salvatores.

"What's taking so long?" Damian asked.

Luca let go of me and fixed his suit jacket back into place. "Nothing. We're leaving now."

W e boarded a private jet at JFK Airport. Marcello dealt with my bags while Luca spoke to the pilot. Bastian followed me into the large cabin with his hand on my ass.

Long, black leather benches and wooden tables rounded out each side of the plane. They even had a bedroom at the back.

I shivered at the thought.

Bastian guided me to a table with four chairs. Damian sat across from us, Luca at his side. Marcello lounged on the bench to my left and stared out the window, shoving a hand through his thick black hair. It was usually messy and falling onto his forehead. I wanted to push it out of his eyes every time I looked at him.

Luca removed his cell phone from his pocket and quickly typed out several text messages. His jaw ticked, annoyed by something.

Probably me.

My hands trembled uncontrollably. Trapped between the Salvatores on their private jet, there was no escaping them.

But at least Aiden was safe. As long as I followed the rules, he would remain unharmed.

I clasped my hands together to steady my nerves. Bastian moved his big hand to my thigh, his long fingers etching into my bare skin with rough possession. Ignoring him, I stared out the window at the lights illuminating a path to the landing strip.

He inched his hand higher up my thigh, taunting me to stop him. Not this time. They all loved the fight. So I would bore him to death and pretend he didn't exist.

His fingers grazed my thong, and my heart sped to an impressive rate. Damian tapped a platinum ring with onyx chips that formed a snake on the wooden table. Luca, Marcello, and Bastian wore the same one. The serpent was part of their family crest.

"I'm living at Wellington Manor," I told them once we were in the air.

Luca leaned back against the leather chair and smirked. Damian's ring hit the table again, and my heart thumped louder. He stared through me as if he couldn't even see a person sitting across from him.

I seriously wondered about Damian and his mental state. While Luca looked down-right possessed by the devil, his usual wicked glare in place, I wasn't so sure Damian even had a soul.

I expected one of them to respond, but Bastian said, "Sick of us already, Cherry? The fun hasn't even begun."

"You don't have a choice," Luca said, speaking for the first time in a while. "Our estate is your new and permanent home."

Bastian tightened his grip on my thigh, lifting my leg, which was on top of his. "We own you now. You're ours to do with as we please."

I snorted. "Keep telling yourself that, Bash. I hope you enjoy fucking corpses because I won't enjoy a single second of you on top of me. In fact, why don't we go into the bedroom and get this over with, so I can go home?"

Damian pushed up the sleeves of his jacket and rested his tattooed forearms on the table, his eyes burning through me like lasers. I thought he would say something clever, but he surprised me by waiting for Bastian to comment.

"You make my cock so fucking hard, Cherry."

With our mouths inches apart, I said, "Let's get something straight. You don't scare me. I don't care if I have to fuck all of you. Threaten me all you want."

Marcello ignored our conversation. He leaned back on the bench across from us, his shoes off and long legs stretched out as he played a game on his cell phone.

"I hate you. All of you. You're fucking deviants."

Damian rolled his shoulders and laughed. He enjoyed being a piece of shit and didn't feel remorse for what they were about to do to me. Bastian wasn't as cold and closed off as Damian. At least I thought he wasn't like him.

Luca tipped the glass to his lips and drank the rest of his scotch. "We all have to be something. Might as well be someone everyone fears."

"I don't fear any of you. I despise you. There's a difference."

"You came with us too easily," Luca said in a cold, deep tone. "As Bash said, you didn't even fight us." He shook his head, amused. "At the very least, you could have screamed or begged. You handed over your virgin pussy to the men you pretend to hate." His gorgeous mouth curled up into a crooked grin. "Now, the real question remains. Which one of us will claim you first?"

Chapter Three

ALEX

W e couldn't fly directly to Devil's Creek, so we boarded a helicopter in Hartford. I was thankful we had to wear a headset. Only the pilot spoke when we left the airport and then again right before landing on the helipad at the Salvatore Estate.

The sprawling estate had an incredible view of the bay and looked like an old castle. They were the princes of Devil's Creek and probably the world. With all of their money and power, they did anything they wanted.

They even got away with murder.

Bastian lifted me from the helicopter and helped me down to the blacktop. Electricity skated up my arms from his touch and spread throughout my body. I hated how my body responded to him. And I hated he knew how much he affected me.

He smirked as I rubbed my hands down my arms. Then he slid his arm behind my back to lead me toward the house.

There was a large veranda that stretched across the back of the mansion. Arlo Salvatore waited for us with his hands stuffed into his pockets between the open patio doors.

Even for a man his age, he was attractive and had passed

down his good looks to his sons. Luca and Marcello were around the same height as their dad but thicker in the arms and chests. The only difference was their eyes. Arlo's were as black as coal, while the boys had blue eyes that reminded me of the bay at night. A trait they inherited from their deceased mother.

"Welcome back to Devil's Creek, Alexandrea."

I pressed my lips together and nodded. "Mr. Salvatore."

Arlo glanced over my shoulder at his sons. "Show our guest to her room and then join me in my office. We have business to discuss."

"Let's go." Marcello groaned as he passed me. "Your room is on the second floor."

Arlo patted his son's shoulder.

I followed Marcello down the long tiled hallway. Luca disappeared in the opposite direction with his father, while the adopted Salvatores stayed on my tail.

Marcello led me to the Tuscan-style entryway on the east side of the house. A monstrous crystal chandelier hung overhead the ornate wooden staircase with the same Salvatore serpent carved into the railing.

Without breaking stride, Marcello carried my suitcases upstairs. He didn't speak a single word, which only caused my heart to pound as adrenaline flooded my veins.

Marcello rolled my suitcases down a beautiful Brazilian walnut floor that was polished to perfection on the second floor. A dozen doors, most of which were closed, spanned the length of the corridor. There were four floors, not including the basement and attic.

Marcello stepped through the open door at the end of the hallway. Bracing myself for my new life, I sucked in a few deep breaths. The room had a high ceiling, an ensuite bathroom, and a four-poster bed with tons of pillows. Straight ahead, the French doors opened onto a large balcony.

Marcello left my suitcases in front of the closet door. He

swiped the fallen strands of hair off his forehead as he walked toward me. "Get comfortable, princess. You're not leaving your tower."

I closed the distance between us and lowered my voice. "Marcello, I know you're not like them."

He considered my words for a second, then laughed. "You know nothing about me or my family."

"I'm good at reading people. You don't want to be here any more than I do."

"When my father makes a deal, it's unbreakable by the other party." His jaw hardened as our eyes met. "Defy him, and he will make you regret it. No matter how smart you think you are, he's smarter. He's stronger and faster and has more money and connections."

"So this is it? I'm stuck here."

Marcello shrugged. "Might as well settle in and take advantage of the perks."

I chuckled at the ridiculous concept. "Yeah, right? Like what?"

"You can have anything you want. You only have to ask. Money is not an object."

I had a trust fund from my grandfather that I refused to spend. So I worked tirelessly, dividing my time between my job at the coffee shop and my art. I hoped to one day sell enough paintings to be free.

"So I could ask for a car, and your dad would buy me one?"

Marcello shook his head. "You don't have that kind of freedom. We have drivers who will take you wherever you want." He dipped his head down to match my height, his deep blue eyes meeting mine. "We arm our drivers. You can try to run, but you won't get very far."

"I'm failing to see the perks, Marcello."

"If you could have anything, what would you wish for?"

"Freedom," I said without hesitation because it was something I never had.

"Sorry, we can't offer you that." He lifted his shoulders an inch, the same expressionless mask on his face. "You should unpack and get some sleep."

Marcello left my bedroom without another word. I looked out the open French doors, surprised the windows didn't have bars.

Someone cleared their throat.

Before I glanced at the doorway, I knew I would find Bastian's hauntingly beautiful gray eyes peering back at me.

Bastian gripped the door frame, and his muscles bulged beneath the suit jacket. He rolled his tongue across his bottom lip as he studied me. With one look, the air drained from my lungs.

A dimple in his right cheek popped against his gorgeous olive skin when he smirked at me. Then my focus shifted to the devil's spawn beside him. Despite Damian's pretty-boy looks, he intimidated me whenever he stared directly at me.

When his eyes met mine, he looked through me. I had always wanted to know what had made him so cruel.

"Get in bed," Damian ordered.

Standing in the middle of the room with my hands on my hips, I glared at him. "No."

"It's your bedtime, Pet." He inched into the room, keeping his distance from me. "You need plenty of rest."

Bastian moved toward the patio doors and stood between them. His back and shoulders looked powerful in the tailored suit that molded to his body.

Damian sat on the mattress and patted the space beside him. I shook my head to get under his skin.

"If I have to come get you, Pet, you won't like what happens next."

"Are you going to spank me again?" I sauntered over to him, maintaining my distance. "Huh? Maybe Bash can tie my hands behind my back while you smack my ass for being a bad girl."

His eyes sparkled as if he liked the idea. "Get over here."

I moved my hands to my hips and glared at him. "Make me."

What was I doing?

He would only make it hurt worse for my insubordination. With every act of disobedience, I would get another whack. And yet, I didn't completely hate the idea, which could only mean one thing—there was something wrong with me.

"Get in the bed," Bastian said before scooping me into his arms. "We've had a long day, Cherry. We're not in the mood for games."

"You're not getting in the bed with me."

"This is our house." He dropped me onto the mattress and climbed in beside Damian and me. "We'll sleep wherever we want."

I slid my ass across the silky comforter until I hit a wall of pillows at the head of the bed. Their eyes darted between my thighs.

Bastian slid his thumb across his bottom lip. "Fuck, Cherry. I can't wait to bury my cock in your tight pussy."

I slapped my legs closed, and Bastian pulled them apart. Damian held my arms down, the two of them working as a team.

"What are you doing?"

I tried to kick Bastian in the face, but this only gave him more encouragement. "Stop it! Get off me!"

He laughed, the same evil cackle that reminded me of a villain from a horror movie. Then he pried my legs open with his big hands, his lips inches from my aching core. Bastian breathed deeply, and I wondered if he could smell my desire.

His hot, wet tongue traced the length of my inner thigh. I moaned when he did it again, and my eyes slammed shut.

"Have you ever let a man taste you, Cherry?" Bastian

spoke the words over the top of my soaking wet panties. "Answer me."

"No," I breathed.

His tongue darted between my folds, pushing my panties inside me. I arched my back and cried out as he sucked on my clit.

"Bastian," I whispered. "Stop."

"Your words say one thing," he taunted with his eyes on me. "But I think you want me to give you an orgasm." Then his eyes shifted to Damian. "What do you think, D?"

"She's begging for it." Damian bent down and shoved his fingers into my mouth. "Isn't that right, Pet? You want my brother to lick your pussy, don't you?"

I sucked on his fingers, which was kind of hot. He asserted his dominance and control over me, making me suck until he was happy. When he removed his fingers from my mouth, I gasped for air.

Damian moved down my body, slipping his hand between my thighs. And unlike his brother, he didn't bother to ask me what I wanted before he plunged the same fingers he shoved into my mouth into my pussy.

I cried out from the insane amount of pleasure that swept over me. "Oh, my God." I found Damian and Bastian staring at me. "No more," I said, even though I didn't mean it.

"How else are you going to handle our cocks?" Bastian asked with a serious expression on his face. "We need to break you in first."

"No," I whimpered. "I don't want you to break me." I breathed through my nose. "Mmm…"

Why did this have to feel so damn good?

"I'm not ready."

"Liar," Damian taunted. "I can feel your pussy squeezing my fingers, begging for more. You want this, Pet."

"Stop calling me Pet, and maybe I would want you."

What am I saying?

He removed his fingers, and I already missed his touch. I blew out a breath of air, attempting to regain my bearings. Damian slid off the bed and shook his head in disapproval.

Come back, I wanted to say. *Finish what you started.*

If there was a female equivalent of blue balls, I was getting it. My body ached for more of their skilled hands, tongues, and fingers. I wasn't sure which one I wanted more.

"Where are you going?" I asked as Bastian hopped off the bed and followed his brother toward the door.

Damian exited the room.

Bastian stopped at the entryway and glanced over his shoulder at me. "Go to sleep, Cherry. You have a big day tomorrow."

Chapter Four

MARCELLO

My brothers were sick, demented assholes. I shouldn't have left Alex alone with Damian and Bastian. I could not trust them with any woman, especially not one as important as Alexandrea Wellington.

I heard Alex yell, then moan through the open door at the end of the hallway. Either she was enjoying herself or being tortured. With my family's legacy on the line, I couldn't take any chances with her life. We needed the merger between our families.

Damian and Bastian stepped into the hallway with satisfied grins as I rushed toward her bedroom. Bastian pulled her door closed and tapped Damian on the shoulder, whispering into his ear. Whatever these psychos were plotting would not end well for Alex.

"What did you do to her?"

They met me in the middle of the hallway, dimly lit by wall sconces. A yellowish glow illuminated their mischievous faces.

This house reminded me of a medieval castle, a home fit for a knight. As a child, I knew I would become a member of

The Devil's Knights one day. I used to think the secret society was more like a chivalrous guild.

But I was so wrong about that.

We would pretend we were knights from medieval times when we were kids. Until we grew up and learned the real Knights were the corrupt bankers of the criminal underworld.

Damian slid his thumb across his red lips, giving me one of his usual creepy smirks. He was mentally unstable and emotionally bankrupt. Most people kept their distance from Damian. You could see the madness dancing across his emerald eyes. His sanity was dangling by a thread at all times, and only my father and Bastian could control him.

"We were just saying goodnight to our pet," Damian remarked, his voice filled with evil laughter.

Bastian patted me on the shoulder and smirked. "Don't worry, Marcello. We took good care of our girl."

"She's not yours."

Their real last names had secured their futures.

Damian Townsend.

Bastian Kincaid.

Legacies at any club on the planet. Like Alex, they were American royalty, direct descendants of the United States' founding fathers. Billionaires with more money than they could spend in their lifetime. Their parents had died in a plane crash when they were nine years old. My father had adopted them, thinking they would be helpful in the future.

But he didn't foresee us needing Alex. He didn't know that making them Salvatores would also put them in the running for Alex's hand in marriage. The Salvatores founded Devil's Creek, but our bloodline didn't trace back to the Founding Fathers.

Our control over The Devil's Knights, and the powerful alliances my father built, kept us in the good graces of The Founders Society Elders. But we were running out of time. We couldn't be part of their elite club if we didn't marry a

Wellington. Alex was the only woman from a Founding Family of marrying age and our only hope of survival.

Sure, we would still be billionaires if we didn't marry a Wellington. But we would lose our connections and alliances and control over the criminal underworld. My father collected secrets, and those secrets had allowed us to maintain our foothold for years. And now that others knew those secrets, he was losing his grip.

"Afraid of a little competition?" Bastian laughed. "Always so serious, Marcello."

They didn't need her, not like Luca and me. So one of us had to marry her. One of us had to produce an heir with the Big Pharma Princess. The Wellington dowry, and all the rewards that came with it, would set up the Salvatores for hundreds of years.

Alex's grandfather was one of the wealthiest men in the world, third on the Forbes Billionaires list. One of the five Elders who ran The Founders Society. The secret society governed the smaller ones, including The Devil's Knights. He had direct authority over the organization my great grandfather had founded after he moved to the United States from Italy.

But we had one bargaining chip, a secret my father held over Carl Wellington's head. And that secret gave us Alex.

It gave us another chance.

"Of course not," I tossed back at Bastian. "But none of us can marry her if she's damaged goods." Stepping closer, I lowered my voice. "She has complex PTSD. Without her brother around to control it, she's going to unravel. It's only a matter of time. So don't fuck with our plans."

"We don't take orders from you," Damian said as he walked past me.

Bastian moved with him, then hesitated for a moment. He placed his hand on my shoulder and squeezed. "I won't let him hurt her."

"He lost control last week," I pointed out. "We all saw it. Damian isn't right in the head."

"Let me handle it. He'll be back to normal soon."

Normal? Damian didn't know the meaning of the word. He hadn't been normal for a single day of his life.

Bash had a brotherly bond with Damian and knew when he was teetering on edge, ready to snap.

After they retreated to their rooms, I opened Alex's bedroom door. She sat on the four-poster bed at the center of the room, arms crossed over her chest in defense. Her pale blue eyes were red and glassy.

What the fuck did they do to her?

The guest room was five times the standard size of a bedroom, with a high ceiling and an ensuite bathroom. I walked toward the balcony set between tall windows that overlooked the bay.

The French doors were open. I stood between them, staring down at the water crashing against the rocks for a moment. Then I closed the doors and pulled the drapes over the windows.

"What do you want?" Alex asked, her voice shaky.

Turning to face her, I loosened my tie and approached the bed, tugging on the silky blue fabric. "Calm down, princess. I won't hurt you."

Her eyes widened when I dropped my tie on the table by the window. "This house has enough beds. You're not sleeping in mine."

Working on my top few buttons, I sat in the armchair across from the bed. "I haven't slept in over thirty hours. I'm not in the mood to argue over something that doesn't matter."

"No," she yelled, cheeks flushed. "After what those monsters just did… I'm not sleeping with any of you."

"What did they do?"

Alex blew out a deep breath. "They forced themselves on me."

I slipped off one wingtip, then another, setting them under the table. "Did they hurt you?"

"No, but…" She bit her lip. "They're animals."

"Did you like it?" I shrugged off my suit jacket and draped it over the chair. "Is that what bothers you most?"

She pressed her lips together and looked away. In her last year of high school, Damian and Bastian had tormented her every day. Physically. Mentally. Emotionally. They touched her, teased her, tasted her, and did almost anything they wanted.

Except fuck her.

That was our one rule.

Luca had acted as if she didn't exist. He used other women to make Alex pay for disrespecting him on her first day at Astor Prep. My older brother even forced her to watch him fuck a cheerleader over the bathroom sink. Alex pretended not to care, but I knew she had feelings for each of us.

She wanted us.

Shirtless, I stood up and fumbled with the zipper of my dress pants. Her eyes traveled up and down my muscled abdomen. She bit her bottom lip, then rolled her tongue across it. I had dozens of scars marring my chest, some of them dipping beneath my waistband.

Cigar burns.

Knife marks.

Two from bullet wounds.

I was head of security at Salvatore Global. The team of mercenaries I commanded handled high-risk jobs around the world. In my line of work, it was important not to have attachments. But Alex was a weakness all of us shared.

I stripped off my pants and laid them on the chair back. Alex's head snapped to me as I approached the bed in a pair of black boxer briefs. Desire scrolled across her face. Her gaze flicked between my chest and my cock, which was getting hard with each sexy look she gave me.

"I won't hurt you," I promised and meant it.

I'd never forced myself on her, never even kissed her. Bastian and Damian didn't hold the same grudge against her family as Luca and me. The Wellingtons had taken something precious from us. Something no amount of money could fix. That was why Carl Wellington had agreed to the union.

It wasn't her fault, but I still wasn't ready to let go. Neither was Luca. His rage fueled him and made him hate even the sight of Alex. She was only here because we were running out of time and options.

After Wellington had struck a deal with my father, he plucked Alex and her twin from a small town in the Midwest. She lived with her abusive mother, who Carl had disowned when she married outside the Founding Families. They lived a life of poverty. Her mother was a struggling artist, her dad an architect who couldn't draw a straight line.

Alex was like my mother.

A natural, talented.

Her childhood had fucked her up, and much like my mother, she had her moments. It took little to trigger her PTSD. A sound. A smell. The slightest thing could garner a reaction from Alex.

We had to be careful with her.

This time, she might break.

I lifted the duvet and slipped beneath the sheets. "I'm staying for your protection, Alex. I won't touch you."

She rolled onto her side to face me. "Why are you being nice? Do you want something? Is this part of some master plan?"

"No."

I reached over, flicked off the lamp on the bedside table, and a whimper escaped from her lips.

"Can you light a candle?"

The dark terrified Alex, a side effect of her mother locking her in closets and dark spaces. She may have hated my brothers and me. Maybe she even hated her grandfather. But her new life was a vast improvement from the one she had before she met us.

"Close your eyes," I told her. "It's time to get over your fear."

"I need music to fall asleep," she lilted. "Can you at least put something on from my Spotify playlist?"

I knew everything about Alex. It was my job to watch over her and ensure she was safe. For years, she'd fallen asleep to Tchaikovsky's Swan Lake every night.

I slid off the bed and grabbed the phone from my pants pocket. Seconds later, orchestra music floated through the speaker.

"This is my favorite ballet," she said as I set the phone on the table and got back into bed. "The story is so heartbreaking. When I was younger, I compared myself to Odette, the swan maiden. I dreamed of a handsome prince that would come save me."

"You got your wish," I told her. "You got four handsome princes."

She sighed. "Lucky me."

By the time the waltz ended, she was dead to the world.

Chapter Five

ALEX

The darkness swallowed me as I sank to the floor and pulled my knees into my chest. I blinked a few times to clear my vision, pinching the skin on my forearm.

"Wake up, Alex. Not real," I whispered, but it was no use.

Nothing.

Same as the last time.

And every time before it.

This was my Hell.

Tears fell from my eyes, coating my cheeks as I screamed for someone to let me out. I begged for anyone to come to my aid. I pounded my fists against the wooden door until my knuckles cracked open, and my hands were numb.

I got on my hands and knees and felt around the cramped space. My chest heaved as I struggled for air, fighting the wave of anxiety that ripped through my body like a hurricane.

I hated the dark.

Hated small spaces.

Desperate to escape, I clawed at the molding. Anything that could provide me a way out. But no matter how hard I tried, I could never get out of the closet.

This was my punishment for taking everything from her.

My mother.

She blamed me for everything that didn't go her way. The woman should have loved me. And yet, she had never shown me an ounce of love. She never cared about me. When she looked at me, she saw everything I stole from her.

Youth.

Beauty.

Money.

Her father's love.

My mother had locked me in a tiny closet for most of my life. I didn't have to do anything to deserve her punishment. Just existing was enough for her.

Someone shook my shoulder, and strong arms wrapped around me like a warm blanket. "Alex, wake up."

My eyes snapped open. A soft breeze from the bay flew into my bedroom through the French doors. I listened to the water crash against the beach, and my heart stopped racing, and my hands stopped trembling.

"I got you," Marcello whispered into my ear. He leaned back against the headboard with his muscular biceps holding me in a vise. "You're safe, Alex."

I laid my head on his chest and let out a deep breath. "Marcello." I slid my palm onto his chest, right over his heart, feeling his heartbeat beneath my fingers until my body relaxed. "My nightmares went away… until you brought me back here."

His fingers lightly ghosted my skin as he tucked my hair behind my ears. He sat up, bringing me with him. "Time to get up, princess."

"I need coffee and a shower."

Marcello tipped his head at the silver tray on the writing desk. I slid my legs off the bed, stretching my arms above my head, and yawned. Marcello's eyes darted up and down the length of my body, and he licked his lips. Ignoring his heated gaze, I sauntered over to the desk and poured myself a cup of coffee with my back to him.

I sat at the writing desk and buttered a slice of wheat toast, topping it with a heaping spoonful of jam before stuffing it into my mouth.

"In one hour, you have a fitting at the boutique in town and then a meeting with Luca."

I added cream and sugar and sipped from my cup. "For what?"

Marcello locked onto me with his usual stern expression as I bit into the toast. "Luca wants to talk to you about the Franco Foundation."

His mother's charity.

I smiled so wide my cheeks hurt. What could Luca possibly want from me? The Franco Foundation had tons of talented artists in their employ.

I glanced over at Mr. Broody, who glared like I was wasting his precious time. "You should smile," I said with a mouth full of food. "It wouldn't kill you."

Leaning back in his chair, he ignored me. He acted as if he hadn't climbed into bed with me to pull me from my nightmare. Like this was a normal thing we did.

He typed a new message with his eyes pointed down at his cell phone. I studied his profile, noting the strength in his jaw and the hardness of his features. He had the perfect bone structure and flawless skin. I wanted to paint him so badly that my fingers itched for the chance.

The Salvatores were cold and cruel. But they were also beautiful.

"Did your mom ever paint you?"

He greeted me with more silence.

I was not giving up without a fight. Ideas for paintings raced through my mind, and I needed his cooperation to bring the concept to life.

He seemed okay with sitting still for hours at a time.

Maybe with a little convincing, he would let me sketch him. I already had the Many Faces of the Devil series. Lonely Boy could be the first in the Lonely Hearts collection.

Yeah, that could work.

I finished my second slice of toast before strolling over to my handsome captor. "How about we make a deal?"

He glanced up from his phone. "For deals to work, you must have something to offer."

I inched my shirt up my stomach. "There must be something you want from me."

A defiant smirk crossed his sexy lips. "I could bind your hands and mouth and leave you to rot in this room." He grinned like the Joker. "How does that sound, princess?"

I shook my head, disappointed with the sudden change of events. What happened to the man who held me in his arms and whispered I was safe? It didn't take long for him to disappear.

Shoving my hand through his thick hair, I pulled on the ends, forcing him to look up at me. "You're a real jerk, Marcello Salvatore."

A sexy one.

He pushed my hand away and went back to typing a text message with one hand. "If you want to shower, get moving. You're not making us late for our appointment."

When his cell phone rang, he answered in Italian. I'd learned a few words and phrases from spending time with the Salvatores. Still, I wasn't well versed enough to understand, not when he spoke so damn fast.

Marcello pointed at the bathroom door as he left the room, issuing a silent warning to get ready.

I locked my bedroom door and headed into the bathroom.

Ten minutes alone.

That's all I need.

The Salvatores were suffocating and intoxicating. As much as I hated them, I also couldn't get enough of them.

Desire laced with anxiety flooded my chest as I thought about Damian and Bastian and what they did to me last night. They could use and abuse me, but they would never own my heart. I would never fully be theirs, no matter how much my grandfather owed them.

I stripped out of my clothes and stepped into the glass-tiled shower, closing my eyes as the water washed over me. The rainfall shower head was the perfect amount of pressure. Slowly, the tension ebbed from my muscles, working its way out of my system.

I took my time washing my hair and cleansing my skin of those dirty boys. The thought of them had me all hot and bothered, my clit throbbing with need. How could I feel such attraction to men I hated?

Leaning against the tiled wall, I slipped my hand between my thighs and massaged my clit. I closed my eyes and imagined their hands on my legs, prying my thighs apart. Bastian looked so fucking sexy last night as he kissed my sensitive skin.

My mind drifted to dirty thoughts of Damian forcing his fingers into my mouth. And then, those same fingers pushing inside me, filling me up. A moan slipped from my lips.

They felt so good, both of them at the same time. It didn't take long before my orgasm swept over my body, rocking me to the core. I hated myself for getting off to them, for wanting more.

After I came down from my high, I was ready to start my day. I pushed open the glass door, and steam gathered around me, filling the bathroom. The hot water burned away the dirty memories of Damian and Bastian.

I grabbed a towel from the hook and wrapped it around me. Even their bath towels felt like silk.

Only the best for the Salvatores.

I moved in front of the mirror that spanned the wall and wiped away the condensation. A gasp slipped from my throat as my eyes met Damian's. My heart pounded so hard that I had to press my hand to my chest to calm myself down.

He sat on the closed toilet lid, shirtless and only wearing a pair of black boxer briefs. Dark tattoos covered his arms and muscular chest and dipped below the waistband of his underwear. His cock was hard, the head poking through the slit in the fabric.

I bit my lip to stifle the scream that desperately wanted to break free. He made no move to shove his giant cock back into his boxers. I couldn't see much of him, but what I could see was thick and touched his stomach when he leaned forward.

Please save me from this beautiful monster.

I spun around to face him, clutching my towel. "What are you doing in here?"

"You're in my bathroom," he said, devoid of human emotion.

"What?" I shook my head. "No, you're in my room."

He pointed at the open door that adjoined our rooms. The house had more bedrooms and bathrooms than an old castle. So why the fuck did they have to give me the one attached to his?

Even Bastian would have been a better choice. He didn't scare me as much as Damian. But when I looked at Damian, I knew something was off about him. I could feel it deep in my bones, my body sending off warning flares to get the fuck away from him.

I held onto my towel for dear life, approaching him with caution. "How long have you been in here?"

Damian smirked. "Long enough."

He studied me with his usual hunter's eyes. My skin sizzled from the heated gaze that traveled up and down my body. I hated how my stupid body responded to him.

"There's no point in hiding from me," he growled. "I've already seen every part of you."

I flung my hand at his bedroom door. "Get out!"

He shook his head, then rose from the toilet seat. I didn't have time to run before he lifted me on the vanity and moved between my thighs.

His hand slid between my breasts and up to my throat. "What were you thinking about when you made yourself cum?"

Blush dusted my cheeks, spreading down to my chest. "I don't know what you're talking about."

"I saw you." My eyes widened as his hand closed over my windpipe. "Tell me, Pet. Did you think about me?"

"Damian, please," I choked out.

His face lit up as he wrapped his long fingers around my throat and squeezed. "Or was it my brother you thought about as you fingered your tight pussy?"

Firmly holding my throat, he reached between us and ripped off my towel. His eyes lowered over my naked body, and he bit his lip so hard I thought he would draw blood.

"Damian," I rasped. "Stop it."

His fingers trailed up my inner thigh, slowly inching toward my throbbing core. "Are you wet for me, Pet? Huh?" He dipped his head down, so our lips brushed. "Do you like it when I dominate you?"

"You're a monster."

A creepy smirk pulled at the corner of his mouth delicious mouth. "I'm worse than a monster."

"Get your hands off me." I slapped him with all of my energy, barely able to breathe with his hand around my throat. "Please, Damian. Stop fucking with me."

Begging was not the route to go with Damian. He enjoyed it too much. So I readjusted my plan and went limp in his arms. I stopped struggling and slumped against the mirror.

We stayed like this for at least a few minutes until disappointment tugged at his mouth. He had the face of an angel attached to the body of a smoking hot demon. It wasn't fair for someone to look like him and be so vile.

His grip loosened on my throat, and then his hand fell away from my body. My gaze dipped to his hard cock, half of which poked through his boxers. He was so thick I wondered if I could get my tiny hand around him.

He grabbed my hand and slid my fingers up and down his shaft as if he read my mind. "Is this what you want, Pet?"

"Damian, stop calling me that."

He dragged his teeth across his bottom lip, staring through me. "You want to know how it feels to get fucked?"

"I don't want to get fucked."

I wanted him, even though I knew he was wrong for me on so many levels. Damian was the last person I should have desired, and yet my body hummed whenever he was around.

He fisted his cock and rubbed the tip between my wet folds. "Yes, you do."

My eyes slammed shut. "Oh, my God." After the initial shock wore off, I opened my eyes and looked at him. "Damian, no. Not like this. Bastian will kill you."

He stopped rubbing my slit and stepped backward. I knew that would snap him out of his head, bring him back from whatever dark place he'd just gone.

His cold, green eyes seared through me like a hot poker, igniting a fire beneath my skin. He pointed his finger at the door. "Get out."

I slid off the counter, leaving the towel behind, thankful to escape his clutches. Damian was dangerous. Not to be trusted. I had to keep reminding myself that every time I let him touch me.

"I better not catch you wearing that slutty underwear," he threatened.

I spun around with my bare skin on display for this delicious predator. "Then what should I wear?"

"Check your closet," he said before he pushed me out the door and slammed it in my face.

Chapter Six

ALEX

I was running behind schedule. But at least I'd dried and styled my curls into a more manageable look. My curls never seemed to stay put. They were natural and easily knotted, especially with how long my hair had gotten over the past year.

Curls flowed halfway down my back, stopping right beneath my first rib. Aiden kept his hair short because of all the kinks. I should have done the same. The last time my hair was this long, Luca fisted it and pushed me to my knees in front of everyone in the school cafeteria.

I didn't miss him or this fucking town. Being back in Devil's Creek stirred up all the bad memories I'd spent years trying to forget.

A bang sounded throughout the room, the sudden noise ripping a scream from my throat. Was that a gunshot? The towel fell to the floor at my feet, and when I spun around, my bedroom door was open.

Marcello stood in the doorway. He ran a hand across his jaw, studying my naked body as if he were committing every detail to memory.

I covered my lady parts with my hands, though it didn't conceal my nakedness. "Get out, Marcello."

He sat in the armchair next to the window, ogling my body with a vacant expression on his face. I could never tell what he was thinking. Unlike his older brother, I couldn't read his emotions.

Luca was usually angry about something. His rage bubbled up inside him, ready to spill over at any moment. The other two were still a bit of a mystery but still much easier to read than Marcello.

He was my sad, lonely boy.

Except he was a man now.

Tall and handsome, Marcello had grown into an irresistible billionaire I wanted to know. I'd come to terms with the arrangement over the years. It wasn't worth fighting against the current. One day, I would marry a Salvatore. There was nothing I could do about it.

Cheeks flushed, I stood naked in front of Marcello. I'd never been with a man, never even kissed one that didn't bear the last name Salvatore. Years ago, Luca and Bastian had claimed my virginity. But Marcello and Damian never seemed all that interested. Maybe they didn't care about being my first.

Desperate for privacy, I entered the walk-in closet. It reminded me of the one Mr. Big built for Carrie in Sex and the City. Shelves, drawers, and shoe racks rounded out the space. Dozens of dresses and skirts hung from silky hangers.

I had shirts of every style and color, designer jeans, and shorts that cost more than most people's yearly salary. Sandals, boots, and heels of varying styles and heights sat on display shelves. Thanks to my kidnappers, I had everything from lacy underwear to thongs and boy shorts.

Not like I needed their charity.

I flipped through the hangers, searching for something modest to wear. Unfortunately, most of the clothes were too short and too revealing. I wondered if the fabric would even cover my ass and tits. When I moved to Devil's Creek, I was skinny and malnourished from living with my parents. But after Pops started feeding me gourmet meals and gave me anything I wanted, I finally grew into my body.

Luca liked women with a lot of curves. That was something he'd made clear back in high school. And now that I had them, his eyes rarely left my body. I looked like the woman he desired. Yet, he still hadn't touched me.

Marcello's fingers dug into my shoulders, snapping me out of my thoughts about his brother. His hands slid down my body, his rough touch possessive and sensual.

Like his older brother, Marcello had never touched me. He never even tried to kiss me. Instead, he watched as the others humiliated me. It was as if Luca and Marcello wanted me to suffer.

Marcello slid his hand up my throat, tapping his fingers against my skin, feeling my pulse pound. "Wear the navy blue dress."

"I'll wear whatever I want."

His grip tightened as his fingers skated down my arm, creating tiny bumps in his wake. "I know what my brother likes. And what makes his cock hard will make him happy."

"Would that dress make your cock hard?"

A guttural sound escaped his throat as his lips brushed my ear. He flattened my back against his chest, forcing me to feel how much he liked this dress. His fingers branded my skin as I tilted my head to the side to give him better access to my neck. Too stubborn to take the bait, he released his grip on me.

Damn him.

I lifted the hanger from the rack and spun around to face him. Holding the wrap dress in front of my body, I stared into the mirror. The navy blue chiffon stopped mid-thigh with a thin belt tied around the waist.

"You'd only have to tug here." I pulled on the belt. "And it would fall off."

"If I were Luca," he said as his eyes raked over my body, "I wouldn't even bother with the belt."

I licked my lips. "I'm not talking about Luca."

Marcello shook his head. "Get dressed. Before you meet with Luca, we're going into town."

I flashed a grin, excited by the thought of fresh air and sunshine.

"Don't get any ideas," he said with an attitude. "I can see the wheels turning into that beautiful brain."

I gave him an angelic smile. "I wouldn't dream of it, boss man."

We rode in silence through Devil's Creek, with Marcello behind the wheel and 90s rock music floating through the speakers. His band choice told me something about him, though Marcello Salvatore was still a mystery. Unlike his older brother, he was quiet and reserved.

Kurt Cobain's voice belted through the car, and I tapped my fingers on my thigh to the beat of "Heart-Shaped Box" by Nirvana, one of my favorite bands.

I leaned on the armrest as we rode into town, invading Marcello's personal space. "Why is there a gate separating our houses from The Hills? This wasn't here before."

Marcello pointed at Beacon Bay, the small coastal community to the right of Devil's Creek. Locals called it Beggars Bay because of past incidents and the significant difference in wealth.

"My father used his political influence to put gates around

Devil's Creek to keep out the beggars. We had too much crime from the surrounding towns."

We rolled through a guarded gate, and Marcello waved at the man sitting in the booth.

"Are you sure it's not so your father can control who's allowed in and out of Devil's Creek?"

"That too."

From the outside, it looked like a wealthy neighborhood. Devil's Creek was a way of life for these people with its sprawling mansions and manicured lawns. Like me, they lived in their gilded cages disguised as mega-mansions, all under the pretense that following Arlo's rules would get them what they wanted. But this kind of happiness had a steep price.

Marcello drove for another ten minutes in silence with his eyes on the road. He parked in front of a boutique called Ciao Bella.

"Let's go," he said as he opened his door.

"What are we doing here?"

"Luca ordered you new clothes."

I climbed out of his Maserati with a groan, still tired from my lack of sleep. "I have enough clothes in my closet. I don't need any of Luca's charity."

Marcello yanked on my arm and dragged me toward the door. "It's not charity. You need to look the part."

"Please keep manhandling me," I deadpanned. "Because I love it so fucking much."

A middle-aged woman with long black hair, wearing a tight red dress that stopped at her knee, strolled over to us with a bright smile. She was pretty and polished. Her smile widened as she appraised Marcello, who looked like he'd just fallen out of a fashion magazine.

"Mr. Salvatore," she cooed. "Welcome back to Ciao Bella." Then she turned her gaze to me. "And this must be the lovely Alexandrea. I've heard so much about you." She extended her hand to me. "I'm Domenica Gallo, the owner of this boutique."

I shook her hand. "Nice to meet you."

She steered me toward a quaint sitting area at the center of the room. "I set aside Mr. Salvatore's order. He's very particular, as I'm sure you know."

"You mean Luca?"

"Yes." She pressed her lips together, smearing her red lipstick. "Mr. Salvatore called this morning. He said you needed a new wardrobe."

The smile I forced burned my cheeks. "I can't wait to see what Luca picked out for me."

The Salvatores controlled every part of my life. So why would my choice of clothing be any different?

"Give me a few minutes to grab everything, and I'll be right back." Domenica headed toward the back of the store and called out, "Valentina, champagne for our guests."

Racks and shelves rounded out two sides of the boutique, with a long row of fabric couches and tables interspersed down the center aisle.

A young brunette emerged from behind a velvet curtain with a silver tray in her hand. "Mr. Salvatore, welcome back to Ciao Bella."

I assumed this was Valentina, who handed a glass of champagne to Marcello. He took it with a thankful nod and passed it to me, waving her off when she offered him another drink.

"Alexandrea," she beamed. "Everyone in Devil's Creek has been talking about you."

I sipped my champagne and nodded. "I'm sure they have."

When Domenica reappeared, she had at least two dozen items draped over her arms. She called out to Valentina for help, and the pretty brunette rushed to her side, taking some clothes from her. Domenica slid a plush curtain along a metal bar, and the women got to work hanging everything from dresses and skirts to jeans and expensive shirts on hooks.

The modest-sized dressing room had a comfortable-looking bench, and a floor-length mirror spanned most of one wall. Valentina told me about each piece's designer. I loved art, not fashion, and zoned out halfway through her speech.

My clothes had paint or chemicals on them most of the time, so I stuck to cheaper brands. I would never order a five hundred dollar shirt for myself.

Ridiculous.

"If you need different sizes, let us know," Domenica said before exiting the dressing room.

I tried on a skirt that clung to my thighs, pairing it with a sleeveless pale pink top that showed some cleavage. Domenica was spot on with my sizes.

I stuffed my feet into ballet flats, jeweled sandals, and heels of varying heights. Then I changed out of a pencil skirt and blouse and grabbed a lipstick red dress with a small bow on the right hip. The fabric stopped mid-thigh, leaving little to the imagination.

It was cute.

My breasts were too big for the top, and when I reached behind me, I couldn't grab the zipper. I slid the curtain to the side and beckoned Marcello with my index finger. He moved toward me without complaint and shut the curtain.

With my back facing him, I pointed to my zipper. "I need your help."

Marcello pressed his hand on my lower back. "You look like a present," he said against the shell of my ear, caging me against the mirror with his muscular body.

"Maybe you should unwrap me," I quipped.

His fingers traveled up and down my spine as he pulled up the zipper. I held my breath as our eyes met in the mirror. He looked so much like Luca. And for a second, I wondered if they tasted the same.

I shook the thought from my mind. Marcello was no better than Luca.

"Looks like Luca ordered the wrong size," he said in that sexy voice that made my pulse pound as his fingers swept across my breasts.

It seemed to please him that Luca messed up my size. Mr. Perfect was always right about everything. He made sure of it because there was no room for error in his carefully curated world.

"Turn around," Marcello instructed.

I spun around to face him, and he moved his hand to my waist, fingers digging into my hip. His eyes traced up and down my body, settling on my breasts, which spilled out from the tight top. My heart raced as he stared at my lips, eventually looking into my eyes. Every inch of my skin was on fire, tingling with desire.

Marcello's cell phone beeped. His fingers flew across the keys, one message coming in after another. Then he took a few steps back from me and raised the phone to snap a few pictures.

"Are you planning to jerk off to that later?"

He ignored me and hit send.

"Get dressed," he said on his way out of the room. "We're leaving."

Chapter Seven

LUCA

Alexandrea Wellington turned me into a fucking psychopath. Yet, beneath all of our hatred, there was a burning desire inside us. The first time I saw her, I wanted to wrap my fingers around her throat and choke the fucking life out of her.

Even as a child, I knew I wasn't normal. But I had one good thing in my life—my mother. She was a famous painter —the most incredible woman to grace this shithole planet.

Alex's family had taken everything from me.

My mother.

My soul.

My humanity.

I would have killed her years ago if we didn't need an heir from the Wellington bloodline. Of course, she wasn't responsible for her family's actions, but that didn't make me hate her any less.

Hate was a powerful emotion.

I wielded it like a weapon and used it against her whenever I got the itch to touch her. To fuck her. I was incapable of intimacy or any real feelings. Hate, anger, lust, I understood perfectly. Blood and destruction tainted my entire world, but with Alex, I wanted to feel something.

Anything to feel alive.

She was the first and only woman I ever kissed. It was too personal, too intimate. I hated when women tried to run their fingers down my skin and press their lips to mine. The idea made me sick to my stomach.

I kissed Alex once and hated it. Except I didn't, not really.

I just hated her.

And her family.

Phone in hand, I leaned back in the leather chair. My cock was like a steel rod thinking about Alex, dreaming about fucking her tight pussy. I couldn't even focus on the meeting and continued texting my brother.

Years ago, I'd almost dismissed Alex as another pretty face. But then, our families introduced us, and I knew she was the woman I would marry. Her grandfather had given her a choice between my brothers and me—but I was winning this competition.

My brothers didn't have shit on me. I was the oldest, the smartest, the most ruthless. None of them stood a chance when I set my mind to a goal.

Alex was beautiful and damaged. I liked broken things, and I wanted to break her some more.

Like calls to like.

My enemies had gotten to Alex a few weeks ago. Thankfully, Marcello had intercepted the threat before she noticed someone was following her home. If my brother weren't good at his job, Alex would have been around the world by now—another casualty of human traffickers.

I thought she was safer away from Devil's Creek. My business often overflowed into my personal life, but none of that mattered until the Russians discovered my obsession with Alex.

I typed a quick message to Marcello.

Luca: Don't let her out of your sight.

Marcello: I'm head of security. Let me do my job. I'm handling the Volkovs.

Luca: We can't afford to lose her. The F Society wants the deed done.

Marcello: Chill. She's safe.

He sent a picture of Alex in the red dress I'd picked out for her. Fuck, she looked so good, like a present I wanted to unwrap.

Despite what she thought of me, I brought her to Devil's Creek for her protection. Because the wrong people knew she was *our* weakness.

Chapter Eight

ALEX

After Marcello hung my new clothes in the closet, I grabbed the leather portfolio from my bed and tucked it under my arm. I had five minutes until I met with Luca. Unfortunately, we'd spent more time in town than my stupid schedule allowed.

Marcello ushered me to the end of the hallway. We took the stairs to the third floor, where Luca had an office and bedroom. As far as I knew, he occupied the entire floor, while Marcello shared the fourth floor with his father. Bastian and Damian were down the hall from me, which meant more torture in the future.

I was easy prey for them.

Marcello was quiet as usual, his stony demeanor in place. We stopped at the end of the hall in front of a tall wooden door with an ornate gold handle.

He balled his hand into a fist and knocked. Seconds later, Luca appeared with a maniacal grin, staring at me with those haunting blue eyes. Luca Salvatore was like a dirty dream wrapped in an expensive suit, dipped in nightmares, and sugar-coated with sex appeal.

His hair was as black as ink, cut short on the sides, and

spiked in the front. The severeness of his jaw matched his expression.

It said *fuck with me, and I'll slit your throat.*

He stepped forward, studying my face before he turned his gaze on his brother. "What took you so long?"

Marcello gave him a bored look, shoving his sleeve up as he glanced at his Chopard watch. "We're on time."

He flung out his hand. "Leave us."

Marcello rolled his eyes and walked away without a word.

Luca wrapped his fingers around my wrist, pulled me into the room, and slammed the door so hard I jumped. He moved his hand to the side of my face, tilting my head to both sides as he examined me. Was he looking for an imperfection? A blemish?

He wore a bespoke navy blue suit that molded to his body as if sewn onto him. Fear shot through my body, my heart pounding as I stood before my cruel prince.

Luca's fingers moved from my throat to my chest, dipping between my cleavage that spilled from the low-cut dress. My skin burned where he touched, my body confusing my fear for desire.

An amused smirk tipped up the right corner of his mouth. He raised his hand and beckoned me to follow him.

"Why am I here?"

Luca sat behind the desk and tipped his head to my portfolio. "Is that for me?"

He took the book from my hand and scanned the pages. Luca didn't seem the least bit impressed with my paintings. I stood in front of his desk, my pulse pounding in my ears, sweat dripping down my back.

The bastard didn't even offer for me to sit. Instead, he ignored me as if I were as insignificant as the furniture in his office. I'd endured tons of interviews, everyone from gallery owners to artists I admired. But this was, by far, the most brutal.

Luca looked at me, his hand on a particular page at the back of the book. It was a piece I called *The Devil's Unfinished Work*.

A mixture of black, red, and orange paints created an Art Deco-Cubism theme. You could see a man's face within the shapes, though you couldn't make out all of his features.

That was the point.

I wanted people to talk about whether they thought the man was the devil himself or just a man who sinned. His mother had inspired the painting. Years of studying Evangeline's work had filtered into my own.

I wondered if he noticed the similarities between our paintings. Could he see how much she influenced me?

Luca's eyes flicked from my face back to the page. He rested his hand beneath his chin and sighed. "This one interests me most of all."

"How so?"

He slammed the book shut and shoved it across his desk. "I have interviewed over three hundred applicants for the Franco Foundation. Some of them have over thirty years of experience under their belts." Luca nodded at the chair across from his desk, and I sat without further instruction. "I only have one question, and then you can leave."

"I don't understand why I'm here."

He steepled his hands on the desk, his face expressionless as he fixed his intense blue eyes on me. "To celebrate the fifteenth anniversary of my mother's death, we're planning an event to showcase modern recreations of her work. The Franco Foundation has been looking for someone with her skill for over a year."

I narrowed my eyes at him. "So this is a job interview?"

Ignoring my question, he leaned forward, his voice deep and smooth. "What qualifies you for this position?"

"Are you serious?"

He nodded.

"Okay," I muttered. "Um... Your mother is my favorite artist," I said, speaking from the heart. "I may not be as talented as my peers, but I can capture what you're looking for."

He shook his head and kicked his dress shoe up on the edge of the desk. "I disagree. Your work is far superior to Madeline Laveau and Dean Rochester. They can sell out galleries worldwide, but neither of them can capture my mother's spirit. Not like you, Drea. You understand the heart and soul of her art."

As he leaned forward, he rested his elbows on his desk. A chill rushed down my arms from his sudden closeness. The five feet which separated us didn't feel like enough when he looked into my eyes, studying my face.

I sat up straight and grinned. "Does this mean I have the job?"

He rose from the chair and tugged at his gold tie. "My father is hosting a party next weekend at our estate. I've invited all the applicants. Attendance is mandatory."

"I never applied for the job," I cut in, voice trembling. "I didn't even know it existed until now."

"One of the many benefits of being my wife."

My lips parted. "I never agreed to marry you."

"You have to choose, Drea. Why do you think you're here? By the end of the summer, you will pick one of us. I'm only making it easier for you to decide."

"I don't want a pity job. You can keep it." I shot up from the chair with my portfolio clutched under my arm. "I'll see myself out."

Luca raised his hand. "I spoke to your grandfather. Carl assured me you would be more compliant this time. Are we going to have problems, Drea?"

I drew a breath from between my teeth, gripping the leather portfolio. "No."

"Your first solo exhibition is at the Blackwell Gallery in one month."

My lips parted in shock. "Blackwell? Are you serious?"

Luca nodded. "It's not the Museum of Modern Art, but it's a start."

"Thank you." I covered my racing heart with my hand, feeling each beat beneath my palm. "Wow. I don't know what else to say."

"Say you'll prepare for the showing." He moved around the desk until he was standing before me. "Don't embarrass me. I had to pull a lot of strings to make this happen."

"I appreciate your help. But what I don't appreciate is your attitude. You've been rude from the moment I walked into your office."

He scratched the corner of his jaw. "The children always pay for the sins of the parents."

Am I here because of my mother?

She hated Evangeline Franco with unbridled passion. Years ago, my mother was engaged to Arlo Salvatore. And after she walked away from the marriage and lost everything, she regretted her decision. Then Arlo married Evangeline and made her one of the most famous artists in the world. It only fueled my mother's rage, and she took all of her anger out on me.

I followed Luca to the entrance doors, sick to my stomach over his strange behavior. Instead of opening the door, he leaned against the wood and turned to face me. I almost crashed into him and grabbed his shoulder for support.

My pulse raced as the scent of sandalwood invaded my senses. He smelled so good I wanted to lick his skin. Instead, I bit my lip to stop it from trembling, and his face contorted into something sinister.

His eyes dropped to my mouth like he wanted to take my lip between his teeth. A man like Luca wouldn't give me a sweet kiss or a peck on the cheek. He would make every second hurt as he branded my lips with his sinful touch.

I swallowed the lump forming at the back of my throat. "If we're going to work together, we should get to know each other."

"I know everything about you."

"Well, I know very little about you."

"Our families decided our futures a long time ago." He grinned like a megalomaniac plotting his next move. "A union between our families will secure world domination for the Wellingtons and Salvatores."

"I don't want to marry you."

"People like us don't get to choose," he said with zero emotion. "I grew up knowing my father would choose for me. You should come to terms with the arrangement now."

Luca gripped my curls and pulled my face closer, his lips pressed into a thin line. His expression was unreadable, as if he'd gone to another place in his mind while his body was still very much present and pressing up against me. I felt the warmth and strength of his chest against mine. An uncomfortable silence fell over us, my nerves shaking through me as he held me in his firm grip.

"I like games. And you won't like how this ends," he growled against my lips.

His words sounded like a threat. What had made him so cold and hateful?

Even with my horrible upbringing, I still cared about others. But Luca was long gone, replaced by a monster with teeth and claws. I felt like he would suck the life from my body if I didn't get away from him. Every second in his presence had me falling deeper under his spell.

Damaged and broken, Luca was the shell of a gorgeous man with a wicked slant to his mouth and blue eyes that sliced through me. He was trying to intimidate me.

But I didn't understand why.

For a second, I closed my eyes and drank in his essence. Every warning signal in my brain fired at once, but my body didn't get the memo. Luca was a cruel billionaire who got what he wanted.

He would go to any length to win this game.

"We're done talking, Miss Wellington," he whispered, speaking to me as if I were some unknown job applicant. Then he reached around me to open the door, pushing me into the hallway. "Your five minutes are up."

Chapter Nine

ALEX

Marcello pulled up in front of a tall wrought-iron gate with a massive W at its center. Wellington Manor. We passed rows of maple trees as we drove onto my grandfather's property. Memories of my brother floated into my mind. The first summer we spent in Devil's Creek, we camped out under those trees.

Our grandmother hated us and made it known we were not welcome in her home. So we spent most of our time outside. We had so much fun before we understood why our grandparents had invited us to live with them back then. By the end of the summer, I realized my rags to riches fairy tale was a lie. My grandfather only wanted to use us as pawns.

It didn't feel right being here without Aiden. Even though it was only one night, I missed my twin.

We parked in front of a sprawling mansion with a circular driveway. I flung open the door, one foot out of Marcello's Maserati, before he grabbed my wrist.

"I'll be back at three o'clock. You won't like the consequences if I have to hunt you down."

"You don't own me, Marcello."

I slammed the door and walked toward the house. In his

late sixties, a man dressed in a black suit and armed with a warm smile greeted me.

"Alexandrea," he said with his head lowered. "Welcome back to Wellington Manor."

"Thank you, Charles."

Charles had worked for my grandparents since he was my age. During my first summer at Wellington Manor, he'd made me feel at home. He never yelled at Aiden and me and always fixed us snacks. They treated us like teenagers who desperately needed parents.

I stepped into the house and glanced over my shoulder at Marcello as he drove away. Good riddance. For the first time in twenty-four hours, I breathed easier without someone on my ass.

I walked toward the sitting room, noting how the interior didn't fit my grandfather's personality. Wellington Manor was cold and sterile, with its white walls and floors. Minimal color unless you counted black and cream. Even the expensive paintings couldn't bring this place to life.

We entered the formal sitting room. Perched on a white leather couch that looked as stiff as its occupant, Blair Wellington—my grandmonster from hell—pursed her lips. Her eyes lifted from my hands to my face with a disapproving look. I always had paint or charcoal on my skin and clothes.

Occupational hazard.

She had raised my mother with impossible standards no human could achieve. So it was no surprise that my mother ran away. I hated Blair with a passion and avoided her at all costs.

"Founders take pride in their appearances," Blair said sharply. "You would be wise to remember that. We can't have you embarrassing us in front of our peers."

"I'd be more than happy to return to Brooklyn," I fired back.

"Leave the poor girl alone." My grandfather yelled at her

from a small sofa at the far end of the room. "She has enough to worry about without you jumping down her throat. Go entertain yourself until we serve lunch."

He tipped the snifter in his hand to his mouth and winked at me.

"I'm going to freshen up," Blair said.

She left the sitting room, heels clicking on the tiled floor as she stormed down the hallway. I didn't need a lecture from my grandmonster. That mean ass bitch could save her advice for someone who cared.

Pops shook his head, annoyed. "Don't listen to her. Blair is a snob."

I crossed the room and hugged him. Carl Wellington III was a powerful man who sold me to the Salvatores, but he was the only family I had left, apart from Aiden. My parents were dead to me the day I became a Wellington.

He patted my back in a soothing, circular motion. "How are you holding up?"

I settled on the cushion beside him and shrugged. "Okay, I guess. I've been through worse than the Salvatores."

Pops sipped his brandy, one eyebrow raised. "How are they treating you?"

Did he care? Doubtful. My grandfather was very good at playing the game.

"Marcello took me shopping today."

He nodded in approval. "Marcello's a good man."

"You think so?"

"I prefer Marcello over Luca. He's more like his mother and will take good care of you."

"He's not much better than his brothers," I pointed out.

"People like us don't have as much say in our lives as others. Marriage is about power, not love. I know it's hard for you to understand this concept, but I didn't marry Blair for love."

I snorted. "It shows."

He smiled, then tipped the glass to his lips. "Blair's family is more connected than the Wellingtons. My father forced me to marry her before I graduated from medical school."

Most of the men in my family were doctors. My grandfather owned Wellington Pharmaceuticals, a company that had been in our family for over a hundred years. Pops had high hopes for Aiden, but he was an artist and would never change.

"The Salvatores are bullies and monsters. I think they enjoy torturing me."

"Arlo is stepping down from Salvatore Global and must choose a successor. If you were to marry Damian or Bastian, that would complicate matters for Arlo."

I narrowed my eyes at him. "Why?"

"Because they're not Salvatores by blood. Damian Townsend and Bastian Kincaid are direct descendants of the Founding Fathers. They can move up the ranks to The Founders Society without a marriage."

"What would happen if I married Bastian?"

"He would become the new Grand Master of The Devil's Knights," Pops explained between sips of scotch. "Your children would become legacies. The same would apply to Damian."

"What would happen to Luca and Marcello?"

"They would lose any claim to the Knights. The Founders Society would shun them. Losing that kind of power..." He breathed deep, eyes downcast. "I don't even want to think about how Arlo would retaliate. It would start a war."

"The Salvatores need a marriage into a Founding Family to legitimize their position. I get that. But I don't understand why they have always been so mean."

His lips parted as if he were about to say something, and then he snapped his mouth shut. He drank from his glass, eyes out the window.

What was he keeping from me?

I'd always felt like I was missing something with Pops. He

saved me from my mother, but it wasn't out of the kindness of his heart. Where was he for the first eighteen years of my life? Where was he when we needed him?

"Years of physical and mental abuse from Arlo hardened those boys," he said after a long pause. "He forged them into men. Made sure they understood the cost of failure."

"I don't want any of them," I said without hesitation. "They're all jerks."

"If they hadn't watched over you for all these years, I don't know where you would be right now."

My jaw dropped at his confession. "What's that supposed to mean?"

"Nothing." He turned away, avoiding my gaze. "I'm thankful they worry about you as much as I do. That's all."

I almost laughed.

Since when did anyone in my life, apart from Aiden, worry about me? Which reminded me... I hadn't heard from Aiden in close to twenty-four hours. That wasn't like him.

"They have no reason to worry about me," I told my grandfather. "I'm boring. When I'm not working at the café, I mostly sit inside with Aiden and paint."

"Speaking of your brother." He set the empty glass on the table, then fixed his deep brown eyes on me. "Before you marry into the Salvatore family, Aiden needs to accept his place with the Knights."

"He doesn't want to join them."

"I fear what Arlo will do to Aiden if he keeps resisting." Pops reached over and placed his hand on mine, holding it against the couch. "We made deals before you were born. They are unbreakable and enforceable under a different set of laws."

I was so confused. My grandfather was one of the five Elders of The Founders Society, the organization that oversaw the other societies under their control.

"Can't you make new rules? Aiden doesn't have to become a Knight."

Pops shook his head. "Arlo is the Grand Master of The Devil's Knights. Whoever you marry will succeed him."

"Why does it matter who I choose?"

He reached over and tucked a loose curl behind my hair. "Because, my dear girl, you will become their queen."

A shiver shot straight down my arms, the hairs standing at attention. "Queen?"

Pops smiled so wide it reached his eyes. "The Knights have waited a long time for you, Alex. It's time for you to learn your true power."

I bit the inside of my cheek, still stunned by his confession. "What makes me their queen?"

"Thirty years ago, I made a similar deal for your mother. Savanna was supposed to marry Arlo Salvatore, and she backed out of the engagement. She disgraced the Wellington name. If Savanna had married Arlo, she would have become the Queen of The Devil's Knights. And now, the responsibility falls to you."

"Why does an all-male secret society need a queen?"

None of this crazy shit made any sense to me. Not this arranged marriage to my high school bullies or any of the arcane secret society bullshit.

Pops laid his palm on the couch and drew a breath between his teeth as our eyes met. "I didn't trust Arlo's father. But to ensure he would protect your mother, I forced him to agree to my terms. The Salvatores needed a marriage into a Founding Family to maintain their position with The Founders Society. Lorenzo would have given me just about anything, and I wanted to ensure our family's legacy remained intact. This is the first time a Wellington will marry someone outside of the Founding Families."

"So that's why I'll become their queen?"

He bobbed his head. "It's written in the charter. You will

be the first-ever queen, giving you an incredible amount of power. The Devil's Knights have hundreds of members throughout the country. They have taken an oath to kill for you, die for you. They take this oath seriously. So it's imperative you choose between The Salvatore boys soon. Becoming their queen offers you a lot of protection."

For most of my life, I had felt powerless. Just the thought of having control over the Salvatores filled me with excitement. I didn't understand what it meant to be Queen of The Devil's Knights. But a small part of me wanted it.

I wanted the power.

Fanning myself with my hand, I rose from the couch, overwhelmed by the shocking news. "I need some fresh air before we eat."

Pops nodded. "Take your time."

I left the sitting room, power-walked down the hallway, and flung open the front door. I walked across the grass with my flats in one hand and my cell phone in the other.

Why hadn't Aiden called or texted in the last twenty-four hours? Not even to see if I'd made it to Devil's Creek. I'd completely forgotten with all the drama last night. It was hard to breathe around the Salvatores, let alone make calls.

I hit Aiden's name on my speed dial and put the phone on speaker. An automated message said The number you're trying to reach is no longer in service.

"What the fuck?"

Bile rose from the back of my throat as panic flooded my veins. This had to be a mistake, so I tried dialing his number directly. But again, I received the same message.

Is my phone broken?

I hadn't received a single call since I'd arrived in Devil's Creek. So I called the pizzeria near my house to check my cell service. A young woman answered on the second ring. I apologized for dialing the wrong number and hung up.

Okay, so my phone works.

Now what?

I moved toward the entrance gate, needing an escape from the confines of my life. Two hours of freedom. That was all I had until Marcello would be back to collect me.

I stopped in front of the fence and then remembered I needed the access code to open it. Pops changed it once a week. Unlike the Salvatore Estate, armed men didn't guard Wellington Manor, but it had on-site security.

Fuck this shit.

Something was wrong with Aiden. I wasn't staying in this town without knowing my brother was safe.

I shoved my flats through the slats in the fence, committed to my mission. The guard watching the security feed was about to get one hell of a show. My inner Spider-Man senses awakened as I gripped the metal bars and found my groove, scaling the tall fence like a superhero. Sharp bits of iron poked my palms, the pain so intense I almost let go halfway.

Slinging my leg over the fence, I mounted the brick post with my thighs spread, and my dress hiked up to my waist. As I stared down at the pavement, nausea swept over me. It was at least a twenty-foot drop.

I drew in a few deep breaths to still my pounding heart.

I hated heights.

What was I thinking?

A car horn blared down the street, startling me. I used my forearm to shield my face from the sun and gasped. Marcello drove onto the flagstones and parked his black Maserati Gran-Turismo in front of the gate.

He popped his head out the window. "Where the fuck do you think you're going?"

Chapter Ten

ALEX

My plan was an epic fail. I hadn't even made it over the front gate before Marcello caught me in a compromising position. I had my dress hiked up to my waist, my legs dangling from the brick post like branches hanging from a tree.

Fear was a motherfucker.

If I hadn't taken in the twenty-foot drop, I would have been long gone, on my way to freedom.

I was so close I could taste it.

As Marcello parked his black Maserati on the flagstones, I yanked my dress down to my knees. Of course, he'd seen me naked already, but I wasn't trying to make it a regular habit. I had to maintain some decency, after all.

But who was I kidding?

My body responded when Marcello was near, like his cock was a beacon, sending signals to my undersexed lady bits.

He popped his thick head of black hair out of the driver's side window. "Where the fuck do you think you're going?"

I rolled my eyes at the prick. "Nowhere, I guess, since I can't get away from you."

My mouth watered as he brushed his hair off his forehead.

His messy-on-purpose look had me itching to run my fingers through his hair. But unlike Luca, who knew he was god's gift to women, Marcello was oblivious to his sex appeal... and the effect he had on me.

Marcello opened his door with an irritated groan, placing one foot on the ground. "Can you get yourself down from there?"

I held up my hands and shrugged. "There's an upside to falling."

Marcello got out of the car. "Can you get down or not? If not, I'm coming up there to get you." He moved onto the grass below me. "Jump. I'll catch you."

"I was never good at the trust fall thing in gym class."

"I got you," he growled. "Get your ass down here."

"You have such a way with words, Marcello. I bet you could charm the chastity belt off a nun."

"Look who's got jokes." He shook his head, his jaw set hard enough to cut through steel. I rolled my eyes, and he raised his hand in the air, wiggling his fingers. "You have two seconds before I climb up there, princess."

"Fine," I agreed. "Make sure you catch me."

"Turn yourself around." He made a twirling motion with his fingers. "Use the brick post as an anchor point and then jump into my arms."

Trusting people gave me fucking hives. That was not something I freely tossed around to anyone. I tore a hole into my cheek from deliberating my next move. Getting up here was easy, but my throat closed up every time I glanced at the ground.

For a moment, I was back at the ski resort in the Pocono Mountains. Aiden had talked me into separating from the group so we could check out the slopes on our own.

He always sought danger.

We'd ventured to the black diamond slope. But unfortunately, we learned the reason for the closure too late. They were replacing a fence that kept skiers from falling off the mountain. If Aiden hadn't grabbed my arm when he did, I would have plummeted to my death.

"Stop fucking around," Marcello said with an attitude.

"I'm afraid of heights."

I followed his orders and turned, so my back faced him, giving him the perfect view of my bare ass. It was too late to rethink the thong under my short dress. I lunged off the wall, spiraling down like a plane falling out of the sky. Marcello wrapped his arms around my middle, and the force of the crash knocked us to the ground.

He rolled on the grass, my chest pinned to his. I expelled the air from my lungs, relieved I didn't break any bones. My eyes found his blue ones as his cock grazed my inner thigh through his pants. He was packing some heat below the belt, like a freaking missile aimed at me, ready to launch.

Pressing my palm to his chest, I sat up, the sudden movement creating some friction.

"Fuck," he groaned, reaching between us to fix himself. "Stop moving for a second."

I rocked my hips into his erection, a smirk tugging at the corner of my mouth. "So you're human after all? And here I thought you were a robot."

I laughed, which earned me a scowl from Marcello. His fingers jabbed my sides as he lifted me off his rock solid hard-on, setting me on the grass beside him. He pushed himself up from the grass with the gracefulness of a tiger. Don't let this beast fool you because there was a savage prowling beneath his beautiful exterior.

Marcello ran his hands down the front of his pants, ignoring the fact I gave him a raging boner. He busied himself with cleaning off his pants and jacket. God forbid a speck of dirt violated his carefully maintained layers of perfection.

I crossed over the flagstones to hit the button on the call

box. A man's deep voice boomed through the speaker, asking me to state my business at Wellington Manor.

"It's Alexandrea Wellington."

The gates opened inward.

Marcello closed the gap between us, his dark eyebrows knitted. "What are you doing?"

"I'm having lunch with my grandfather."

He grabbed my arm, his fingers marking my flesh as he dragged me away from the gate. "Only good girls get privileges. You've just lost yours. Get in the car."

He opened the passenger door and forced me inside the car. Marcello was so much stronger, and it was impossible to fight him.

"Try to run again, and I'll handcuff you to the bed."

"Ooh, foreplay," I joked. But as our eyes met, he gave me a stern expression.

I held up my hands in surrender. "Fine. I'll behave myself."

He leaned over me to grab the seatbelt and winked. "Good girl."

Marcello got behind the wheel and flew down Founders Way like we were on the Autobahn. I clutched the door handle and leaned back against the headrest.

There were only five properties on this road, so we arrived at the Salvatore Estate in a flash.

Marcello acknowledged a few of the armed guards, who lowered their heads. Then, a wrought-iron gate opened for us. He drove onto the estate, stopping in front of a covered garage that housed a fleet of cars.

Mario Andretti's evil twin slid out from behind the steering wheel. Within seconds, he ripped open my door and lifted me over his shoulder, dragging me toward the house like a caveman.

I slapped his back, arms, and that tight ass I wanted to

sink my teeth into, my fists pounding with fury. "Put me down! I can walk on my own."

Marcello released a wicked chuckle that sent shivers down my spine as we entered the foyer. I fought him as we ascended the stairs, which was pointless and a waste of my energy until he set me down at the top of the landing.

"Asshole!" I shoved my palm into his chest. "Why are you treating me like a child?"

"Because I can't trust you not to run again." Marcello's cell phone dinged with several text messages in a row, and he read them with a scary smirk. "You shouldn't have run."

I rolled my eyes. "Whatever."

After we entered my bedroom, Marcello inched toward me. I walked backward and groaned when my elbow hit the bedpost. A flicker of desire sparked in his eyes, sending a ripple of pleasure down my arms. He pushed me onto the mattress, moving his knee between my thighs.

Is he going to kiss me?

Marcello grabbed my wrist, raised my arm above my head, and breathed against my lips. "I gave you some freedom, and this is what you do with it."

"Get off me!"

I lifted my knee to kick him, but he was too fast. Marcello grabbed my leg and laughed as I struggled to fight back.

"Think about escaping again, and I'll spank your ass so hard you won't walk for a week."

"Sounds like fun. You going to tie me up and take me over your knee?"

That was about as far as I'd ever gotten with Luca. A kiss, one time, many years ago. He looked disgusted with himself afterward, like the thought of kissing me was repulsive. Then he took me over his knee, bound my wrists and ankles together, and spanked me like a rotten child.

It was hot.

Hell, I even begged him for more. And that was the last time he touched me.

His cell phone dinged with a new text message. Probably another message from Luca, the king of the dicks. A laugh escaped his throat as he slid off the bed. My handsome captor grinned, his eyes traveling up the length of my body.

"See something you like, asshole?"

Marcello glanced at the room's corner. I couldn't see anything past the crown molding, but I assumed there was a camera. He tipped his head, then walked away.

"Wait!" I sat up as he reached the door. "Where are you going? I need to eat."

"You should have thought about that before you ran," he said before closing the door behind him.

The Salvatores had caged me for years. So why did I expect anything different from them?

"Marcello, let me out of here." I balled my hand into a fist and banged on the door until pain shot up my arm. "You asshole, open this door."

As expected, he greeted me with silence... and the sound of water splashing.

The bay.

I spun on my heels, my stomach growling as I flung open the French doors that led to the balcony. Salty air floated into the room, and I drank in the scent. This was Luca's idea to lock me in my bedroom.

Message received, dickhead!

Furious, I turned away from the open doors and flipped Luca the middle finger. Right at the hidden camera.

Anger surged through me, heat rolling off my skin like flames. Those assholes dragged me back to this place, only to lock me up like Rapunzel in her fucking tower. Positive I had Luca's attention, I grabbed an expensive glass vase from the table by the window. I raised it above my head, laughing as it smashed to pieces on the carpet.

Fuck Luca.

Fuck Marcello.

Fuck the Salvatores.

I went around the room, breaking everything but the lamps. It felt good to watch the glass shatter. Like those bastards had done to my heart repeatedly. Years of enduring those insufferable bullies had turned me into a lunatic.

With each valuable I destroyed, my heart stopped racing. My pulse returned to normal with each shard of glass and ceramic that littered the carpet like a fucked up painting.

Like something I would paint.

I smiled at my handwork, proud of my latest creation.

You're losing it again.

No, I'm not.

Maybe just a little.

Some people called me crazy. They said I was just like my mother and another disappointment to the Wellington name. So I had to prove them wrong, show all these rich assholes they had underestimated me.

After my second involuntary stay at the Haven Asylum, the doctors diagnosed me with complex post-traumatic stress disorder. My PTSD wasn't isolated to a single incident. Instead, it was the product of years of trying to escape locked closets, dark bedrooms, and my mother's emotional and mental abuse.

Then, I met the Salvatores.

Four broken boys wanted to take out their pain and anger on me. They had tortured me throughout my final year at Astor Prep. Every single day I dreaded going to school. My twin brother tried to intervene. But my bullies had purposely aligned my classes with theirs so no one could help me.

I ignored the nagging throb at the base of my skull, a clear sign I was about to have an episode.

Not now.

No, I had to fight it and show the Salvatores that they

couldn't hurt me. My head pounded hard and fast, forcing my eyes shut. I clutched the side of my head and groaned.

Fuck this.

I couldn't let my kidnappers see me fall apart on camera. So I spun around and headed toward the balcony. The Salvatore Estate sat at the center of Devil's Creek, overlooking the bay. So I had an unobstructed view of the coastal towns surrounding us.

On the other side of the bay, the lights from Wolf Hallow twinkled like stars in the dark blue sky. Beacon Bay was to my right, hidden by an overgrowth of trees.

Gripping the brick post, I closed my eyes and let the sea glide over my skin. In and out, I took deep, calming breaths and tipped my nose up to drink in the saltiness.

My mind drifted to Aiden and the last time I saw him. He looked tired, his blond curls longer than usual. Dark circles ringed his eyes. I knew he was taking pills and had confronted him about it the night before. He promised he would stop.

Aiden.

I needed him.

His cell phone was disconnected.

How was that even possible?

I paid the bill last week.

It wouldn't have been the first time Aiden owed a drug dealer money. He had a bad habit, but I wasn't exactly in the position to judge him.

Please be okay, Aiden.

Another sharp pain pierced my skull, and my fingers clung to the railing for support. I blew out a deep breath as images flashed before me, unable to stop them from taking my brain hostage.

It was so dark.

Too cold.

Loud screams.

A woman laughed.

My mother.

Then wicked male laughter.

The Salvatore brothers.

Each image flashed before my eyes, moving so fast that I struggled to breathe. My chest felt heavy, as if weighed down with sand. Pressing a palm to my chest, I gasped for air.

I needed to get out of here.

To escape this fucking prison.

Desperate to be free, I slid a chair out from the table on my right and moved it beside the railing. Even though I didn't feel like I was still in my body, I was fully aware of my actions.

Keep going.

I hopped onto the chair, and a cool breeze floated off the bay, blowing my hair in my face. If I could get over the railing without falling to my death, I could hug the brick post and shimmy my way to the ground. At least a dozen men with guns patrolled the perimeter. This place was better guarded than Fort Knox.

I needed to get the fuck out of this place and find Aiden. So I had no choice but to conquer my fear. I pressed my palms to the brick ledge and pulled myself up, arms outstretched to maintain my balance.

Just breathe, Alex.

Don't look down.

What could have been a moment or an hour passed before I finally snapped out of my head, slowly returning to reality. My heart still raced, but for an entirely different reason. Fear flooded my veins as a bitter chill washed over me like breaking waves.

I looked down, teetering on edge, and a shriek escaped my throat. It was at least a fifty-foot drop to the ground.

What was I thinking?

Then, I thought, What would the Salvatores do? They would haul ass over this balcony and disappear like a phantom in the night.

Stick to the plan.

Find Aiden.

I covered my heart with my hand and closed my eyes, feeling each beat beneath my fingers.

You can do this, Alex.

With each breath I took, I convinced myself this was true. But as I hooked my leg over the side, my foot slipped on the spire, and my sweaty fingers slid down the cold metal, throwing me off balance.

At least I will die trying.

Chapter Eleven

LUCA

I was still working from the night before when Marcello called. I never slept. My demons kept me awake at night, taunting me. Besides, the Devil didn't need sleep.

I answered the call and put it on speakerphone. "I'm in the middle of mapping the trade routes for the cartel. This better be fucking important, Marcello."

"Alex is more important than our business associates."

"Let me guess. She's mad that you locked her in the room. So fucking what?" I leaned forward, elbows resting on the desk. "It's much less than what she deserves for trying to run. If I weren't so busy, I would have spanked her ass for pulling that stunt."

Marcello breathed into the receiver. "She's having night terrors. Maybe it's too soon to take Aiden away from her. If we push her too hard, she'll break."

"Good. I like her broken. She's more fun to play with that way."

"You know what the doctor said," he snapped with venom in his tone. "She can't handle the distance from her brother. Initiation is six months without contacting anyone other than the Knights. When Alex realizes her brother disappeared, the whole plan will fall apart."

"She can handle it," I assured him.

"She needs a doctor," he muttered. "I'm telling you, Luca, she's not fucking okay. Alex is just like Mom. Trust me. I know what I'm talking about."

Why does he always have to bring up our mother? She was the reason Alex was here, the reason I wanted to choke her to death every time I had to look at her.

"I got it under control, Marcello."

I had a contingency plan for my contingency plan. With Alex and her health, I covered all of my bases. I wasn't a man who left anything to chance. We needed her sane and compliant. The Devil's Knights needed their queen, and it was time for Alex to serve her true purpose.

"Fine, but if this goes sideways, we'll lose our status with The F Society."

"Marcello, calm the fuck down. That girl has been ours from the moment we laid eyes on her. She pretends to hate us. But we all know she secretly enjoys playing the game."

"You love the game. Not so much the rest of us."

"Please, Bash and Damian are like cats chasing a mouse. She enjoys the thrill of *their* hunt."

"She's trashing her bedroom as we speak."

Marcello groaned, and even without seeing him, I figured he was tugging at the ends of his hair in frustration.

"Fuck. What do you want to do with her? She's out of her mind."

I shot up from the chair and approached the flat-screen monitors on the wall. We had every angle of the property, every bedroom, even a feed in Alex's old apartment that was now empty.

Damian was in his room, one hand on his cock, the other on the wall. He stared down at a laptop, jerking off to what looked like really hardcore porn. He couldn't get enough of that shit.

Bastian was in his bedroom, fingers on the piano keys, working on the new song he was writing. Marcello sat on the top step of the second landing with his cell phone in hand, eyes pointed down at the screen.

I scanned the cameras until I found Alex's bedroom. "Has she taken her medicine today?"

"I gave it to her this morning with her breakfast."

"Give her a sedative, something to calm her down."

I watched Alex throw a twenty-thousand-dollar vase across the room. Punted an irreplaceable Faberge egg like it was a football. I won that in a game of poker from a Russian mobster.

I shook my head. "It's like she's possessed."

She deserved a good spanking for trying to run from Wellington Manor. But I was short on time and patience. So I figured a few hours in isolation would sort her ass out. It would give her some time to think about what she had done. But as usual, Alex was full of surprises.

"Shit." Keys jingled in Marcello's hand as his breath grew heavier. "Are you looking at the feed in her bedroom?"

I glanced over at the video feed and gasped. Alex moved a chair across the balcony and stepped onto it.

"Marcello, get in there. Now!"

She climbed up onto the brick ledge, arms stretched out at her sides. The wind blew through her hair, strands smacking her in the face. Unfazed, she stood there as if she were invincible.

Did we fuck up already? Did one hour in the room make her want to kill herself?

No, she wouldn't.

I watched as Marcello lifted Alex over the railing and carried her into the bedroom, kicking the patio doors closed behind him.

At least she was safe.

Fuck, that was close.

Relieved, I expelled a deep breath from my lungs. I called it years ago. This woman would be the death of me.

Of all four of us.

"I got her," Marcello said into the phone as he set Alex on the bed.

She blinked rapidly, staring through Marcello like she wasn't in her body. He waved his hand in front of her face, and she didn't even acknowledge him. Lips pressed together, she sat with her palms on her thighs and stared at the wall.

What the fuck?

Stay with us, baby girl.

"What do you want me to do?" Marcello turned his back on her and walked toward the ensuite bathroom. "She's out of it. Unresponsive."

"Plan B."

"Okay," he groaned. "I'll call you when she wakes up."

I hung up and took a long sip of scotch. If anything happened to our girl, we were fucked.

Chapter Twelve

ALEX

The darkness found me again. It always did. *Hello, old friend*, it whispered in my ear. *Welcome back.*

Like most nights, I tossed and turned, forced to endure my own personal Hell. Images flashed before my eyes, colors swirled together, and the room spun around me. Hands slid down my arms, touching me in places my kidnappers had claimed for themselves.

I rolled onto my side, and the hands slipped away. The room spun on its axis. A gray mist swirled around my head, the room replaced by a new nightmare.

A new version of Hell.

My body ached from my feet pounding the cement. Every muscle cried out for me to stop, begging me to slow down. But I couldn't. They were too close, right on my tail.

I ran through the crowded streets of Beacon Bay with a group of men chasing me. They called out my name, taunting me with each step.

Don't stop.

Keep going, Alex.

"You can run, Alex," a man taunted. "But you can't hide. We will find you."

The soles of my sneakers burned as I bolted down a back alleyway, headed toward The River Styx. But when I reached the rundown bar, my feet stuck to the ground. No matter how hard I tried, I couldn't take another step.

Stretching out my fingers, I reached for the door. The handle was right there, just a few more inches.

So why couldn't I touch it?

I heard loud breathing behind me, and a shiver rolled down my back. The hair on my arms and neck stood at attention. Fear rocked through me when my eyes landed on four tall men with broad shoulders.

My mouth dropped in horror at the paint on their faces, one half covered in snakeskin. The tallest of the group had golden scales branding his tanned skin. He looked like a copperhead snake, poisonous and deadly.

But so were his friends.

All of them had tattoos on their necks, arms, and hands. They wore black hoodies and fitted jeans, the right sides of their faces obscured by the paint. The tallest of the group had white-blond hair and raised his tattooed hand to his jaw. He'd painted his skin yellow with white chevrons like a king cobra.

The man on his left had the greenish-yellow hue of a pit viper. They were all terrifying, but the last man was pure evil. His scales were dark brown, and when he opened his mouth, I gasped at his black tongue.

A black mamba.

What the fuck?

But before he could speak, my vision blurred, and someone shook my shoulder. "Alex, wake the fuck up."

My eyes shot open at the sound of Marcello's deep voice. He held onto my shoulder, sitting at the edge of my bed. Concern scrolled across his face. I attempted to speak, but my mouth was so dry my tongue stuck to the roof of my mouth.

I closed my eyes for a moment and breathed.

Maybe he wasn't real.

Maybe it was all a dream.

"Look at me." Marcello slid his hand beneath my chin and squeezed, forcing my eyes open. "How long has this been going on?"

"What?"

"Night terrors. They're getting worse."

I blew out a deep breath and shoved his hand away from my face. "Don't act like you care about me, Marcello. You're the one who locked me in this room. I only have you and Luca to blame. I dreamed about the night you and your sicko brothers dragged me out of bed at Wellington Manor. How you dropped me off in Beacon Bay in the middle of the night and let The Serpents chase me until I had a panic attack that hospitalized me for a week."

The Serpent Society was a small gang of unknown men connected to the Salvatores. Their name came from the serpent in the Salvatore crest, so I'd assumed they were related. But no one knew the identities of The Serpents, only their code names—Hades, Morpheus, Charon, and Lethe—named after the most notable personifications of the Greek Underworld.

For years, I had woken up from the same horrific dreams. The dark closet. My mother and her slow, agonizing torture. Those old, painful memories of my bullies and their constant torture.

Aiden had slept beside me most nights when we were kids to help quell the terrors. He would rock me back to sleep and hold my hand to stop the shakes. Then, when we left for college, the dreams stopped.

The distance from the Salvatores had kept them at bay. But after two nights away from Aiden, my mind unlocked my worst memories.

All of my fears.

Marcello grabbed a tray from the table by the window. He set a teacup and a plate of toast in front of me. My stomach rumbled as I looked down at the butter and strawberry preserves beside the toast. The Salvatores knew everything about me.

It was disturbing.

I sat up and hooked my finger through the cup's handle, lifting it from the saucer. "Is this a peace offering?"

Marcello ignored my question, hands on his narrow hips. I drank the tea and shoved a piece of toast into my mouth.

Marcello sat in the armchair by the window with his black wingtip resting on his knee. We sat in silence, which suited me fine. I had nothing to say to his grumpy ass.

After I finished eating, he got up from the chair and moved the tray to the writing desk. "Do you need to use the bathroom?"

"Yes."

Marcello lifted me in his arms like I was a damn baby, crushing me against his chest.

"I can walk," I protested. "You don't have to carry me."

He acted as if he hadn't heard me, focused on the door he shoved open with his foot. We entered the ensuite bathroom, and he set my feet down on the cold tiled floor.

"I'm not peeing with you in here," I mumbled, sleep clouding my rough and scratchy voice. "Get out."

The room swayed in front of me. A flash of colors and lights blurred my vision as a sharp pain pierced my skull.

I pressed my fingers to my temple. "I don't feel good."

My head pounded like a jackhammer drilling into cement. Not a migraine, I thought as Marcello turned his back to give me some privacy. Sometimes the headaches were so bad I threw up for hours. I had fucked up flashbacks and nightmares that made it impossible to tell the difference between fact and fiction.

What happened earlier?

I slid my panties down and sat on the toilet, humiliated with Marcello standing a few feet away. But with the room slipping out from under me, I didn't care as much. I wiped, pulled up my panties, and flushed the toilet before a wave of nausea hit me like a ton of bricks.

Clutching the edge of the sink, I stared into the mirror, seeing two of myself. My reflection on the left gave me a devilish grin. The one on the right blew me a kiss.

What the fuck?

My mind played tricks on me. I should have been able to trust myself above anyone else. But when my dissociative episodes spiraled out of control, I was helpless.

Like right now.

Then I thought about the tea and the toast and wondered if Marcello drugged me.

"What did you…"

As I lost my balance, Marcello scooped me into his arms and whispered, "I got you, princess."

Chapter Thirteen

ALEX

After Marcello drugged me, that bastard left me locked in my bedroom for days. A man with a gun strapped to his chest delivered my meals. He looked scarier than the Salvatores, so I didn't bother fucking with him.

They dosed every other meal with strong medicine that knocked me on my ass. I felt like I was at the Ritz Carlton version of the Haven Asylum, without the doctors, pill-pushing nurses, and group therapy sessions.

While I was sleeping last night, someone left art supplies in my room. If I had to guess, it was Marcello throwing me a bone, so I didn't lose my mind.

I lay on my bedroom floor, my fingers wrapped around a rigger brush, making slow, sweeping movements. In one month, my solo show was an exhibition at the Blackwell Gallery in SoHo. Luca thought he could bribe me into marrying him. So far, he wasn't even a close second.

I painted a man with murderous eyes, his horns sticking up from his thick, dark hair. Smoke and falling ash surrounded his head as if he'd stepped out of Hell. He wore a fitted suit that outlined his strong shoulders, the definition in his arms. It could have been any of the Salvatores.

As the sun was about to set, Marcello unlocked my door. He stood in the entryway with his hands on his hips, pushing his suit jacket to the side to reveal two guns holstered on his chest.

Still mad at him, I turned away and returned to my painting. I saw his shiny black dress shoes before I looked up at all six feet four inches of him. His muscles bulged beneath the fabric stretched across his thick chest. Black messy waves fell onto his forehead.

Marcello stared down at the canvas with a rare smile. "You've been busy."

"There's not much for me to do in my cell, warden."

He stuffed his hands into his pockets and sighed. "Alex, this was for your good. You needed your meds. I checked with your doctor. You haven't refilled the prescription in three months."

Teeth gritted, I looked up at him. "What gives you the right to go behind my back and talk to my doctor? I'm suing that bastard." I shook my head. "So much for doctor-patient confidentiality."

"Your grandfather has medical power of attorney. So he gave his approval for me to speak to your doctor."

"I'm not fucking crazy!" I shot up from the floor. "Stop treating me like it. My grandfather used that stupid document to control me. I only agreed to let him make decisions for a few months. It's been six years."

Marcello slid his arm behind my back and pulled me closer, suffocating me with the delicious citrus scent of his aftershave. "C'mere, princess. Just breathe."

I let him cradle my head against his chest and stroke his fingers through my hair. Even though I hated him, I kind of needed a hug.

I needed Aiden.

"My phone died a few days ago. I don't have a charger and need to find my brother."

He hugged me harder, pressing my cheek against his hard chest. "I'll get you a phone charger."

I lifted my head and looked up at him. "Is my brother okay?"

"Why wouldn't he be?"

I inspected his face for a lie and didn't find a hint of malice.

Marcello studied my painting with a semblance of a smile, and then his eyes met mine. "This might be your best work."

"You think so?"

He nodded. "You have a natural gift. My mom could see the flaws in every person and bring them out." Then he tucked my hair behind my ear, his fingers softly brushing my cheek. "We're eating in the dining room in one hour. Change into something more appropriate."

I lifted the strap over my right shoulder and snickered. "Do my paint-covered overalls offend you, sir?"

He moved past me and into my walk-in closet. Seconds later, he dropped a black dress onto my bed. "Luca wants you to wear this one. Get ready."

Fuck Luca.

I wasn't a Barbie doll for him to dress up. He was sadly mistaken if he thought I would play by his rules.

Marcello walked out of my bedroom and closed the door behind him.

Screw their demands.

I grabbed two paintbrushes from the cup holder on my desk and pinned my curls into a chopstick style. If the Salvatores wanted to control when I ate and what I wore, I could have fun with them. Add some personality to my boring cocktail dress. Plus, I knew it would annoy Luca to see me so imperfect, which gave me another crazy idea.

M arcello escorted me to the main dining room an hour later, commenting about my dress. He warned me not to mess with Luca tonight and begged me to change. The Prince of Hell was in a bad mood.

Tough shit.

Arlo sat at the head of the table. Luca was on his right beside Bastian and Damian, leaving the left side for Marcello and me.

I wore a black v-neck rosette dress that hugged my curves. The fabric stressed my breasts and ass, a slit running down my right thigh. Luca couldn't take his eyes off me. Bastian and Damian undressed me with their minds.

Luca's sinful expression quickly twisted into an angry snarl. "What the fuck did you do to that dress?"

I smiled so wide my cheeks hurt. "You don't like my modifications?"

All of my clothes were plain and blah, typical rich asshole shit. I preferred jeans, tanks, and shorts, but Luca spared no expense, providing the best clothes his money could buy. The dress was beautiful and elegant, but it wasn't me. So I added red and gold streaks of paint and set the acrylic with the hairdryer.

He balled his hand into a fist on the table, teeth clenched. "No, I don't. You ruined a vintage Oscar de la Renta."

I rolled my shoulders, not giving a single fuck. "I'll write you a check."

"I don't care about the money," he shot back.

"Then what do you care about?" I glared at the smug bastard. "Because it sure as hell isn't me."

He shook his head, his top lip quivering. "Keep testing my patience, woman."

"Or what?"

"Basta," Arlo muttered to Luca in Italian, ordering him to stop. His father extended his hand to the vacant chair at his side. "Sit here, Alexandrea. Please."

Marcello pushed my chair into the table before taking his place on my left. He didn't utter a single word to anyone, his expressionless mask in place. Around his family, he was a trained soldier, a weapon forged for their deviant purposes.

Arlo tapped a platinum serpent ring on the arm of his chair and studied me with fascination. He leaned back in the chair and rested his elbows on the arms. "How are your paintings for the gallery showing coming along?"

"Okay, I guess."

Arlo's eyes shifted to Luca, then back to me. "My Eva had her first solo show at the Blackwell Gallery. This could be the start of a brilliant career for you. I hope you're ready for all the attention you'll receive."

I nodded. "I'm working on a few new pieces that will be ready in time."

Arlo drank from his glass, intimidating me with his hardened gaze. His sons had inherited all of his best and worst features. But for a man his age, Arlo was handsome. Maybe even charming, if you could overlook all the horrible things he'd done to keep his power.

"You have a lot to profit from a sold-out show at Blackwell," Arlo commented.

"Art has nothing to do with money."

His lips curled upward. "So much like my Eva. She didn't care about the money."

"No respectable artist does this for the money. Once money gets involved, it sucks the fun from a creative outlet."

"If Eva were alive, she would have been proud to call you her daughter-in-law," Arlo said, his deep voice as smooth as silk. "You have accomplished a lot in a short time."

My mouth fell open from his confession. It was the nicest thing he'd ever said to me.

"I wish I could have met her," I admitted. "I would have loved to paint with her."

"You have a similar style, a mixture of Eva and Jean Metzinger."

"My mother hates Metzinger," I told him. "She also hates cubism and Art Deco. And I hate her. So, naturally, I loved Metzinger, Picasso, and similar artists. And through their work, I found Evangeline."

"Your mother hated Eva, too."

My mother had often voiced her hatred of Evangeline's paintings. She pitched a fit when my grandfather had sent Queen of Nothing to me for my seventeenth birthday, the year before he brought me to Devil's Creek.

I nodded. "One night, when I was sleeping, my mom took a knife to Queen of Nothing, ripped the canvas to shreds. I loved that painting, and she ruined it."

Arlo smirked as if he understood why my mother chose that painting to deface. "Eva painted it for your mother. Your mother and Eva were always in competition."

My mother was a child painting with Crayola watercolors compared to Evangeline Franco. She had no vision, style, or taste. Her work was flat and lifeless with zero emotion —like her.

"My mother was the queen of nothing?"

He nodded, and I burst into a fit of laughter. I'd always wondered why my mom was so mad that she destroyed it.

I smiled. "I made her pay for that."

Outraged, I'd raced into my mother's studio, a converted garage not attached to the main house. I dumped all of her oils on the floor and lit a match, savoring every second as I watched her work burn. After years of abuse, it was the least she deserved.

Arlo flashed a rare smile. "Your grandfather had to pull many strings to make your little stunt disappear."

"I only have one regret."

He cocked his head at me. "And what is that?"

"I should have burned down the studio with her inside."

His gaze traveled over to his sons, who had been quiet, listening to us as they ate their salads. They all gave me pleased looks. I hid my inner crazy behind pretty dresses and fake smiles. But in some ways, I was just like them.

Arlo's dark eyes flared with excitement. "All in due time, Alexandrea."

What the hell does that mean?

"You have a lot more in common with Eva than you think," Arlo confirmed with a somber expression. "She had a lot of fire. Passion."

"Anger fuels my passion."

"Eva wanted a daughter," Arlo said between bites of his salad. "It was the only thing I couldn't give her."

Why did I feel like he softened me up for the final blow? With Arlo, nothing was ever simple. Like his sons, he was only friendly when he wanted something, and he was never this personal with me.

"Perhaps you will have a daughter with Luca or Marcello. It's time for you to choose," he insisted.

At least now I understood what would happen if I didn't pick them.

You have more power than you think.

I shot a glance at Luca. "Your son only wants to possess me like a toy or a pet. Luca doesn't want a wife. He wants someone to control. And Marcello... I'm not sure what he wants."

Luca's demon eyes burned a hole through me.

"Isn't that right, Luca? You just want a plaything. Not a wife."

"Don't tell me what I want," he snapped. "I don't care if I

have to break your finger to put a ring on it. You're fucking marrying me."

A shiver skated down my arms from his threat. "Here, I didn't think you could get any worse."

He slammed his fist on the table. "Don't start with me, Drea."

"What's the rush to put a ring on my finger?"

"Because it's time for us to get this over with," he growled through gritted teeth. "I'm done playing games with you."

I threw my hand over my heart and made a silly face. "Your declaration of love touches me."

He tipped his head back and laughed like a lunatic, like loving someone was the silliest idea he'd ever heard. "Get real. We don't marry for love."

He wanted to get this wedding over, produce an heir, and wash his hands of me. Our marriage was a business transaction—a deal made by rich pricks behind closed doors.

But I wanted his love and respect. I wanted more than he could offer.

Rage stirred inside me like a potion brewing in a cauldron, my anger about to bubble over. "You want someone to boss around," I fired back. "A wet hole to stick your dick in when you're bored. Not a wife. Count me out."

Bastian laughed. Marcello didn't even breathe beside me. Arlo looked so pissed he might explode. And Damian—that fucking psycho—sat back and picked at an onion roll, popping pieces into his mouth like he was eating popcorn at the movie theater.

Enjoy the show, asshole.

Luca held my gaze, his hand curled into a fist on the table. "If I wanted a whore, I'd fuck one."

"You have plenty of them on retainer. Ask one of them to marry you. I'm sure they would love to act out their *Pretty Woman* fantasy with you."

Luca was no Richard Gere. That was for fucking sure.

I lifted the napkin from my lap and dropped it onto the table before shooting up from my chair. "Thanks for the heart-warming proposal, but I'm pretty fond of my fingers. I need them to paint. So if you'll excuse me, I think we're done here."

The legs of his chair scraped across the marble floor. "Sit down, Drea." His words burned with anger. "You can't run away every time shit gets hard."

He rarely called me Alex. So I wasn't sure if Drea was a term of endearment or another way for him to disrespect me.

"You're the one who taught me to run," I yelled, my cheeks flushed with heat. "I never wanted to leave someplace so badly until I met you."

"You think I'm letting you go?" He crossed his arms over his chest and shook his head. "Nah, baby. You're not going anywhere. Sit your pretty ass in that chair." He pointed his finger, reminding me of my first day at Astor Prep when he forced me to my knees. "And take those fucking paintbrushes out of your hair."

I crossed my arms under my breasts, pushing them out. "Nope."

"Drea," he warned.

I waggled my eyebrows to taunt him. "Come over here and make me."

"Just take them the fuck out."

"Why?"

"Because that's how his mother wore her hair when she was painting," Arlo interjected in a cool, calm tone.

None of the boys ever mentioned their mother. Marcello and Luca used to paint with their mom, from what my grand-father had told me. She wanted them to be more like her and less like their father. But after her death, Arlo forbade the boys to paint or even speak about their mother. He closed the doors to her studio and threw away the key.

I plucked the paintbrushes from my hair and dropped

them onto the table with a sigh. My wild curls spilled down past my shoulders.

"We're about to serve the steak," Arlo told me. "You don't want to miss this cut of filet. I had it delivered for the special occasion."

I took my seat and glanced at Arlo. "I'm done discussing marriage."

He nodded.

Servers set plates in front of us, ending our conversation. I tilted my nose up and drank in the delicious scent of the ten-ounce filet mignon served with a baked potato, fresh asparagus, and a side of Béarnaise sauce. My mouth watered as I lifted my fork and knife from the table and cut into the steak.

No one spoke a word during dinner. And when Luca's phone rang loudly in his pocket, his father scowled because he didn't allow cell phones at his dinner table.

Luca ignored the call, then Marcello's cell phone rang. One after the other, they checked their messages.

"Motherfuckers." Luca crushed the phone in his hand. "I'm going to break their fucking skulls."

Marcello stilled beside me, and his eyes pointed down at the screen. He wasn't the type to blow up, not like Luca. So composed and calm, I could see why Marcello handled the security for Salvatore Global.

I attempted a peek at his phone, and he shoved it under the table, out of my view. What the hell was up with them? Luca handed his phone to his father with an irritated look on his troubled face. Arlo read with clenched teeth.

We shoveled food into our mouths at record speed. Everyone refused dessert, which was a welcome relief because I could not wait to get away from the table.

On my way out of the dining room, Luca grabbed my shoulder, my back hitting the wall as he pressed his chest against mine.

I shook him off. "Don't manhandle me, asshole."

Marcello tapped him on the shoulder. "We have to go."

A dark-haired guard appeared beside Marcello. He was a few inches shorter, dressed in a black suit. A gnarly scar ran down his neck, dipping beneath his dress shirt. He whispered something to Marcello with his body angled away from me.

"What's going on?" I asked Luca.

He stroked my cheek with his fingers. "Nothing you need to worry about, pretty girl. Go upstairs and paint."

"Are you in trouble?"

A sexy smirk lifted from the corner of his top lip. "Are you worried about me, baby girl?"

Was I? Maybe. As much as I hated his ass, I cared about him.

"Where are you going?"

Turning on the charm, he gave me a dreamy look and swiped my hair behind my ear. "Paint something for me."

"Stop manipulating me, Luca."

He grabbed my shoulders, forcing me to look at him. "Just do this for me. Stop asking questions."

Marcello's cell phone beeped. "Luca, we have to go. Now!"

"Fuck," he growled.

They walked down the hallway with Damian and Bastian in tow.

"Miss Wellington," the guard said. "Can you follow me?"

I ignored him, unable to take my eyes off my captors. They stopped at a locked room near the front door. Marcello passed guns to his brothers as if they didn't carry enough weapons.

What the fuck?

Chapter Fourteen

LUCA

My blood boiled as I slid into the passenger seat of Marcello's Maserati. Rage was an emotion I felt often. It both comforted and consumed me.

Alex glared at me throughout dinner each time my cell phone dinged with another message. Someone had hacked into our private servers. Even with the best 256 bits of encryption, the Volkov Bratva had stolen some of our data.

The Devil's Knights were already under attack because of our access to the Battle Industries artificial intelligence software. Everyone in the world wanted to get their hands on the software.

Shit was going downhill fast.

We'd lost members of The Devil's Knights last month. War was coming to Devil's Creek.

It was only a matter of time.

The Knights were the bankers of the criminal underworld. We did business with shady people worldwide, which left a constant target on our backs.

"What's the plan?" Marcello asked as he drove off our property with Bastian and Damian following in the Porsche.

"I don't know yet." I stared out the window, my jaw

clenched. "One thing at a time. Just head toward the marina. We have to offload this shipment before we can worry about the Russians."

I scrolled through the message boards on the Dark Web. Below Alex's picture was a short headline: Virgin Queen of the Knights. We still hadn't told Alex about her role and why she was so important to the survival of our family and the future of The Devil's Knights.

In the comments, men from the depths of hell were demanding they add Alex to the next Il Circo auction. Once a month, The Lucaya Group hosted a traveling auction. They were an international criminal organization and the same people who killed Damian and Bastian's parents.

The Lucaya Group was unknown, untouchable. Even the FBI and CIA didn't have enough intel on them. So we only suspected who ran the group.

You had to place a preliminary bid to receive an invitation to get to the main event. They usually held auctions on a private island or at an old mansion, someplace off the grid.

Marcello blew past the guard at the gate, now entering a subdivision of Devil's Creek called The Hills. "I think we're walking into a trap."

"This isn't our first shipment delay."

Gripping the wheel, he took a hard turn around the bend. "The timing is convenient. We've been fielding threats for the past month. Then the cartel changes their plans, throwing off our deals with the Sicilians. If we don't find Volkov's men soon…"

The Volkov Bratva worked for The Lucaya Group. From what we'd gathered, the leader was an ex-KGB. My father had promised Damian and Bastian revenge.

But how do you find a ghost?

"They're trying to sell Alex on the black fucking market. We better find those motherfuckers before that happens."

He tugged at the ends of his hair, then placed his hand

back on the steering wheel. "It's my fucking fault. I'm the head of security. I knew better than to disable the encryption. It was only for a few seconds. I didn't think..."

"We'll fix it," I assured him.

We had the best hackers at our disposal and would find a way around the auction.

"Alex isn't in danger at our estate. No one can touch her while she's under our roof."

"We need more men," Marcello insisted. "I'll double the guards at the house."

"The Five Families will help." I threw out the idea as a last resort. "They hate the Russians more than we do."

"No," he said without a second thought. "They want too much. We will find another way." Marcello flew down the hill, taking another hard turn, and the scent of the bay floated through the windows. "We can't admit any new Knights until *Legare*. And after what you said to Alex before dinner, she'll never agree to become our queen."

"She'll forgive me."

"What is wrong with you?" Marcello shifted gears and punched the gas. "You think a woman wants to hear that you'll break her finger to put your ring on it?"

"Fuck off. Don't talk to me about Alex."

"Your jealousy is fucking with your head." He sighed. "It makes you irrational. She's not yours, Luca. Alex is ours."

"We're done talking about her." I turned up the radio, and "Bring the Pain" by Method Man cranked through the speakers. "Focus on the shipment."

I bobbed my head to the rap beat, ignoring my brother as the marina came into view.

"No, we're talking about her," he yelled over the music.

"Would it make you feel better if we took her to a safe house? Hmm, little brother?"

He turned off the radio and snarled at me. "Don't fucking patronize me. It will kill you if you don't claim her first, won't it? For as much as you hate her, you want her, too. Just admit it, jerk off."

Avoiding his annoying comments, I flipped through my cell phone and opened the security app on my phone. I scrolled through the cameras in the house and searched for Alex and Roman. She lay on the floor in her bedroom, dressed in silk pajama shorts and a matching tank top.

Alex dipped the tip of her brush into a crimson-colored paint and swirled it across the canvas. Another painting. I loved watching my girl create her masterpieces. She was so talented, a natural artist like my mother.

Roman sat in a chair by the door, watching her with his fingers a few inches from his gun. He was the only person on our security team I trusted as much as Marcello, but I needed to see her. To check on her. Stalk her like I had done from a distance for most of her life.

Alex met us right after her eighteenth birthday. But all four of us had known about her for most of our lives. We'd been waiting years for our queen to take her rightful place beside us. That didn't stop us from hating her, from making her life hell.

Bastian and Damian didn't have any personal grudges against Alex. But Marcello and I had every reason to hate her. It surprised me how quickly my younger brother was thawing out. Alex reminded him of our mother, and he wanted to take care of her.

When we parked at the marina, I didn't see the harbormaster.

We dealt with regular shipments at the marina once a week. Most of the time, they went off without a hitch. But for the past week, I'd had to reroute a few of the shipping containers to accommodate last-minute changes from our business associates.

That was why I kept Alex locked in her room for days. All of us were busy trying to make the logistics work and didn't want the stress of having to watch over her. She also needed a steady dose of her meds to level her ass out.

Win-win.

"Volkov's men won't stop until Alex is dead. They want their pound of flesh, and they will try to take it from her."

My brother parked, then snapped his head at me. "Ever since she's come back to Devil's Creek, you're all fucked up."

"Because we can't lose her." I slid my phone into my pocket and opened the door. "She's too important to our survival. We will lose everything without her."

"If we could admit new members, we'd have more coverage across the country. The longer we delay *Legare*, the worse this will get. The Knights need a queen. So put your fucking pride aside, get on your hands and knees, and beg Alex to marry your miserable ass."

"I got her a solo show at the Blackwell Gallery. Isn't that enough?"

He shook his head, a frown in place. "You know what she wants."

Love. Something I didn't understand. My mother was the last person to tell me she loved me, to show me how much she cared.

How could I ever love a Wellington? Not after what they did to our family. It would be a betrayal to my mother and her memory.

"Stop acting like a dick if you want Alex to marry you. Locking her in a bedroom won't change her mind."

I made a deal with Marcello. When we were kids, I protected him from our father. Every beating and punishment I took in stride.

He owed me for my sacrifice.

Alex is mine.

Chapter Fifteen

ALEX

I drifted in and out of consciousness all night, chasing one dream after another. After a while, they all blended, sweet dreams turning into my worst nightmares.

Heavy footsteps tapped the hardwood floor. I followed the sounds, my pulse pounding in my ears, the blood rushing to my head. The room was pitch black except for the light coming in from the balcony.

As I blinked again, a figure emerged from a dark corner.

"Who's there?"

No answer.

I slid off the bed and ran toward the ensuite bathroom, where I'd left my cell phone on the charger. Before I could close the door and turn on the light, someone pushed me into the room. Stumbling backward, I grabbed the edge of the sink for support.

"Get away from me!"

"No," he breathed against my earlobe.

"Luca?" I looked in the mirror and released a relieved breath. "Why didn't you say anything? You scared the shit out of me."

He clutched my wrist, squeezing so hard pain shot up my arm.

"Stop that!"

He lifted me by the hips, his fingers branding my skin as he slammed my butt down on the counter.

"Say something! What's wrong with you?"

I shoved my palms into his chest, hoping he would fall backward so I could slide off the counter. But he was too big and strong to overpower.

Luca grabbed my shoulder and held me in place, the heat from his body radiating off him. "Drea," he whispered as he pressed his forehead to mine. "I need you, baby."

"Luca, talk to me. What the fuck is going on? What happened?"

In one swift motion, he ripped my panties from my body.

"Luca, talk to me. Why do you look like you're possessed?"

I fisted his dress shirt in my hands and shrieked at the liquid on my skin. A candle flickered on the counter. I'd lit it before I went to bed, so I could find my way to the bathroom if I woke up in the middle of the night. Even in the dark, I knew it was blood.

"You're hurt." I shoved his suit jacket off his shoulders. "Why are you bleeding?"

"It's not my blood," he said with a dead look.

"What did you do?"

"Everything I do is for you." He twirled his finger around a curl and whispered, "My Queen D, I won't let anyone take what's mine."

"What are you talking about?"

"Baby, please." He kissed my lips. "Not tonight."

Luca flipped me over, so my stomach was on the counter, my ass up in the air. He ran his palm over my bare ass and pinned my body to the marble. I squirmed beneath him, and he slapped my ass hard.

"This is your fault, D." He spanked me again, and I yelped

from the sudden pain. "You turn me into a monster. Do you know how many men I have killed for you?"

"Luca, stop being so cryptic. Tell me what's wrong."

He ignored me, and by the fifth time he spanked me, the pain turned to pleasure, each slap sending a rush of adrenaline throughout my body. Liquid heat pooled between my thighs with each whack of his palm.

I liked when he dominated me.

He scared me, and I wasn't sure I could handle him most days, but it felt good when he touched me like this. My whines turned to moans, riding out an orgasm until the bitter end. After he fed his demons, Luca smoothed his palm over my backside to soothe my throbbing skin. I watched as he unbuttoned his shirt and dropped it onto the floor.

Blood streaked his chest.

At least it wasn't his.

He stripped off his belt, and I met his intense gaze in the mirror, daring him to continue.

Luca doubled the belt in his hand and rubbed it along my backside. "You like getting spanked, baby girl?"

"Yes," I choked out.

His hand covered my ass cheek, his fingers rubbing against my slit. "You're so fucking wet." He licked his lips and spread my thighs, staring at my pussy. Luca slid his long finger inside me, grunting as he broke through my inner walls. "Fuck, you're so tight."

After adding another finger, he wrapped his other hand around my throat and squeezed. I craved this side of him: the hunter, the monster, the devil in all of my dirty fantasies. My insides clenched around him as I rocked into his hand. Each wave of pleasure rolled down my arms and legs.

Luca's usual scowl turned into a wicked grin that reminded me of the Joker. My villain. He stared into the mirror, his eyes wild and on fire with desire.

Pain and torture.

That's what got Luca off.

He squeezed my throat hard enough to make me gasp. I slapped his hand away, which earned me a laugh in response. His fingers were still inside me, spreading me open. Fuck, it felt good when his fingers dragged along my inner walls.

He leaned forward, brushing my earlobe with his lips as he tightened his grip on my throat. I knew what he wanted. He was waiting for me to permit him.

"Luca, not like this."

Luca flipped me over and hooked my legs around his back.

"Talk to me. What's wrong?" I shoved my hand through his spiky black hair, forcing him to look at me. "What happened tonight? Whose blood is on your clothes?"

His lips crashed into mine, his tongue aggressively sweeping into my mouth.

He hadn't kissed me in years.

Just that one time.

He stole one kiss after another. The devil I craved claimed me like he needed my last breath to survive. Plagued by whatever he'd done tonight, I let him use me for his twisted purposes, forgetting about our issues for the moment.

I closed my eyes and scraped my nails along his skin. Luca growled as I clawed at his back, biting his lip as we fought a silent war.

Luca looked at me, his eyes even more haunted than usual. "I know you hate me." He sucked my bottom lip into his mouth. "But you have to marry me. It's the only way I can keep you safe."

"Safe from what?"

"Not tonight, baby." He held my hand on the countertop. "That's a conversation for another time. You need your rest."

After Luca attacked me in the bathroom, he kissed me one last time and put me to bed. But, of course, he didn't stay with me. Intimacy was too personal for him.

I rolled over the following day to the sunlight shining through the French doors on my face. It was after eight o'clock. So I quickly showered, dressed, and headed downstairs for breakfast.

On my way to the main dining room, I heard voices.

"You're an idiot," Luca boomed.

He fired back a few more insults before Marcello's voice projected loud enough for me to hear him.

"They will sell her," Marcello said in a stern tone. "We can't afford to sit on our asses. This needs to be done now."

Adrenaline shot through my body, forcing my heart to pump harder, my head spinning from the blood that rushed through my veins.

Was he talking about me?

I leaned closer to the dining room, and my sneaker screeched across the tiled floor. Then, all life inside the dining room ceased.

Shit.

They heard me.

My stomach twisted in knots as I stepped into the dining room. Luca sat at the head of the table with Bastian and Damian at his sides. Marcello was at the other end of the table. He stared down at the newspaper on the table in front of him with a coffee in hand.

"Look who's joining us." Luca smirked. "Did I wear you out, baby girl?"

"Luca," I warned. "Don't start with me before I've had my coffee."

He scanned every inch of me with his cup raised midair, his eyes traveling up and down my body. I wore a pair of black spandex shorts, but he looked at me as if I stood before him naked.

Luca beckoned me with his finger, and I moved toward him like I was under a spell. He dug his fingers into my hip and shoved me onto his lap. "I'm leaving after breakfast." He brushed his lips against mine. "I'm going to New York. I have to deal with something for work. Marcello will stay with you until I get back."

"What about the Franco Foundation gala this weekend? Will you be home in time?"

"Of course." He tugged on my curls and moved my mouth to his. "Where's my goodbye kiss?"

I leaned into Luca, and he grabbed the back of my head, fisting my curls in his hand. His lips crashed against mine, rough and possessive, so hard and fast he sucked the air from my lungs.

Luca released his grip on my hair when our lips separated, his haunting blue eyes laser-focused on me. He rolled his thumb across his bottom lip, a sexy gesture that would have made most women melt.

Luca raised his hand, and the butler appeared at his side. "We'll have a plate of fruit, no pineapple. More toast, fresh butter, and preserves."

A few minutes later, the kitchen staff appeared with fresh fruit plates cut into perfect slices and a stack of toast with all the fixings. My stomach rumbled as they set the food on the table in front of us.

Luca moved the fruit plate in front of him. "I'm hungry."

"So eat."

He stuck out his tongue. "Feed me."

"You have hands."

He tipped his head at the plate. "Start with the grapes."

I snarled at him. "I want to poke your eyes out with a knife and shove them down your throat."

Annoyed, I lifted a bushel of grapes in my hand, knowing he would only become more of a thorn in my side if I fought him. It was breakfast. I could pop a few grapes into his mouth and send his miserable ass on his way.

Luca buttered a piece of toast. I plucked a grape from the vine and pinched it between my fingers. He opened his mouth, licking my skin as I dropped the grape onto his tongue. His touch sent a bolt of electricity up my arm.

I continued the charade until Luca licked my fingers clean. Then, he hooked his arm around my back. As I reached for the plate of eggs, my shirt rode up my stomach. Luca slipped his hand beneath the fabric.

I knocked his hand away.

Luca moved the plates toward the center of the table, sending silverware crashing to the floor. He raised his hand to dismiss a servant who attempted to clean up after him. The man exited the room in a hurry.

Clutching my hips, Luca lifted me and dropped me onto the table in front of him. He spread my thighs apart with his hands. The chair scraped the tiled floor as he moved between my legs.

"Luca, what are you doing?"

Ignoring my question, he pushed me down on the table until I was flat on my back. My chest heaved with a mixture of fear and desire. He yanked my shorts down and kissed my inner thigh, up to my throbbing core. His eyes met mine as he breathed over top of my lace panties.

"Luca," I moaned. "This is so inappropriate."

He released a wicked laugh. "I'll tell you what's appropriate, Queen D."

I rolled my head to the side and caught Damian and Bastian staring at me. Bastian licked his lips, heat flickering in his gray eyes. Damian bit down on his fist like he wasn't sure if he could control himself. Marcello looked like he wasn't breathing behind the coffee mug in front of his mouth.

I attempted to sit up, and Luca pushed me back down. "Are you mine, Drea?"

"No."

Luca inched my panties down as his brothers watched us. He slid two fingers inside me, and I gasped from the sudden pressure. "You can pretend I disgust you, but we both know you're always wet for me." Luca thrust harder. I cried out as his fingers rubbed my inner walls. "Even when you can't stand the sight of me, your pussy craves me."

Luca held me down on the table and sucked my clit into his mouth. My legs trembled as he ate my pussy like I was his meal. I squirmed, and he tightened his grip, devouring me like a starved man. I should have pushed him away, but it felt too good to make him stop.

Damian rested his elbows on the table. His suit jacket slid up his forearms, revealing sleeves of tattoos as he leaned forward. "Spread your legs wider, Pet," he growled with an evil look. "Let us see you."

"She has a pretty pussy," Bastian commented.

Marcello grunted in agreement.

"She tastes good, too," Bastian told him.

Damian leaned forward to grab my thigh, pulling my legs apart so he could get a better look at Luca's tongue sliding between my wet folds. He pinched my nipple over the fabric of my thin tank top, tugging so hard I whimpered.

"You gonna come for us, Pet?"

A wave of heat spread down my arms and went straight to my toes. "Oh, fuck." My eyes slammed shut, and a hiss escaped my lips. "Mmm… I'm going to come."

All eyes were on me.

They looked like predators focused on their prey, waiting to go in for the kill. A wave of excitement shot down my arms as my cheeks heated with warmth, which spread down my chest.

Gripping Luca's dark, spiky hair, I leaned back on my elbows and watched him work his magic between my thighs. He'd never touched me like this. Not even once after all these years. Something changed inside him last night. Like a switch flipped in his brain, and now he was all-in with me.

It was confusing as fuck.

I felt like I had whiplash from all the mind games and misdirections. Whenever I got closer to any of them, they always pushed me away.

"Luca," I moaned, rocking my hips to get more of his tongue, on the verge of an earth-shattering orgasm.

As if my words snapped him back to reality, he stopped licking my pussy. He looked at me with those dark blue eyes that gutted me every time. His breath on my wet, sensitive skin made my toes curl, and I wanted to scream from all the pressure building within, only for him to deny me an orgasm.

I kicked his chest with my sneaker. "Asshole, I was about to come. Why did you stop?"

He cupped my sex like a savage. "You better remember this belongs to me while I'm gone. Mine, you got that?" He shot up from the chair, his cock so hard it looked like it was about to poke a hole through his pants.

I fixed my panties and slid off the table to grab my shorts from the floor. "Why are you acting like a caveman?"

After pulling up my shorts, he wrapped his fingers around my neck. He didn't squeeze as hard as he did last night. But it was still enough pressure to make me gasp as he kissed me like he wanted to consume me.

Our lips separated after a heated battle of wills, our tongues warring against the other.

Luca lowered me into his chair, holding my back against his chest. "Fuck, baby girl. You taste good."

I elbowed him in the chest and scowled. "I hate you for not letting me come."

He snaked his arm around me and smiled against my cheek. "I want you to think about me for the rest of the day. Think about how much you want me to finish the job when I get back."

"I'll just ask one of your brothers," I said to piss him off.

His eyes darted across the table at each of them as if he were issuing a silent warning.

The butler popped his head into the room and cleared his throat. "Mr. Salvatore, Ms. Laveau is here to see you."

My jaw nearly hit the table. "As in Madeline Laveau?"

The famous painter, art restorer, and one of my idols.

"I have to go," Luca said with a bite to his tone, setting me into the chair beside his. "I don't want to be late for my appointment with the new director of the Franco Foundation."

My heart sank to my stomach like an anchor hitting the ocean floor. If Madeline Laveau was the new director, I didn't get the job.

That fucking bastard.

I should have known all the affection and attention was to distract me. Another trick. A tactic. He rarely touched me, and he always left me hanging when he did.

As Luca walked into the hallway, I wanted to use his head for target practice. He made me believe I had the job at the foundation. Was anything real with Luca, or was it all a lie?

Sell her dreams.

Give her nightmares.

That was the Salvatore way.

Chapter Sixteen

ALEX

After Luca exited the dining room, Marcello moved beside me. He drank his coffee in silence so he didn't interrupt his brothers.

Damian was on a conference call with someone from another country. He spoke an unfamiliar language while Bastian sat on his right and took notes. They each owned half of Atlantic Airlines and ran the company together.

Marcello chugged the last of his coffee, then offered me his hand. "I want to show you something. I think you'll like it."

He led me through the house until we were standing on the veranda at the back of the estate.

"I'm going to show you something only the Salvatores know about," he said as we veered toward the center of the property.

"So it's a secret?"

"Don't even think about attempting this on your own. It's dangerous."

"Danger is my middle name," I joked.

Marcello shook his head and steered me past the helipad and the Olympic size pool, yanking on my hand as we passed the staff living quarters. Their backyard—if you could call it that—was the size of a city block.

Men with guns lined the perimeter, making it clear I would never leave here on my own. So I was a prisoner in this castle for the foreseeable future.

We stopped in front of what looked like an indestructible metal shed. My eyebrows knitted together as he lifted a panel on the wall, revealing a digital scanner. He held his right palm against the glass that flashed green as it confirmed his identity.

Inside, it didn't look like much—steel walls with monitors, a long desk on one side of the room that had at least a dozen more screens. I moved toward them, staring in disbelief at the live video footage.

"What is this place?" I asked, bewildered by all the secret spy shit. "Do you watch me from here?"

He shrugged, unaffected by my last question. "It's where I work when I'm home."

At least now I knew for sure there was a camera in my bedroom. There was footage of all the founders' mansions, including Wellington Manor. At least twenty feeds, some of which were of my apartment in Brooklyn.

A chill rolled down my spine as if someone had thrown a bucket of ice water on my head. I looked up at Marcello. "How long have you been watching me?"

He rubbed a hand across his chin and glanced at the monitors. "Years."

"Why?"

I was afraid of the answer but needed to know the truth.

"Because we have a lot of enemies. You don't want to know how many times we've come close to losing you."

"Why would anyone want to hurt me?"

Marcello turned to face me, staring at me with those beautiful but sad blue eyes. "Because the future Queen of The Devil's Knights holds a lot of power in our world. Men who are not used to taking orders from women will answer to you. They will fight for you, die for you, be whatever you need. We are all at your beck and call. It's our duty to serve you."

"So my grandfather wasn't making that up?"

He shook his head. "We need you, Alex. Our lives are in danger. There are certain rules, a code every Knight must follow. Even in times of war, we can't break the rules."

"Then why have all of you been assholes to me for years?" I threw my hands onto my hips and held his gaze. "You guys could have been nicer if I'm so important to you."

He let his eyes lower to the ground and sighed. "Have I ever hurt you?"

"Not physically. But you've hurt me in other ways."

"It was never my intention." He tucked a loose curl behind my ear and rubbed the pad of his thumb across my cheek. "I'm not like my brothers. I don't take pleasure out of other people's suffering."

"I know. But you locked me in my room for days."

"I did that for you, Alex."

He stared at my mouth and wet his lips. For a moment, I thought he would kiss me. Not once had he ever tried, and I'd always wondered how he would taste.

Marcello pulled away as if this was too much intimacy for him, dropping his hand to his side.

He dropped to his knees in front of a steel door built into the floor. I watched as he turned the wheel on top of the door, spinning it with a groan.

"Stand back," he said before the door crashed to the ground a few inches from my sneakers.

I poked my head inside the hole, surprised to find a metal ladder attached to the wall. "Who are you people? This is like something from a James Bond movie."

Marcello chuckled. "My family is full of surprises."

"I bet this house has tons of secret passages."

He winked to confirm my assumption but offered no additional information. Then, he said, with his arm extended, "After you."

"No way! For all I know, there are snakes and alligators down there. And I hate the dark."

"Alex, it's just stairs. Do you think I would take you down here if I thought you would get hurt?"

Would he? The jury was still deliberating on that one.

He noticed my hesitation and jumped to his feet, brushing off his pants. "I'll be a few rungs below you. If you fall, I'll catch you."

I glanced down at the ladder and cleared my throat. "Um... I don't know about this. I hate heights and dark spaces. How deep does this tunnel go?"

He pointed his finger into the cave of wonders. I couldn't bring myself to look again, too freaked out about being buried alive in the dark.

"It's only a twenty-foot drop," he said like it was nothing, and I rolled my eyes at his use of the word only. "Then it's about a two-minute walk to the beach."

"Do we have to do this in the dark?"

"It's time to get over your fear." He rubbed circles over my shoulder blade, giving me one of his tempting smirks. "How about we start now?"

I bit my lip to stop it from quivering. "I don't know."

Marcello pulled me into his arms, stroking his long fingers down my back. "You're the most important woman in my life. I won't let anyone hurt you, princess."

"I'm trusting you, Marcello. That's not something I often do."

He grabbed my hand and kissed the top of it. "You can trust me with your life. Now let's go."

Marcello climbed into the mysterious hole. When he was a quarter of the way down, I wiped my sweaty palms down the front of my shorts.

"You got this," Marcello said from below, his deep voice

reminding me I wasn't alone. "I'm right below you. Just take a few steps."

Following Marcello's voice, I moved down the ladder with caution. This reminded me of an episode of Lost. The one where the survivors of Oceanic Flight 815 found the underground bunker with the countdown timer.

Every moment with the Salvatores felt like a ticking clock. Like I was seconds away from losing myself.

Marcello hooked his arm around me and lifted me off the ladder when I was close to the bottom. A proud smile pulled at the corners of his mouth. "You did good, princess. But, see, it's all in your head. You can do anything if you put your mind to it."

My smile mirrored his. "That was terrifying, but I'm glad you pushed me to do it."

He moved his hands to my backside, pressing my chest against his. "The rest of the way is a piece of cake."

As his delicious citrus scent washed over me, I thought about kissing him. I wanted to claim him for myself. My heart raced abnormally fast, thumping in my chest like a drum. I clutched his thick bicep to steady myself, still slightly shaky from my nerves and the climb. He must have sensed my desire because he stepped back, his hands falling away from my body.

Marcello wanted me.

But he was loyal to Luca.

He tipped his head. "Let's go."

We strolled into the dark passage, and goosebumps dotted my flesh. My nose turned up at the earthy scent mixed with the saltiness of the sea. I covered my nose and mouth, sneezing several times.

Stupid allergies.

"We're almost there," Marcello said after the fifth time I sneezed.

I couldn't wait to get the hell out of there. Between the

darkness and my allergies, I was seriously regretting this trip. But at least I was leaving the estate. Until now, I had felt like a prisoner.

The Salvatores didn't share their secrets with anyone. Marcello was trusting me. I just had to play the game and make him think I'd accepted my fate.

The passage dumped us out at the far end of the beach, closer to Wellington Manor. I could see my grandfather's estate looming above us. Founders Way only had five houses on the entire block. The Salvatore estate was at the dead center and reminded me of a medieval castle, complete with towers and parapets with armed guards.

Wellington Manor was to my left. An old mansion that looked like a Southern plantation. Then there was the Cormac Compound on my right. A stone monstrosity that looked like something from Coastal Living.

Made primarily of glass, the Battle Fortress looked like Tony Stark's Razor Point mansion in the Iron Man movies. At the far end of the street, Fort Marshall stood at the edge of the cliff. Everyone called it that because the Marshalls were an old money military family.

"Tell me something, Marcello. I've known you for years, yet I know more about your mother than all of you combined."

He sipped from a water bottle, eyes on the water. "My mom wasn't like us."

"Obviously." I chuckled. "She seemed so full of life, carefree."

"She wasn't like that all the time," he said in a hushed tone, his expression darkening. "Some months, she would fall into such a deep depression we couldn't get her out of bed. My father would beg her to get up. He'd try almost anything to get her back to normal, but even he couldn't help her. We learned how to ride out the waves of her moods."

"Did she need to be hospitalized?"

"Sometimes," he admitted. "Your grandfather was a huge help. He treated her privately and prescribed all of her medications under an alias so that no one could link them back to her."

"Why was her illness a secret? Plenty of artists struggle with mental health issues."

"She wanted to maintain her legacy without people thinking she was like van Gogh."

I laughed. "She wouldn't have cut off her ear."

"Some days, I didn't know if she was coming or going. She was unpredictable." He glanced down at me. "Kinda like you."

"I didn't know," I whispered. "No one ever told me any of this."

"We wanted you to believe my mother was perfect. You admire her so much. Knowing the truth would have ruined the image of your idol." Marcello's gaze lowered to my lips. "My dad says any woman worth chasing is a little crazy. I think he's right."

"People with mental illnesses don't like being called crazy."

"How about passionate?" He smirked. "Everyone has a weakness. My mother didn't want the world to know about hers."

"What's yours?"

Marcello stared at the water. "Feeling out of control."

"Like Luca."

"That's not Luca's weakness. He thrives in chaos. Luca gains control from feeling out of control."

"Then what would you say is his weakness?"

"You."

Laughter spilled out of me. "If you say so, Marcello."

We walked for another hour in near silence, only exchanging a few words occasionally. Neither of us needed to fill the void, which was nice. I enjoyed being with Marcello, allowing the energy between us to charge my mood.

When we reached the spot, Marcello clutched my shoulder and turned me, so we were facing his estate. The sky was a faint blue, still a little dark in some places.

"Beautiful," I whispered.

He cupped my shoulders with his strong hands and rested his chin on my head. "I thought you might like this."

A sudden calm washed over me as I relaxed in his arms, consumed by the high this man provided me. For years, I thought he was just like Luca. But Marcello Salvatore was full of surprises. Sure, he had a darkness inside him. We all did. Beneath his chiseled exterior was more than a man capable of violence and cruelty.

"Marcello, I need to know something."

His body tensed against mine as if he was anticipating this question.

"Is my brother okay?"

I felt him slowly slipping away from me, physically and emotionally. What we shared a moment ago almost seemed like a distant memory as his hands fell from my body, leaving me desperate for his touch.

"Why do you ask?"

"I haven't heard from Aiden since we left Brooklyn. Something is wrong."

His fingers dug into my hip, and he spun me around. "I'm sure he's fine."

"Can you check your spy cams? I saw the one for my apartment."

He nodded. "I'll look into it." His words said one thing, but I could see that he was hiding something from me in his eyes. "Are you ready to head back? You need to try on your dress for the Franco Foundation gala this weekend."

Chapter Seventeen

LUCA

I sat on the throne at the front of the ritual room in The Devil's Knights temple. The local Knights gathered before me, with Aiden Wellington at the group's center. Dirty and exhausted, he could barely open his eyes as he shoved his long, blond curls off his forehead.

His sister came with us willingly. That was part of the deal. Once Alex was ours, Aiden belonged to the Knights.

This was his future.

He'd just begun his initiation into The Devil's Knights and wouldn't be the same man Alex knew at the end of the six months. Aiden Wellington no longer existed. I was a bastard for keeping them apart, but we had rules all Knights had to follow.

Like me, most Knights joined us after they turned eighteen, right before the start of their first year of college. A six-month process similar to pledging a fraternity. Except you could only speak to the men within our organization.

We couldn't admit new members outside of the initiation phase, which was a pain in the ass because we needed to rebuild our ranks after losing men in various battles over the past few months. The Lucaya Group and the Russians had infiltrated some of our cells. And without crowning Alex our queen, we couldn't replace the men we'd lost.

Aiden was the only exception.

I'd endured challenging tasks with the men in this room, bonding experiences that not only indebted us to the Knights but also brought us closer. Marcello followed in my footsteps two years later. He went through the arduous process with his best friend, Sonny Cormac. Luckily for me, I was initiated with Damian and Bastian. We weren't brothers by blood, but they were as much a Salvatore as me. Forged by bloodshed and violence, we were now weapons capable of disposing of our enemies.

Aiden wasn't the pussy I once thought. He also had a particular skill set. I discovered his hidden talent when he sought a local gang called The Serpents. Of course, he didn't know that we controlled The Serpents. They worked for us. Even their name came from the serpent on the Salvatore crest.

"Your sister is in danger," I told Aiden. "She will be listed at the next Il Circo auction."

As part of his initiation, Aiden would spend one month with a different group of Knights throughout the country. He was at their beck and call, performing whatever duties they required. Aiden was only here until the end of the month, long enough for him to watch Alex's gallery opening from a distance.

Aiden scratched at the stubble on his jaw, his eyes downcast. "Where is Alex right now? Is she okay?"

I nodded. "Physically, yes."

Aiden stepped closer to the dais. "And mentally? You know she can't survive six months without me."

"She's fine," I assured him. "Your sister is much stronger than you think."

"Alex has a mental illness, Salvatore. She may seem okay now, but what will happen to her once she doesn't hear from me? You can't keep my initiation from her. It will kill her." His nostrils flared. "And if anything happens to my sister, I'm coming for you."

Marcello had the same concerns. He knew firsthand that people with severe PTSD could flip the switch. Years of pain and suffering at her mother's hands had fucked up Alex.

With all the shit I'd endured from my father, I had my issues.

No feelings.

A black heart.

I didn't have flashbacks or triggers, but I had moments of pure rage. No doctor could fix me. Even if they could, I wouldn't want to be normal.

My anger was a weapon.

Aiden stuffed his hands into his pockets, surveying me with suspicion. He was right not to trust me. Salvatores did anything to achieve their goals by any means necessary.

Aiden was a necessary evil.

Marrying Alex was another.

Aiden shifted his weight from one foot to the other, biting the inside of his cheek. "How is Alex handling our separation?"

"Not well," Marcello admitted. "She wakes up screaming your name at night."

Aiden scrubbed a hand across his face and sighed. "Six more months," he groaned. "She won't last until then. You don't understand what losing me will do to her. My sister needs me."

He was right. All the men standing at my sides knew this to be true. But we had rules we couldn't break—not even for our future queen.

"We're at war," I told him. "The Volkovs tried to grab Alex. So far, they have been unsuccessful. But they're ramping up their efforts, finding new friends among our allies."

He rubbed his tired eyes. "How can I help?"

"Sonny and Drake will explain on your way to New York. Try not to get yourself killed."

He lowered his head, keeping his opinions to himself. When we kidnapped him from Brooklyn, he made smart-ass comments. Now that he understood the structure of our organization and the role his sister would play, he was more compliant.

Aiden had orders to follow.

After Aiden left the room with the rest of the Knights, I looked at Bastian, Damian, and Marcello. "Go get Alex. It's time to prepare our queen."

Marcello gave me a weary look. "How far are you going to take this?"

With our enemies getting closer, we had little time. The Knights needed a queen. I needed Alex to marry me so that I could become the Grand Master.

I'd been patient for too long.

"As far as we need to go."

Chapter Eighteen

ALEX

R ough fingers slid down my thighs as I drifted in and out of consciousness. A man cradled me against his hard chest with his hand on the back of my head. I couldn't find the strength to move as he carried me down a flight of stairs.

The man laid me on a soft bench, and leather mixed with the saltiness of the sea filled my nostrils. Someone sat beside me and brushed my hair off my face.

"Close your eyes," he whispered.

We moved forward, and the man placed his hand on my back. His feather-light touch sent a shiver down my arm. I rested my head on his thigh as he tried to coax me back to sleep.

What felt like a few minutes passed before the car stopped. A door opened, and I heard water splashing from a distance. He carried me in his muscular arms, headed toward the water. Fear rocked through my body, sending a ripple of nervous energy down my arms.

Several pairs of shoes tapped the cement behind us. Instead of heading toward the dock, we took a set of stairs that tunneled underground. We stopped at the bottom of the encasement.

"Where are you taking me?"

No answer.

The sound of heavy footsteps filled the silence that hung in the air between us like smoke. We halted in front of a brick wall. A man wearing a black cloak with the hood pulled over his head removed a brick from the center of the wall, revealing a hidden lock. He slipped his hand into his pocket, produced a skeleton key dangling from a silky red string, and slid it into the lock.

"Where am I?" I attempted to roll onto my back to look up at the man cradling me, but as I moved, he tightened his grip, smashing my face against his hard chest. "This is some Skull and Bones meets Harry Potter shit," I muttered. "Are the Death Eaters on the other side of this wall?"

A man laughed behind me.

I struggled to break free from the man restraining me, but it was no use. The harder I fought him, the more he tightened his death grip.

As the man in front of us removed the key from the secret lock, another person stepped to his side and helped him push the wall inward, revealing a private entrance hidden beneath the town.

"What the fuck is this place?"

Dead silence.

We stepped into a cramped passage that smelled like mildew, salt, and earth. No one even breathed as we rounded a corner, then another.

I tilted my head to the side to look at the stone walls with iron lanterns built into them, the dim light casting a soft glow. Symbols on the walls looked like markings in a Masonic temple.

Except these were scary.

Skulls with knives driven into the bone. Knight helmets with blank faces and the eyes of a demon. A knight in full armor was holding the Scales of Justice. The weight was unbalanced, dipping to one side with a giant serpent holding it down, slithering up the arm of the knight.

A few minutes passed before the man in front of us opened a door. We stepped into a massive room with a high ceiling that seemed impossible this far underground.

My captor set me down, and I staggered to the side, forcing me to grab his arm before I fell to the hard floor. He moved behind me and grabbed my hair. Straight ahead, two thrones sat atop a dais. A man dressed in a long black cloak sat on one of the thrones, a hood covering his face.

I blinked a few times to clear the sleep from my eyes. Men in black cloaks hid under their hoods. The man before me rose from the throne, tall and imposing, with his cloak fanning out around his ankles.

I stared up at him, but the hood covered his eyes. He stepped off the dais and moved in front of me. The man behind me forced my head down, holding my hair.

"What do you want from me?" I asked, my voice sounding distant.

Two more robed men surrounded us, creating a circle to trap me inside. My breath caught in my throat. I could hardly function with my heart hammering out of my chest, on the verge of a panic attack.

Were these men going to kill me?

Rape me?

Torture me?

I had no fucking clue.

"You brought me here," I muttered. "What do you want? What is this place?"

No one spoke.

Was this all a dream?

Wake up, Alex.

I dug my fingernails into my forearm, clawing at my skin to help me wake up.

This had to be a dream.

A new version of hell.

I raked my fingernails up and down my vein, trying to free myself from this prison. "Wake up, wake up," I whispered, repeating the same motion.

Why wasn't it working?

Not real.

Not real.

Wake up, dammit.

Black wingtips stopped in front of me. A man grabbed my wrist, his fingers digging into my flesh with force. I slapped his hand, and he released me, taking a step back.

I looked at each of the hooded men. There was a gold knight's helmet with crossed swords over the left breast of their robes.

That's when it hit me.

I was with The Devil's Knights. This was their Billionaire Bat Cave.

I shoved my palms into who I assumed was Luca's chest, and he stood there, allowing me to pound my fists. But not for long. He wrapped his long fingers around my wrists and squeezed.

"What do you want from me?"

The room was so quiet I could hear myself breathing.

"Why am I here?"

No answer.

He turned on his heels, and the men parted for him. Luca sat on his throne, the hood still in place. I moved toward the dais. "What the fuck is your deal?"

More silence.

Fueled by my rage, I shouted, "Explain why you brought me here in the middle of the night." I smacked his chest. "Say something, you sick motherfucker. Do you want to play games? Bring it, asshole. I'm so fucking ready to play."

Luca leaned forward, his elbows resting on his thighs, the hood covering his face. "You know why you're here."

"No, I don't."

I scanned the room, wondering what they did with the altar. These sick assholes probably performed satanic rituals and made offerings to their gilded gods.

Luca glared at me, studying me with curiosity. Though he should have been more concerned that I would claw his eyeballs out with my fingers and feed them to him. I was sick of him and his stupid mindfuckery.

"Look, Luca, I'm tired. And I'm not in the mood to play beer pong with your frat bros. So we can keep doing this dance, or you can let me go."

One man snickered. Maybe he wanted to play beer pong with me. I almost laughed at the ridiculous thought.

What the hell did they do down here?

Jerk each other off.

Fuck women.

Worship the Devil.

Who knew?

I wasn't sticking around to find out.

Luca's gaze met mine, and a shiver rolled down my spine. My dark prince was terrifying on a typical day, but tonight, he looked possessed. "It's time to accept your place with The Devil's Knights."

"I never agreed to join your secret society, Luca."

He smirked. "You never had a choice, baby girl."

"Because you never gave me one."

He pointed his finger at the back of the room. "Go! If you want to leave, we won't stop you."

Without a second glance, I spun around and hopped off the dais. Marcello blocked my path with his chest. His head was down, but I knew his scent. Why did they even bother with this arcane bullshit?

It was fucking stupid.

I stepped around Marcello, and he didn't stop me this

time. Before I left the room, I glanced over my shoulder. All eyes were on me, but only Luca's face was visible.

I took one last look.

Luca was so damn beautiful my heart ached when our eyes met. His upper lip twitched as if he were about to explode at any second. The rage was always present, brewing at the surface. He did his best to contain it, but I knew him well.

I ran from the room so fast that my bare feet ached as they scraped the rough stone. I stopped at the end of the dark hallway, feeling like they were closing in on me. Hand over my heart, I blew out a deep breath and tried to control my rapid pulse.

Why would they bring me down here? What the fuck were they thinking?

I had to get out of there.

Away from these psychos.

I walked in circles, taking one turn after another, my head spinning with each turn. Where was the exit? They opened the secret door by removing a brick from the wall.

But which one?

They all looked the same. I spun in circles, trying to retrace my steps. Panic bubbled up inside my chest, the dark walls suffocating me.

It was too dark.

Too cramped.

Too damn cold.

Sinking to the floor, I leaned against the wall and took a few deep breaths, reminding myself to calm down. I needed to find a way out of this creepy ass cult hideout. Luca knew I would not get far. That had to be why he let me go without having me followed. He did nothing without a plan.

Get up.

Keep going.

I pushed myself up from the ground. Every bone and muscle in my body ached as I walked down the long hallway. The ceiling and walls felt like they were closing in on me. I could hear my heartbeat in my ears, my pulse pounding out of my skin.

I swayed from side to side and pressed my hand to the cold, rough wall for support. A chill rolled through the dense passage, the scent of moss filling my nostrils.

As I rounded another corner, I stopped dead in my tracks. Four men with hoods hiding their faces stood in front of the double doors. They were about a hundred feet away, their gazes locked on me.

The one at the center, who I assumed was Luca, beckoned me with his index finger.

I shook my head.

My heart raced as he approached me. The narrow passage blurred before my eyes, and now there were two of him. I slumped to the side and grabbed the wall so I didn't crumple to the ground.

Fuck panic attacks.

Just breathe, Alex.

Breathe.

"When will you learn?" Luca said in his usual cold tone. "You can't escape fate, baby girl."

My fingers slid down the wall, and as my feet slipped from under me, I saw Luca's pretty blue eyes.

Then I lost consciousness.

Chapter Nineteen

MARCELLO

A lex was the one person who linked all of us. She was the answer to our current problems, the queen who would balance the power scales in our corrupt organization. But unfortunately, our queen could never go with the flow. She had to fight against the current and refused to follow orders.

In silence, we stood in front of the altar, a moment of acknowledgment passing between us. I knew all of my brother's secrets, and they knew mine. There were no barriers between us.

Except for one.

I wanted to marry Alex.

But I had made a promise to Luca when we were teenagers, an unbreakable vow. Back then, I didn't know what he was asking of me. Knowing Luca, he knew when he would ask for that favor. My brother did nothing without a plan.

He had taken most of the abuse from our father. He shielded me from the violence as much as he could. He even jumped in front of me and let our father whip him, cut him, whatever Dad needed to satiate his dark desires. And even though it killed him, he had to relinquish some of his control to The Devil's Knights.

She was their queen, too.

Alex rolled onto her back on the ceremonial altar and groaned. Her chest heaved with each deep breath she took, then her eyes opened. She stared up at the ceiling with her hand over her heart.

Luca and I moved closer to the altar. Our sudden movements turned her attention to us. Her eyes widened as she scanned our faces, then her gaze swept over the room.

She shot up from the table. Without a bra on, her nipples poked through the thin fabric of her pajama top, her big tits bouncing. I loved her tits. When we first met her, she was skinny and malnourished. Now, she had curves for days and a thick ass I wanted to slap.

My dick strained against my pants.

Fuck, I wanted to devour her.

We'd all agreed we would share her, but it was different with Alex. She could marry any Salvatore, but we would lose our birthrights if she didn't choose either Luca or me.

We would lose everything.

Bastian and Damian would never allow that to happen. So they constantly pushed her out of her comfort zone and made her feel like a toy.

A pet.

I wanted to throw my hat into the ring, but Luca would win the game. And the stupid deal I'd made... I didn't have a choice but to let him have her. It was only a piece of paper. Nothing more than a merger of our families.

She would still be a Salvatore.

"What the fuck is wrong with you?" Alex's top lip quivered. "Why did you bring me here?"

Luca placed his hand on her thigh. "You need to learn more about the Knights."

She scanned the room with suspicion. "What is this creepy-ass place? It's freezing down here. Couldn't you have asked me to come with you in the daytime? When I wasn't fucking sleeping."

"We don't allow outsiders to see the entrance to our temple," Luca told her, trailing his fingers down her thigh.

Only the town's founders and the Knights knew about the underground tunnels beneath Devil's Creek. The catacombs connected each of the founders' houses to the temple and The Founders Club. Alex would have spent hours chasing her tail if we hadn't come to rescue her. By the time she passed out in Luca's arms, she had looked like she'd gone mad from spinning in circles.

She wiped the sweat from her brows, breathing heavily. "What the fuck is going on, Luca? You said I could leave."

He clutched her thighs, moving between them, his fingers sliding up her smooth skin. "It's okay, baby. I got you."

"What do you want from me?"

"You."

My brother was slowly coming around. After I yelled at him on our way to the marina, he took my advice about Alex. Maybe it was because we walked into an ambush and were lucky to leave with our lives. Or perhaps it was the fact we had a ticking clock dangling over our heads.

Our time was almost up.

She grabbed Luca's hand, slid it up her leg, and stopped right at the seam of her shorts. He continued his slow exploration of her beautiful body, shoving her shorts and panties to the side so I could see her pretty pussy.

Fuck.

She was perfect.

I could see her juices glistening on her wet slit, even in the dim light. She could hate us all she wanted, but she was always wet for us.

"You want Marcello to touch you, baby girl?" Luca whispered the words, his lips inches from hers. "How about Bash? Damian?"

Alex studied his face as if she thought Luca was baiting her into a trap. Then she looked at me like she wanted to lick every inch of my skin. A look I returned with even more intensity.

I would tear her apart if I had her first. Years of wanting to fuck her had turned me into a fucking animal.

Alex glanced over at Bastian and Damian. Her tongue rolled across her bottom lip as she surveyed their faces. They looked like savages, ready to attack. She leaned back, resting her palms on the altar, and spread her legs wider. Her chest rose and fell as she sucked in shallow breaths.

Without speaking, she communicated she wanted this. I'd never had a problem sharing women with my brothers. They were all disposable.

But Alex was special.

My blood felt like it was boiling beneath the surface, my skin so hot I felt like I was on fire. Alex was beautiful, her body pure fucking perfection. I loved her curves, every single one.

We just stared at her like four wild animals on the hunt. She didn't even bat an eyelash. There wasn't an ounce of fear on her face.

As she stripped off her shorts and panties, Alex held my gaze. Luca tugged on her right thigh and Bastian on the other. They spread her legs wider so Damian and I could see her pussy. I stood there, knowing I had to watch, waiting not so patiently for my turn with our queen.

A moan escaped her lips as Luca dragged his finger along her slit, and her eyes slammed shut. Bastian moved his hand beneath her chin and rubbed his thumb across her bottom lip.

She wet her lips.

Alex stripped off her pajama shirt, baring her beautiful body to us. Damian made a hissing sound now that all her curves were on display.

I'd never been so fucking turned on, seeing Alex wild and

out of control, finally accepting her place. She'd fought us for years. And now she wanted it.

She wanted the power.

My cock was so hard I couldn't even think straight. She knew this was dirty and sick, but she wanted us anyway because she was dirty and sick like us.

Bastian inched his hand up her thigh, apprehensive at first as if he were waiting for her permission. In this room, the queen made the rules. Soon, she would choose us at *Legare*. Then, we would complete the ceremony that would crown Alex our queen.

She locked eyes with Luca and leaned back on her palms, giving us the perfect view of her pussy. Alex looked good enough to eat. And I wanted to do just that.

Bastian and Luca's hands were too big. So they had to divide and conquer, Luca taking the lead, plunging two fingers into her soaking wet pussy. Alex cried out, her legs trembling as Luca stretched her out.

I forced myself to watch what he was doing to her, seeing how much she enjoyed my brother making her come. Bastian rolled his thumb over her clit and kissed her sexy lips as he worked her inner walls.

She opened up for him, and her tongue swept across his bottom lip. Bastian pulled her mouth to his, crushing her lips with a kiss. My heart pounded so fast that it felt like it was about to punch a hole in my chest.

Alex made me feel alive.

Made me feel out of control.

She brought chaos to my life.

Out of breath, Alex stole her lips from Bastian's. Her eyes darted down to their hands between her legs, both of them spreading her wider. She panted so hard that her tits bounced with each thrust of their fingers.

"You like this, Cherry?" Bastian growled. "Do you like it when my brothers watch?"

Alex nodded, her body trembling as Luca switched between pinching and rubbing her clit.

"Feel good?" Luca added another finger, slamming into her. "You want us to make you cum again, baby girl?"

"Yes." She rocked her hips to shove Luca's fingers farther inside her. "Harder."

"Do you want my brothers to join?" Luca clutched her chin and then licked the length of her neck. "Hmm? Do you want all four of us?"

"Not yet," she whimpered. "I want Marcello and Damian to watch."

Damian groaned beside me. I felt his pain. My cock throbbed, desperate to be inside her tight virgin pussy.

Only one of us could claim her.

We still couldn't agree on who would strip Alex of her innocence. Luca, that greedy motherfucker, wanted her virginity, firstborn child, and the right to call our queen his wife.

Not fucking happening.

If he wanted to be the Grand Master of The Devil's Knights, he had to give up something. Marrying Alex would give him what our father had trained him for since birth.

Bastian wanted her cherry.

I wanted to knock her up.

Not surprisingly, Damian wanted something sick and twisted from Alex. It involved blood and shit that would turn her stomach.

Bastian dipped his head down, sucked Alex's nipple into his mouth, and tugged on it with his teeth. She moaned, tracing the pad of her thumb over the hard bud as our eyes met. Then, she looked at my brothers as they wrecked her from the inside out.

Luca swatted her hand away and grabbed her tit. He massaged her for a second, but not gently. Fucking her with his fingers, he twisted her nipple, stealing a scream from her lips.

"More," she moaned.

"So demanding, woman," Bastian taunted with the click of his tongue. "Our sweet little virgin isn't so sweet anymore."

Withdrawing his fingers, Luca added a third and slammed back into her pussy. "She's never been sweet. Isn't that right, baby girl?"

She bobbed her head and moaned. "If I was sweet, do you think I would let four devils steal my soul?"

Luca's wicked laughter pierced the air.

"We're taking more than your soul, Cherry." Bastian thrust into her harder than the last time. "Every part of you belongs to us."

She dragged her teeth across her bottom lip. "Mark me, Bash."

He fucked her pussy up, slamming his fingers beside Luca's so hard she screamed. "Wait until I put my cock inside this pretty pussy. You'll never forget who owns you."

"I'm gonna come," she whined, holding my brother's shoulders for support.

Alex wanted it hard and rough. She was in luck because that was our specialty.

"Jesus," Damian muttered as he grabbed his cock over his robe. He looked over at me. "We need to take her to The Mansion. Break her in so we can play with her."

I nodded in agreement.

We had plans for Alex and her virginity.

As my brothers tag-teamed Alex, they fell into a familiar routine, as if they could anticipate each other's next move. Thrusting her hips into Luca's hand, Alex licked her bottom lip and milked his fingers. I'd never seen her so in her element. Our girl was fucking beautiful on her worst days and a goddamn goddess as she chased her high.

She tilted her head toward the ceiling as her orgasm peaked. "Luca," she muttered, and then, "Marcello." My cock jerked, wanting to say hello to her pretty mouth as she whimpered, "Oh, my God. Bash... Damian... I'm coming."

"That's it, Cherry." Bastian moved his free hand to the back of her head and forced her to look at me. "Come for us."

"Squeeze my fingers, pretty girl." Luca dipped his head down and bit her lip. "Scream for us."

Breathing hard, she looked into his eyes and moaned each of our names. She looked so fucking wild and beautiful, possessed by the orgasm spilling out of her in violent waves. One moan after the other ripped from her throat. Alex muttered our names again, repeating them until her body stopped trembling.

"Fuck," Luca grunted.

Alex studied my brothers as they licked her juices from their fingers. Our little sinner wrapped her fingers around their wrists and glided her tongue over the wet fingers they had inside her.

"Damn, Cherry," Bastian groaned. "I can't wait until my cock is dripping with your cum."

Luca tucked her blonde curls behind her ear and brushed his thumb across her cheek. I watched this rare show of affection from my brother. I'd never seen him like this with anyone.

We'd never even hugged, not once in our lives. All four of us were here because Alex had the power to bring us together.

"Get dressed," Luca said before he sucked her bottom lip into his mouth. "We're done playing for tonight."

Chapter Twenty

ALEX

O n the Franco Foundation gala night, I wore a red strapless gown that cost more than my car. The Salvatores had spared no expense for their captive. They wanted everyone to think they were taking good care of me. To show me off to their wealthy friends.

As I entered the great hall, a tall blond approached me. He was lean but muscular, dressed in a black tuxedo. Shane "Sonny" Cormac IV was Marcello's best friend and the oldest son of a shipping tycoon. And he wasn't afraid to tell you about his family's billions.

Sonny's gaze moved up and down the length of my body. "Look at you." He shook his head. "You are fuck-hot and don't even know it."

"Still a charmer, I see."

He bent down to my height, a smirk tugging at his mouth. "I own the biggest yacht in the marina. Take a ride with me next weekend."

I laughed. "Does that pickup line work on girls?"

Sonny winked. "Wait until you see my yacht."

"So, where's your date?"

He sipped from the highball glass, scanning the crowded

room. "Currently unattached. I wouldn't want to give my parents the wrong idea by bringing a woman to a social event."

"Afraid of commitment?"

His eyes found mine. "Haven't met the right woman."

"Your parents don't meddle in your love life?"

"We're Irish," he said as if that explained everything.

Bastian and Damian entered the room from the private entrance wearing tuxedos. My heart raced at the sight of them. They looked like dark, scary versions of James Bond as they approached Luca.

Luca looked like a king, flanked by Bastian and Damian, leaning against the wall as if his shoulders were holding up the damn thing. The Salvatore men were beautiful.

Bastian's dark brown hair was messy as if he'd rolled out of bed and somehow still looked hot. He scrolled through his cell phone with a smug expression on his gorgeous face.

None of them ever smiled.

Damian's shirt was untucked, a few buttons open, revealing the dark tattoos on his chest. A gold silk tie hung loosely around his neck. From across the ballroom, I could see Damian's chest rise and fall when he locked eyes with me. He looked like he wanted to know everything that made me tick. Like he wanted to throw me over his shoulder and drag me upstairs.

I spotted Pops across the room. He wore a tuxedo and styled white hair to hide his receding hairline. Blair drank champagne at his side, chatting with her friends. The cold bitch stood ramrod straight like she had a pole shoved up her ass.

"I think it's time you meet your new subjects," Sonny said.

I raised an eyebrow at him. "Subjects?"

"Someday, you'll be the Queen of The Devil's Knights, making you a powerful woman."

"I'm not interested in power."

Sonny offered me his arm, and I latched onto him as we moved throughout the ballroom. "The sign of a true queen."

"I hate politics," I groaned. "And all the bullshit in this town."

"If you want out, there are ways to leave Devil's Creek… if you know the right people."

"And you're the right person?"

He gave me one of his golden boy smiles and winked. "I have my ways." Sonny swiped two champagne glasses from a server's tray, handing one to me. "You look like you could use another drink."

"Do you read minds?"

"I read faces," he countered. "Don't worry. This will all be over soon. Just smile and look interested. Everyone is watching you."

I looked around the room and found Luca staring at me. He sat beside his father at the front of the room on a chair that looked like a throne. The chairs had high backs with intricate symbols carved into the wood. An S with a snake wrapped around it.

Luca rested his elbow on the arm and spoke to his father, who gave him a curt nod. Then, his terrifying gaze swept over the room and landed on me.

Were they talking about me?

Sonny moved his hand to my back and sipped from his glass. "Rule number one, Little Wellington. Never let them see you sweat."

"I'm not sweating."

"You look like you're about to crawl out of your skin."

I looked up at him, inspecting his handsome face. "What's your secret? You're too happy to be a founder's son."

He shrugged. "Lots of alcohol, loose women, and the feel of the open sea on my face."

"How did you get the nickname Sonny?"

"Because of my last name. Mac is Irish for son. My father

is Shane Cormac III. I'm the fourth." He rolled his eyes as if it annoyed him to share the same name as his relatives. "Since my family owns Mac Corp, my uncle thought he was funny and started calling me Sonny Mac. It was already getting too hard to tell all the Shanes apart. So the rest of my family started calling me Sonny, and the name stuck."

Luca appeared at my side as if he'd materialized out of thin air. His cold, hard stare rocked me to the core, settling deep in my bones.

He extended his hand. "Dance with me."

I took Luca's hand, and he hooked my arms around his neck. His hard body felt incredible against mine, which I tried to ignore as his fingers jabbed my hipbone. We moved to the song's beat, acting like a couple. Like he wasn't holding me in his death grip with a forced smile for our audience.

"You've spent most of your night with Sonny," he said midway through the song. "Do you prefer his company over mine?"

"It wasn't intentional. You were busy with your family."

"You are my queen." His breath ghosted my lips, so close we could have kissed. "It's time we make it official."

"If you want a wife and a queen, you better treat me like one."

"That mouth of yours," he growled, his voice deep and smooth.

Licking my lips, I stared up at my handsome prince. "Maybe you should do something about my mouth."

Luca smirked, then rolled his thumb across my bottom lip, smearing my lipstick. "Perhaps I should."

After years of fighting with him, I knew he would only respect a woman who made him work for it. He was one hundred percent alpha male. Intimidating and scary in every way, his cock got hard for mouthy women.

He stroked my cheek with his fingers, staring at me as if

we were the only people at the party. "Come to my room tonight for a drink."

"No."

His eyebrows rose in surprise. "You don't say no to me."

"No, sir." I chuckled. "Is that better?"

Luca shook his head at my defiance. He dipped his head down, his lips soft and warm against mine. "It's time for the big announcement."

"What are you talking about?"

He pressed his lips to my forehead, then slipped from my grasp. "After tonight, your life will forever change."

Chapter Twenty-One

LUCA

S onny led Alex by the hand through the great hall. He showed her to everyone in town like she was a prize he had won. She laughed and smiled, covering her mouth with her hand every time Sonny cracked a joke.

In a perfect world, she would marry a guy like Sonny. He had more freedom and control over his life. She could spend months on his yacht, sailing across the Atlantic Ocean.

But she was a Wellington.

And she was mine.

I moved to my father's vacant chair at the front of the ballroom and tapped Marcello's arm. "What are you and Cormac up to?"

He rolled his eyes. "Nothing."

"Bullshit," I snapped. "If either of you fuck with my plans, I'll slit your throats and paint the town with your blood."

"I'd like to see you try, brother."

Marcello was a trained killer, skilled with weapons and hand-to-hand combat. No one sane would mess with him. But sense had left my crazy ass a long time ago.

My younger brother led a team called Alpha Command at Salvatore Global. They were a group of mercenaries and thieves our clients employed for their illegal businesses. On the books, they handled security for my family's company.

I watched Alex with Sonny. She flicked her curls over her shoulder and laughed. He held our queen close, keeping her safe from the other monsters lurking in the ballroom. The Devil's Knights would die for Alex. We would do anything to protect her from our enemies.

"We need to escalate our plans," I told Marcello. "What we've tried so far isn't working."

"What do you have in mind?"

"She thinks Wellington is innocent. Her precious Pops plays his role so well." I shook my head, disgusted. "Look at him."

Our gazes shifted to the dance floor, where Carl led his granddaughter away from Sonny. They engaged in a heated conversation as he spun an upset-looking Alex in circles. Angry scowl in place, her lips moved as if she were arguing with him. Carl bent down to whisper in her ear, and then her dark expression changed to her usual sunny demeanor. A master strategist, Carl knew how to play the game.

I raised a glass of scotch to my lips. "She thinks she's doing him a favor. Wait until she finds out why he brought her here."

An evil grin turned up the corners of his mouth.

"Any updates on the next shipment? The Basiles called last night. They want to add to their usual order."

"I'm still waiting for confirmation."

I leaned into him and lowered my voice. "We need her compliant. If Alex tries to run again, throw her ass in the shipping container. That would give her a good scare, don't you think?"

He scanned the room for Alex. "She'll behave. I'm making headway with her. Give me more time. Alex will learn to trust me."

"We locked her in her bedroom for days. She's biding her time until she can run again."

"I think she learned her lesson the first time."

But did she?

The orgasms we'd given her in the temple weren't enough for her to stay. But after the announcement tonight, she would never want to leave. It would change the game for her, for all of us.

Marcello's phone rang with a new message. He read it, committing the cipher to memory, then held the screen in front of me. It was the date and the coordinates of our next shipment.

We partnered with Mac Corp and Battle Industries to provide weapons and illegal technology to our business partners. They were sniffing too close. And with the Bratva's attention aimed at Alex, we needed all the friends we could get.

Marcello deleted the message and shoved the phone into his pocket. "How many containers are we adding to the usual shipment?"

"Four more to accommodate the Basiles. Coordinate the shipments with Sonny."

"You wouldn't put her in a container, would you?" Marcello's eyes narrowed as he looked at me. "Because we could lose her forever. She's afraid of the dark and confined spaces. You saw how she reacted in the catacombs."

I waved my hand to dismiss his concern.

"I'm managing her PTSD," he said in a fiery tone. "But something that traumatic could trigger the wrong response. I've seen what happens with soldiers. We don't have time to play games, Luca. She needs to marry one of us before we fuck her up even more."

"I have the situation under control. She'll be kissing my feet after Dad makes the announcement."

A smile tipped up the corners of his mouth. "Alex deserves this. Admit it, you smug bastard."

I nodded in agreement.

His cell phone rang with a new message. Marcello studied

it with his teeth gritted, his other hand balled into a fist on the table. "Fuck."

"What now?"

"Someone attacked the men at our safe house in Beacon Bay." He rose from the chair. "I have to go."

"No." I threw my arm out in front of him. "Send Roman and his team."

"But," he protested. "This is my job."

"Not tonight. If you leave, Alex will wonder where you went."

Marcello's fingers moved across the keypad of his phone. "Done."

"They're getting closer." I stood beside him. "It's only a matter of time before they come for her, Marcello."

He stuffed his hands into his pockets and sighed. "The Founders Society will deal with the Bratva. After we complete *Legare* with Alex, everything will go back to normal."

I almost laughed at his suggestion. "Normal? Like we know what that means."

"The Charter forbids us to admit new Knights until after *Legare*. So we have to speed up the process."

His gaze shifted to the right side of the ballroom to The Serpent Society. Hades leaned against the wall, a drink in hand as he spoke to Morpheus. Charon was on his right, chatting with a pretty brunette dressed in a pink gown. Tall and imposing, Lethe loomed over the girls attached to his arms.

They all used nicknames associated with the Greek Underworld. Hades, the God of Death. Morpheus, the God of Sleep. Lethe, the River of Forgetfulness. Charon, the ferryman of the underworld.

They lived up to their names.

The Serpents would do anything we asked of them. Unlike other secret societies, they operated under a different set of rules. But at least they were under our control.

I tapped Marcello's shoulder, eyes on the men across the

room. "Talk to Hades. We'll need The Serpents' help hacking the Il Circo website."

He bobbed his head. "Anything else?"

"Bring Alex to my bedroom after the party."

Marcello's eyebrows rose.

"Don't worry, brother." I squeezed his shoulder. "You'll get your turn with our queen."

Chapter Twenty-Two

ALEX

People whispered my name, rumors spreading across the ballroom like smoke in the wind. Everyone knew my backstory—every detail of my life. Whenever our gazes met, they offered fake smiles.

"That's Alexandrea Wellington," a blonde woman said.

"She's beautiful," another woman commented. "But I heard she's crazy like her mother."

My cheeks flushed with heat.

"She'll probably run like her mother," a red-haired woman said about me, flicking her long locks over her shoulder. "The Salvatore men can't keep the Wellington women around long enough to produce an heir."

A pretty blonde in her late forties tipped her head back and laughed. "If she's anything like her mother, she won't last until the wedding day."

I craned my ear to listen, but the loud orchestra music drowned out their voices. Men gawked at me while women studied me with curiosity and disdain. Someone tapped a microphone. Everyone in the room turned toward the stage, where Arlo stood in front of a podium.

"On behalf of the Franco Foundation, I would like to

thank you for coming tonight," he said, projecting his deep voice throughout the ballroom. "Your support of the arts has kept my late wife's legacy thriving for fifteen years. Tonight, I've asked all of you here to announce the new director of the Franco Foundation. Please help me welcome world-renowned painter and fresco restorer Madeline Laveau."

A round of applause swept across the crowded room as a short, middle-aged woman with cropped brown hair climbed the stairs. She wore an elegant black gown that brushed her ankles. Glowing brighter than the sun, she took the microphone from Arlo.

Madeline was one of my idols.

She'd risen to notoriety around the same time as Evangeline Franco. They were both experienced painters who were also skilled with frescoes. I'd wanted to learn the techniques and would have given anything to study under a woman like Madeline.

After Madeline gave a short speech, the crowd clapped again. Then she raised the microphone to her mouth once more. "I was very close with Evangeline Franco. She was an esteemed colleague and a dear friend. She used to say that a true artist can capture the very essence of a person with the swipe of their brush. Anyone who can expose a person's flaws and see into the depths of their soul will forever be a legend in the viewer's mind. There's no doubt Eva was a legend."

More applause filled the room. Then Madeline smiled as her eyes shifted to me. "For my first order of business as the director of the Franco Foundation, I would like to welcome our newest artist to the team. Someone who captures the spirit of Evangeline Franco in each of her paintings. Alexandrea Wellington, would you please join me on stage?"

My jaw nearly hit the floor.

She said my name.

My name.

Oh. My. God.

I snapped my head to the right as my eyes filled with tears, knowing I would find all four Salvatore boys staring at me. They clapped with proud smiles on their handsome faces, even Damian, who usually looked like he wanted to murder me.

Luca had made it seem like I wasn't qualified to recreate his mother's paintings. I thought his hiring of Madeline meant I was out of the running.

I forced myself to move forward, my body on autopilot as I climbed the stairs and shook Madeline's hand. None of this felt real. Like I was outside of my body watching myself perform the motions.

I didn't have a speech planned. Thankfully, I didn't have to give one. My heart pounded as I stared out at the crowd. The overhead lights heated my skin, the brightness blinding me.

"The Salvatores have a real eye for talent," Madeline said into the microphone. "Just like Eva and me, Alex is a graduate of the Rhode Island School of Design. She's a rising star, known for her devil-inspired paintings. The moment I saw her work, I thought of Eva. She would have been thrilled to let her future daughter-in-law recreate her notable works for the fifteenth-anniversary celebration at the end of this year."

Daughter-in-law? Who did she think I was marrying? Luca probably fed her lies, so I would look like a fool if I married anyone but him.

In awe of this moment, I stood straight, unable to move, barely able to think. My heart pounded so loudly I wondered if Madeline could hear it trying to climb out of my chest. I kept my eyes on Luca and his brothers, attempting to steady my breathing. This wasn't the life I had envisioned for myself. But maybe the Salvatore brothers weren't so bad.

After Madeline said her final words, we spoke offstage, promising to meet next month to discuss my new job. It was too good to be true. Everything was finally falling into place.

Perfect timing.

My deviant boys were desperate for me to choose, to get me down the aisle. Luca would have done just about anything to win the game. My virginity, my hand in marriage.

I lost sight of the Salvatores.

They were in the ballroom one minute and gone the next. It was hard to see through the sea of people. Though, I could always find my devils.

Where the hell did they go?

I spotted a tall man with blond curly hair on my way to the bar. He wore a black suit, his back to me. Either I was losing my mind, or my brother was here in Devil's Creek.

Aiden.

I pushed my way toward the ballroom entrance. The man slipped out of the room and ventured down a long tiled hallway. Everyone from van Gogh to Metzinger donned the walls.

I followed the man as he ascended the long staircase to the second, then the third floor. He was too quick, moving with a purpose. Walking as fast as my feet would allow, I rushed upstairs and searched for him.

Where did he go?

Am I hallucinating?

Midway down the hallway, a flash of light seeped out from one bedroom. The double doors were open, wide enough to see a tall, muscular man rip off his suit jacket. He had black hair and tanned skin. With his back to me, I couldn't tell if it was Luca or Marcello. They were only eighteen months apart, but they looked like they could be twins.

He stripped off his shirt and dropped the white oxford on the floor with a silk tie. My mouth fell open as I stared in disbelief at dozens of scars on his back. Then, a gasp ripped from my throat, and he spun around.

Luca Salvatore was possibly the most gorgeous creature I had ever seen in my life. He grabbed the shirt from the floor and slipped it on, his muscular stomach equally scarred.

Luca flung open the door and pulled me inside with a snarl. "What did you see?"

"Nothing."

"Bullshit." His mouth twisted in disgust. "Why are you up here? Are you spying on me?"

Luca slammed the door, caging me inside his bedroom. He pushed me onto his bed, and his eyes traveled over the front of my dress before settling on my face.

"No, I'm not a spy. I was looking for someone."

He stood between my legs and clutched my chin, tilting my head back until our eyes met. "Who?"

"My brother."

Luca's eyes narrowed. "Your brother isn't here, Drea."

"I know what my brother looks like."

"You must have imagined him. It wouldn't be the first time."

I snarled at his rude comment. "Ten minutes ago, I liked you. Now, not so much."

"Shame," he taunted.

"I haven't been able to get a hold of Aiden. His number is disconnected. He hasn't tried to call me. It's been two weeks."

"I'm sure he's fine."

His thumb grazed my bottom lip, and my pulse raced as the scent of the sea and sandalwood invaded my senses. He smelled so good that I wanted to lick his skin and taste the cocky asshole who held me captive.

"Are you afraid of me?"

"No, you won't hurt me."

He raised an eyebrow and smirked. "What makes you so certain?"

I bit my lip to stop it from trembling, and his face contorted into something sinister. His eyes lowered to my mouth, and he gave me a seductive look like he wanted to take my lip between his teeth.

"Use your words," Luca demanded. "Answer me, or I'll have to punish you for being a bad girl."

"I'm not a bad girl," I shot back with fire behind my words.

His eyes flickered with desire. "No? Because I think there's a little devil hidden beneath your beautiful exterior." His long fingers inched down my arm, flames scorching my skin. "And I think she wants to come out and play."

I cleared my throat, ignoring his last statement. "I know when someone wants to hurt me. You won't hurt me, Luca." I shoved his hand away from my face. "So cut the shit and let me go."

Unfortunately, I had learned this lesson the hard way. Most of the people in my life had tried to hurt me over the years. Because of them, I wasn't a delicate girl who handed out her trust to anyone.

I could spot a snake a mile away, and I knew Luca did not want to cause me physical harm despite his intimidation tactics. But what he was doing to my emotion and my body.

Well, that was another story.

A moment of silence passed between us. Luca inspected me like he was peeling back my skin, looking beneath each layer. Like it wouldn't satisfy him until he discovered my darkest secrets. But I could tell even my worst ones wouldn't compare to what he was hiding.

He couldn't fool me. I'd known enough evil people to see right through him.

Luca was rotten to the core and didn't give a shit what anyone thought about him. He wanted people to see the ugliness inside him. I knew from firsthand experience it was easier to push someone away before they got too close than to let them into my life, only to end up disappointed.

"What happened to your back?"

He turned away from me, his eyes on the balcony to our left. "You don't want to know."

A warm breeze blew in through the French doors, leading to a large patio overlooking the bay. My fingers itched at the chance to sketch every detail of his face with my charcoals.

"Art tells the truth, even when people lie," I said to quote his mother.

Luca's head snapped to me, and heat rushed down my arms. I couldn't tell if he wanted to kiss me or kill me.

"You don't have to hide from me, Luca."

Standing painfully still, he clenched his fist, and his jaw tightened.

I shot up from the bed, now standing in front of him. Feeling brave, I slid the dress shirt over his strong shoulders. "Let me see you."

I wasn't talking about the scars on his back. I wanted to know what made Luca Salvatore tick. What were his hopes and dreams, his strengths and his weaknesses? I wondered why my heart beat differently when I looked into his eyes, why I felt connected to him in ways I could not explain.

"I see you too," he said. "You know what it's like to hide the truth."

I nodded. "I won't hurt you, Luca."

Madness danced across his blue eyes. "Maybe I want you to."

He turned his head to the side, unable to meet my gaze, and the fabric bunched around his muscular biceps. Then he shook the shirt off, letting it fall to the floor. I smoothed my fingers over his marred skin.

My parents never laid a hand on me, but I had endured years of neglect in my version of Hell. Aiden was the reason I made it through those painful times. So who did Luca turn to? His brothers were not the comforting types.

I stifled my gasp, the sight of his scars up close heartbreaking. My mind drifted to someone hitting him with the buckle of a belt until his skin cracked open—someone slashing into his flesh with knives. A few were from cigar burns.

I closed my eyes and cringed, wondering how he had survived years of torture. He flinched and hissed when I placed my hand on his lower back. The worst scar ripped a tear from my eye, wetting his skin.

Luca groaned, then pulled away.

"I'm sorry. I didn't mean to…"

He spun around, studying me with a strange expression on his face, and then swiped his thumb beneath my eye. "Don't cry for me, baby girl. I don't deserve your tears."

Luca buttoned his shirt, staring down at me as if he were deciding what to do with me. Then he grabbed my wrist and yanked so hard I tripped. My cheek smashed into his hard chest.

He opened the door and led me into the hallway, squeezing my fingers as we descended the stairs to the second floor.

"Where are you taking me?" I slapped his arm, desperate to get away from him. "Let me go, Luca."

He grinned like a maniac. "It's a surprise."

Chapter Twenty-Three

ALEX

L uca tugged on my hand and picked up his pace. My feet hurt from walking so fast, but he wouldn't slow down until we stood in front of the elaborate French doors at the end of the long hallway.

"This is my mother's studio," he said with his eyes on the doors. "No one has been inside for years." He snapped his head at me. "I thought you'd like to see it. You'll need to understand her better to recreate her paintings."

He opened the door. My jaw dropped as we walked into a massive room with a domed ceiling, hand-painted by the legend herself. Dozens of emotions poured out of me as I spun in circles, studying every detail of Evangeline Franco's masterpiece.

"Wow," I whispered. "I'm speechless."

"My mother had that effect on many people."

"She did this by herself? It must have taken her years."

He nodded. "She started after Marcello was born and finished a few months before her death."

"That's some serious dedication."

I stopped in front of Evangeline's self-portrait and stared at her in awe. She was gorgeous, with flawless skin and long black hair that looked like fine silk draped over her shoulder. Her sons had inherited her big sapphire eyes and long, black eyelashes.

"How did she capture the detail so well in her face?" I mumbled without meaning to speak aloud.

"My mother sat in front of the mirror." He pointed to the exact spot in the room's corner. "She memorized every detail of her face before her brush moved across the canvas." He smiled at the painting. "She wore a simple but elegant black Chanel dress and her favorite Mikimoto pearls. The entire time she laughed and smiled, cracking jokes about how vain she must look painting herself."

I chuckled. "She was an amazing woman."

"Everyone loved and adored her," he said as his eyes met mine. "Even people who didn't know her."

Luca moved to the next canvas on the wall.

"I have this painting," I told him. "It was the first Evangeline Franco piece I owned. Pops surprised me with it."

"My mom painted a second edition for Carl. They were good friends."

I raised a curious eyebrow. "They were?"

He nodded. "My mother hated your grandmother, but she was close to Carl. She had a lot of pain in her joints from painting. He prescribed her medications to help. She also suffered from migraines from breathing in the fumes."

We stared at the canvas splashed with reds, yellows, blues, and greens. I could make out the shape of a face, but I couldn't tell if they were male or female. Her style was a mixture of Cubism and Art Deco, the two I also favored. Evangeline titled it *The Truth About Liars*, my favorite piece in her collection.

Luca pointed at a long bench next to an easel covered with a tarp. "I sat there when she painted it. She was so mad that day, even though she tried to hide it. I helped her choose the paint for her palate, and then she started flinging her brush at the canvas."

"I'm sure there was more skill than throwing paint."

He shook his head. "I'd never seen her like that. She was so angry with my father over something. They fought a lot in the last few years before her death. I thought she'd lost her mind when she started screaming, 'I will always tell the truth even when you lie.' I think she was talking to my dad."

"Some of the best art comes from pain. That's when the muse takes over."

Luca studied my face, and then his eyes slowly drifted down to my lips. "Congratulations. You earned this position, Drea. The board of the Franco Foundation unanimously agreed you are the most qualified."

"And you? Did you give me this job to make me change my mind about you?"

He shook his head. "No. I would never let someone who wasn't talented imitate my mother's art. You'll start at the foundation after your exhibition at the end of the month."

"Thank you," I whispered, even though I hated having to thank Luca for anything.

Moving toward the center of the room, I glanced up at the ceiling, taking in every detail. My heart thumped in my chest as I absorbed her sad story. The hidden meaning behind her work was heartbreaking.

"This is incredible," I whispered, still in disbelief at her fresco skills. "Your mother's story is so vivid."

He narrowed his eyes at me. "What story?"

"You don't see it?" He shook his head, and my eyes filled with more tears. "When did your father adopt Bastian and Damian?"

"Six months before my mom died."

"That makes sense. When they came into your lives, things got messy." I stared up at the ceiling, unable to meet his gaze. "I studied Christian Lit because I wanted to better understand artists like da Vinci and Michelangelo. Christian artists use numbers and symbols in their work that correspond to the Bible."

He cupped my shoulders, holding me at arm's length. "Stop rambling. What are you talking about?"

"I don't have it all figured out." I raised my hand and pointed at the far right corner to the first pendentive. "You can see the start of her journey. Beneath the red and gold geometric shapes, there's an Art Deco woman hidden in the puzzle pieces."

He tilted his head to the side. "How did you see that?"

Because it was how I taught myself to paint. I hid my emotions with the swipe of my brush, so others could interpret my art however they liked. Concealing pieces of yourself in your work took a lot of skill.

"It's easy to miss," I assured him. "Your mom hid her story well. Do you see how she used lines and shapes to make it look like one unified piece?"

Luca nodded, and I motioned to the next set of images. "See the woman holding a baby in her arms in a fancy dress? She looks like the typical Art Deco woman. So does the man wearing a top hat beside her. She's showing her transition from a girl to a woman and from a wife to a mother."

I grabbed his hand, leading the way as we strolled across the tiled floor. "She's older in the next image. And now, she's kissing a baby boy with another one hugging her leg. She starts with who she was before she met your dad. The number one represents creation and the start of her art journey. The number three relates to the divine, like the Trinity. And then she had Marcello, the number four representing the totality of her creations."

"Keep going," he urged.

"Are you sure?" I cocked an eyebrow at him. "You won't like how it ends."

"I'm sure."

I motioned to the next pendentive, where two more boys stood at the man's side. The woman hugged her children and turned away from Arlo and his adoptive sons. She was full of life in the previous images, but now dark storm clouds separated them.

"Your mom wasn't happy about adopting Bastian and Damian. Six is the sign of the devil, a symbol of imperfection. Damian and Bastian disrupted the unity in your family."

He expelled a deep breath of air as he studied the fresco. "My mom spent a lot of time in her studio after my dad adopted them."

"It shows." I tugged on his hand, and we moved across the floor. "See the faces in the broken pieces of the mirror?"

"No."

"Focus, Luca. They look like rectangles, joined to form one piece. But they're shards of glass, and if you close one eye, you'll see the stained glass has the shadow of a man's face."

He craned his neck to get a better look. "Now, I see it."

"Your mother was so talented."

He nodded.

"This is where it gets super dark." I pointed at the most devastating images. "There are seven mirrors. All of them have the same man's face."

"My father?" Luca guessed.

"It's not obvious the man is your dad… but yeah, who else would it be? An outsider would look at this and think nothing." I released a sigh and continued, "There are seven days in a week, seven virtues, and seven—"

"Deadly sins," he finished with a pained expression marking his handsome features. "Keep going."

"Your dad is wearing a crown with ten points." I motioned toward the last piece of the Salvatore puzzle. "Ten horns, like the red dragon, symbolize complete and total power."

"The red dragon?" Luca's voice lowered as he stared up at the ceiling. "As in the devil?"

I cleared my throat. "Yes. William Blake was a poet and artist known for The Great Red Dragon paintings, commissioned to recreate the books of the Bible."

"I'm familiar with his work."

"See how your dad's face is dark on one side, blocking out the light?" I raised my arm above my head to show him. "Your mom placed you and Marcello where the mirrors cast a yellow glow on your faces, illuminating your golden crowns."

I laughed, enjoying the private joke.

"Don't stop now. What's so funny?"

"William Blake said, 'He whose face gives no light, shall never become a star.' I think she wanted someone to know your dad had gained total power and control, but he would never be a star. No one would see him for his achievements, at least not in the way he wanted."

He smiled at his mother's defiance.

She wanted her work to live on long after her death, and I hoped this gave Luca some closure.

"Whatever he did to get that power." I looked at him, unsure of how he would respond. "She was afraid of your dad, wasn't she?"

"Toward the end, yeah. I never let her out of my sight if I could help it."

Blinking the tears from my eyes, I wiped them away with my finger. "I feel the pain in her art. That's what I love about her paintings." I slipped my fingers between Luca's, and his eyes found mine. "When you look at the walls, what do you see?"

He glanced at the framed oil paintings and canvases hung on the walls and shrugged. "I'm guessing not the same thing as you."

I chuckled. "Probably not."

"What do you see?"

My eyes traveled around the room, and my heart dropped to my stomach. "A cage."

I hated telling Luca the truth about his mother. Years of studying her work made it easier for me to weave the threads of her life together. But you had to know her family to make the connections. She married a man she once loved, and he later turned into the devil.

Luca cupped my shoulder with his big hand. "What do you mean by a cage?"

"I mean a literal cage. Do you see the black panels on the walls?" I pointed at each corner of the room. "They connect at the ceiling."

His mouth widened as he followed my finger up to the domed ceiling.

"She felt like a prisoner. You're doing the same thing to me."

"I'm not caging you, baby girl." He brushed his knuckles across my jaw, and the corner of his mouth turned up into a rare smile. "I'm setting you free."

Chapter Twenty-Four

ALEX

After leaving Evangeline's studio, Luca dropped me off at my bedroom. He insisted I change into something more appropriate and then disappeared.

Marcello waited for me in the armchair by the window. A plunge lace teddy, black with pink fringe, dangled from his finger. "Wear this, princess."

"What if I want to choose my clothes?"

He laughed, as if the idea was ridiculous, and held out the lingerie with a bored expression on his handsome face. I took it from him and headed into the bathroom.

Of course, he followed.

With my back to him, I stripped off my clothes. The other night in the Knights' temple, Marcello didn't touch me. But he watched me gain pleasure from his brothers. Did it turn them on to share? It sure as hell seemed like it.

Marcello stared at me in the mirror, his eyes on my breasts as he slid a silky black robe over my shoulders. Nerves shaking through me, I shoved my arms in the holes and tugged on the belt.

Marcello swept my hair off my shoulder, his fingers

brushing my neck. "Luca doesn't like to wait." He steered me toward the door. "Let's go."

We walked down the hall in silence and climbed the stairs to the third floor. Luca had the entire west wing to himself. I poked my head into a few rooms to see what Luca was hiding, but Marcello pulled on my arm, dragging me toward the end of the hall.

We stopped in front of a set of double doors left open a crack. As Marcello knocked, anxiety bubbled in my stomach. I took a deep breath and prepared to be alone with Luca as he opened the door.

Three walls were white except for the one behind his bed, black to match his headboard and heart. I inched my way into the room, with Marcello behind me. Luca sat in an oversized armchair by the window with a glass of scotch in front of his mouth. His blue eyes looked feral as they roamed up and down my thighs.

Marcello left without a word, closing the door behind him.

"Sit on the bed," Luca ordered.

I glanced at the black sheets and gulped down my fear. Luca sipped from his glass, studying me as I sat across from him, leaving no part of my body uncharted. I wiped my sweaty palms on his sheets, hating how nervous he made me.

He downed the last of his scotch and set the glass on the table. "What's under the robe?"

"Come find out."

He rose from the chair and ran a hand through his dark spiky hair. A rush of adrenaline coursed through my body as he loomed over me with a crazed expression on his face.

Luca slid his hand beneath my chin and lifted me from the bed. A ripple of energy shot down my arms as our eyes met.

Luca Salvatore was a hunter.

This side of him scared me, but it also turned me on. I liked the rush—the feel of my blood pumping so fast that I struggled to catch my breath.

Luca shoved the robe off my right shoulder, exposing my bare skin to the chill in the air. My nipples hardened into points as his fingers danced along my skin.

"Are you going to give me trouble?"

I shook my head.

"Good girl."

He pushed me down on the bed. I laid back on the soft sheets, a moan escaping my lips as he yanked my thighs apart and pulled me closer to him. Luca leaned forward to untie the belt at my waist, revealing the lacy lingerie that hid nothing.

His eyes flickered with carnal hunger as they traveled over my breasts, my nipples sore from his careful inspection. He rolled the pad of his thumb over the tiny bud and groaned.

I soaked through the lace, desperate for him to touch me. After years of hating him, I could not deny how much I wanted him. His anger, his rage, I wanted all of it.

He dipped his head down, the heat from his breath racing up my stomach. I shivered from his touch, and a wave of red-hot pleasure spread down my thighs. His mouth hovered over my nipple. I expected him to suck on it through the fabric, but he just breathed on my skin, teasing me.

"Tell me what you want, Drea."

After years of craving his sinful touch, I wanted him to fuck me until I couldn't walk out of his bedroom. So I moved my hand to the back of his head, gripping his hair. A cocky smirk tugged at the right corner of his mouth as my lips brushed his.

"I want you, Luca."

He pinned me to the mattress with his muscular body, his lips crashing into mine with fury. Sweeping my tongue into his mouth, I tightened my grip on his hair and rocked my hips, desperate to create some friction.

He held me down like he wanted to tear me apart, kissing me with every ounce of hatred I felt for him. I was sick for wanting him. Stupid to let my bully touch me again.

With each flick of his skilled tongue, we fought a war with each other. Luca tasted like scotch and poor decisions. He was the devil in disguise, a man who made me sin and never want to stop.

He claimed my body like a new territory he wanted to conquer, fisting my curls between his fingers as he deepened the kiss. His long, hard cock poked my inner thigh. I fought for control, and he gripped both of my wrists, holding them above my head.

Luca lifted the thin strip of lace over my breast and pinched the hard bud between his fingers. He twisted my nipple harder. "Do you want to know what it takes to be my queen?"

"Yes," I moaned.

He ripped the lace straight down the middle, baring my naked body to him. Pinching my other nipple, he yanked so hard I thought he would rip it off. But with the pain came an intense pang of pleasure.

"Fuck, that feels good."

Luca sucked on my nipple, sending a ripple of electricity down my legs. At first, he soothed my pain, but then his soft licks turned into hard tugs with his teeth. With my nipple between his teeth, he stared at me with a wild look.

"Luca," I panted.

He released my nipple, and then his tongue was on my skin, gliding down my stomach. Every inch of my body heated where his tongue touched, and when he stopped right above my pussy, I cupped the back of his head.

"Please, Luca."

"A queen never begs." Luca slid off the bed and rose to his full height. "She takes what she wants."

I sat up, my entire body trembling with anger. "What are you doing, Luca?"

He stepped backward and shook his head. "We're done. Get dressed."

What the fuck?

I glanced down at my ripped lingerie and sighed. Luca made my head fucking spin with all of his mind games. I was an idiot to think I was finally getting somewhere with him.

He typed a quick text message, then poured himself another glass of scotch before dropping into the armchair by the window. The bastard lit a cigar and looked at me from beneath his dark brows. A plume of smoke gathered around his head. He typed messages and pretended I wasn't in the room with him.

Marcello appeared a minute later. He gave me a concerned look and helped me tie the robe around my waist.

Furious with Luca, I marched over to him, stood between his spread thighs, and smacked his cheek. "That's what a queen would do."

Fuck, that hurt.

As I walked away, I shook out my stinging palm.

Luca roared with laughter.

I stormed out of the room with Marcello at my side. Neither of us muttered a single word until we were one floor below and standing in front of my bedroom door.

Marcello grabbed my shoulder. "What was that about?"

I shrugged. "I'm playing the game."

Chapter Twenty-Five

ALEX

The rest of the week wasn't as dramatic, I barely saw the Salvatore brothers. They were busy running their companies, which left me a lot of time to paint. With my show in a few weeks, I needed to prepare. I couldn't mess up my chance, not after they had done so much to help advance my career.

I hadn't had any more bathroom ambushes from Damian. The few times I saw him, he barely looked at me, let alone tried to touch me. Bastian was also distant. He hadn't even called me Cherry during our brief encounters. Marcello was back to his broody, lonely boy routine. And Luca was nowhere to be found.

Are they bored with me already?

After a three-hour painting session, I stripped off my paint-covered overalls and searched for something to wear. I changed into a pair of skinny jeans and a navy blue top. The clothes molded to my body. Even the Valentino pumps were my size. Dressed in thousands of dollars worth of clothing, I felt like a princess.

I checked my hair one last time and headed downstairs to meet Arlo's driver. We had an appointment at Picasso's Playground so that I could get more art supplies. They were closing the store for one hour just for me—one of the many perks of living with the Salvatores.

I strolled down the main hallway, headed toward the entrance of the palatial estate. Loud voices traveled from a distance.

I stopped outside the sitting room and pressed my back against the wall.

"Her brother no longer exists," Arlo said in a deep tone laced with irritation.

"She's asked about him," Marcello said. "I can't lie to her forever."

"None of that matters," Arlo said in a firm tone. "Luca is marrying Alexandrea Wellington to secure our legacy with The Founders Society."

"What if she chooses me?" Marcello asked.

"Then you will bow out gracefully. There will be other opportunities for you." A moment of silence passed over them before Arlo said, "Alexandrea is a distraction Bash and Damian don't need. But I said I would indulge the two of you. I owe you as much after everything you've given up for this family."

What does Arlo owe them?

They spoke for a few more minutes about business, and then their footsteps approached the entryway.

Shit.

I ripped off my heels and bolted down the hallway in the opposite direction. They would have killed me if they knew I overheard their conversation. I stopped at the ballroom. At least from here, I could pretend I had just come downstairs. So I stepped into my heels, composed myself, and then walked toward them with my head held high.

Dressed in dark, tailored suits, the Salvatores were as intimidating as they were handsome, perfect in every way.

Even Arlo was still attractive for his age. It wasn't hard to see where Marcello and Luca got their good looks.

"Where do you think you're going, Cherry?"

"To get art supplies," I told Bastian.

Arlo moved around his sons in a hurry. Marcello winked as he blew past me, attached to his father's side. At least he wasn't ignoring me.

Luca looked at his brothers, avoiding my gaze. "I have a meeting in ten minutes." He walked away, his hand raised in the air and his back facing me. "Call if anything urgent requires my attention."

He was so damn confusing, the most infuriating of the four brothers. His insistence on pushing me away, treating me like shit, only made me want him more. Maybe I was too fucked up, damaged from years of trauma. That was the only explanation for why I felt the way I did about the cruelest prince.

Bastian gripped my bicep. "We'll take you to the store."

"No, that's okay. Your dad's driver is waiting for me."

Bastian dragged me down the corridor by the arm. "We'll make sure you get there safely."

I wasn't so sure about the safe part, but okay. Not like I had a choice. It was nice having a few days without them. But I knew better than to get too comfortable with their absence.

Without further complaint, I followed them outside. Bastian slid into the driver's seat of a blue two-seater Porsche, forcing me to sit on Damian's lap. He hooked his arm around my middle, and his fingers splayed across my torso.

We drove off the property, the windows down and the wind blowing through our hair. I tried to sit up, and Damian increased the strength of his death grip. The psycho pinned me against his hard chest, his cock pressed into my ass. I felt him growing harder for me with each movement.

"Sit still, Pet," he growled against the shell of my ear.

Then he bit my earlobe, tugging on it like an animal. "Before I punish you."

I didn't want another spanking, so I straightened my back and laid on him like a corpse. Bastian glanced over at me, one eyebrow raised, then he cranked the radio. A rap beat blared through the speakers.

The guard opened the gate for us. Bastian floored the gas as we rode into The Hills, a subdivision of Devil's Creek. The cheapest house in The Hills was five million dollars.

Ten minutes later, Bastian parked in front of Picasso's Playground. He turned down the radio and reached across the center console to put his hand on my knee. "Don't think about running."

"You're not staying with me?"

He shook his head. "Got shit to do, Cherry."

"Where are you going?"

"Out," he said in a dismissive tone. I pushed open the car door, and Bastian clutched my wrist. "We have cameras everywhere." He pointed at a black SUV in the corner of the parking lot. "Your security detail is over there. They will drive you home."

Home. It still sounded weird to call the Salvatore Estate anything other than a fancy prison on the sea.

"Got it." I sighed. "No running."

Bastian's fingers dug into my left thigh, marking my skin. "When I get home, you better be in my bed."

I rolled my eyes and shoved his hand away. "I don't want to sleep with you."

A crazy smirk tipped up the corner of his delicious mouth. "Afraid I'll bite, Cherry?"

I was afraid I might like it, but I didn't let my face show my true feelings for him. So I wore my usual mask.

My gaze moved between them. "I'm not sleeping with both of you."

"Just me," Bastian said, his voice deep and modulated. "Damian sleeps alone."

That was a relief.

"Okay," I agreed since Bastian was the lesser of two evils.

"Wear something tight… or nothing at all." He winked. "Your choice, Cherry."

I slid off Damian's lap and rushed into the store before they could request anything else from me.

Chapter Twenty-Six

ALEX

Around eleven o'clock, I heard Bastian and Damian stumble down the hallway. I kept my door open, so I would know when they were back from wherever the fuck they'd been for the past six hours.

"Cherry?" Bastian called out.

I popped my head into the hallway. "I'll be there in a minute."

"Now." He tapped his palm on his thigh. "C'mon, woman. I'm not in the waiting mood. I told you to be in my bed when I got home."

I stepped into the hallway, dressed in silky black shorts and a matching spaghetti strap top without a bra.

Damian appraised my body for a moment and licked his lips. He had streaks of red on his neck and shirt collar. With his sleeves rolled up to his elbows, I glanced at the dark ink on his forearms. I couldn't get a good look at the detail in the designs, but as I moved closer, I saw more blood on his skin.

My mouth widened as I inspected his body. Then I looked at Bastian, not surprised to find he also had blood on his shirt. However, he wasn't as bloody as Damian.

I inched closer to them, naturally gravitating toward Bastian. "Why are you both covered in blood?"

Damian's lips parted as if he were about to speak, and then he disappeared into the room beside mine. He slammed the door, which caused me to jump.

"What's his problem?"

"Ignore him." Bastian waved off my concern. "He gets cranky when he doesn't get his way."

"You didn't answer my question."

"Don't ask questions," Bastian warned before grabbing my arm and pulling me into his bedroom.

Like my room, this one had a wall of windows overlooking the bay. French doors led to an oversized balcony. A California King, decked in black silky sheets and pillows, sat at the center of the space. Almost everything in the room was black and white. He even had a grand piano by the window.

On a table on the other side of the room, a stack of notebooks sat beside an electric piano. His walls were black-and-white striped, which seemed odd until I recognized the familiar pattern.

"You painted your walls to look like the keys of a piano?"

He smirked. "Didn't take you long to notice."

"How could I not? It's so different. Can you play the piano?"

Bastian nodded, then turned away from me to strip off his suit jacket. "Come here," he said as he entered the walk-in closet.

I followed him inside, and when he raised his hand, beckoning me to come closer, my heart pounded with a strange mixture of fear and desire.

"Take off my shirt," he ordered.

Hands trembling, I popped open the buttons on his white oxford. He was lean and muscular but not as big as Marcello in the arms and chest. Built like an athlete, he looked like he spent all day at the gym.

Only Marcello had played sports. He was QB1 in high school and had the body to match. The other three had spent their days terrorizing everyone at school, smoking weed on the soccer field, and pissing off the teachers. And, of course, tormenting me relentlessly.

Bastian watched me as I helped him out of his shirt, sliding the soft fabric over his broad shoulders. Except for the scattered scars marring his chest, he had tanned, smooth skin. I traced my fingers over the most prominent scar directly over his heart. It looked like an X made with a knife.

I glanced up at him. "How did you get this one?"

He looked away as if he were ashamed. "Don't worry about it, Cherry."

"Tell me."

"No." He gripped my wrists and moved my hands back to my sides. "Go get in bed."

I inched backward a few steps, my body shaking, but it was from the anger swirling inside me this time. "You don't have to be so mean."

His arm shot out toward the door. "Go. Now."

And here I thought we were having a moment of normalcy.

I did as he requested and sat on his bed. The mattress was soft, and the sheets were smooth against my skin.

Bastian emerged from the closet wearing a pair of dark gray boxer briefs that hugged his impressive package. Nothing but muscle graced his toned body that had me begging for a taste.

"Might as well get comfortable, Cherry." He lifted a notebook and pencil from the table. "You're spending the night."

As he approached the bed, my pulse raced uncontrollably. I pressed my lips together and breathed through my nose. Bastian propped his back against a stack of pillows and stretched out his long legs beside me. He rested the notebook on his thighs and flipped through the pages.

Silence passed over us, and as if I wasn't even here, he started writing in his book. I rolled onto my side to see what he was writing.

Music notes.

"You write music?"

He bobbed his head as his pencil moved across the page.

"Isn't there an app or program you can use?"

Bastian sighed, then glanced over at me. "This is how my mom taught me to write music."

His confession shocked me. He was only nine when he lost both of his parents.

"You could write music when you were that young?"

"Yes." Bastian raised an eyebrow. "Any other pressing questions?"

I scooted closer to him, my fingers inches from his thigh. Being this close, I could feel the heat radiating off his body.

"How old were you when you learned how to play?"

He dropped the pencil into the crease of the book and sighed. "Three."

"Wow. Really? So you were... What do they call it?"

I was drawing a blank.

"A prodigy," he answered.

"Yeah, that's it."

Bastian grabbed his cell phone from the bedside table and groaned. "It's almost midnight. Bedtime soon, Cherry. I need to get back to this. Quiet."

"Can I watch?"

He dropped his phone onto the table and tapped the space between us with his palm. "No more questions. I need to concentrate."

As expected, Bastian was much nicer than Damian. He seemed like he could care about a woman, though I seriously doubted he would. I would need the jaws of life to make him open up to me.

I curled up beside him, using my elbow to support my

173

weight. Entranced by how his mind worked, I stared in awe at the music he created. Periodically, he hummed a tune, rehearsing the chords aloud to see if they worked together. It felt like hours had passed before he set the notebook on the bed and leaned back against the headboard.

"Can I hear the song?"

He drew a breath from between his teeth, his eyes on the ceiling. "Not yet."

"Does it have a name?"

Bastian turned onto his side and swiped a strand of hair behind my ear. "You ask too many questions for a girl who's being held captive against her will. Questions in this house will get you killed."

I gasped. "Don't threaten me."

"I'm not." He dipped his head down, our mouths so close I could feel the heat from his breath. "But you need to learn your place. You're not a Salvatore yet."

"You're so heartless."

"Heartless, yes." He laughed at the insult. "I never claimed to have a heart, Cherry. But you seem interested in mine."

"I only asked about the scar."

He rested an elbow on a pillow, and his gray eyes fixed on me. "Of all the scars on my chest, you asked about that one. Why?"

"Because it looks like an X over your heart."

"And you think it means something?" Bastian pressed his lips together. "It couldn't be a coincidence?"

"No. I think you did that to yourself."

He clutched my wrist and placed my palm on his chest, right over his heart. "You feel this? My heart beats just like yours."

"You're not like me, though. Normal people feel compassion for others. Instead, you thrive off my pain. You enjoy watching me squirm."

"Not as much as Damian," he admitted. "We're both sick fucks. You better learn to deal with it."

A trail of heat rushed down my arms, spreading throughout my body like wildfire. I licked my lips. He grabbed the back of my head and pulled my head closer. Of all the Salvatores, he was never afraid to kiss me.

I pressed my lips together, hesitant to let him kiss me. Kissing was too personal. And each time I let him, I felt more of a bond. A spark of attraction. The desire to act out all of my fantasies with him.

I hoped he would go for my lips, but he turned his head and kissed my neck, slowly inching his way up to my jaw. Then, like a starved man, he licked and sucked on my skin, let his teeth graze every inch before he bit me.

Even though it hurt, I was so desperate for more. So I climbed on top of Bastian and rocked my hips into his hard cock.

He sucked my bottom lip into his mouth. "You want me to take your virginity right now, Cherry?" He twisted my nipple over top of the silky pajamas. "Answer me."

I squealed when he pinched me harder. "Not tonight."

"Are you sure about that?" Bastian grabbed my ass cheeks and pushed my pussy into his cock, sliding me up and down until I writhed on top of him. "You're begging to get fucked."

"You won't do it tonight. All of you are saving my virginity for something."

He shoved down my top and sucked my nipple into his mouth. "You'll like what we have planned, Cherry. Trust me. It's worth the wait."

A shiver rolled down my bare arms, and it wasn't from him biting my nipples. "I didn't realize you were so romantic."

"I'm not. Your first time won't be romantic, but it will be memorable."

I took his hand and shoved it down my panties.

A wicked grin illuminated his pretty gray eyes. "How bad do you want to cum, Cherry?"

"Please, Bash." I guided his fingers between my folds. "I want you."

Even if it killed me to say it aloud, it was the truth.

"You're so tight," he hissed. "Fuck, baby. I'm going to tear your pussy up."

I moaned at his dirty words, staring at his delicious mouth as I bounced up and down on his fingers, shoving him deeper and deeper.

"What are you going to do to me?" I rode his fingers hard. "Tell me."

A sexy grin illuminated his eyes. "My little virgin likes dirty talk?"

I pressed my palms to his chest as my orgasm brewed inside me. "Yes," I whimpered. "Talk dirty to me, Bash."

"Ride my fingers like they're my cock." He slid another finger into me, and despite the sharp pinch, I was desperate to reach the finish line. "You're such a bad girl. And here I thought we bought a sweet virgin."

"No, you didn't," I muttered right as I came on his fingers. "You wouldn't know what to do with a sweet girl."

Bastian removed his hand from my panties and licked my cum from his fingers. "Fuck, Cherry. Your pussy tastes so good I don't want to eat anything else for the rest of my life."

I chuckled, then lightly slapped his chest with my palm.

"I'm serious."

He snaked his arm around me and, in one swift motion, pinned my back to the mattress, making room for himself between my thighs.

"Why do you want my virginity so badly?"

He cupped my cheek in his big hand, his long fingers rough against my soft skin. "Who said I'm the one who's taking your virginity?"

"I don't want it to be Damian."

He waggled his eyebrows. "Then that's who will do the deed."

I shoved my palms into his chest. "You had me fooled for a minute. Now that I've come to my senses get off me."

"No can do. I'm not done with you."

"Bash." I squirmed beneath him. "Please. Just let me up. I want to go to sleep."

He slid down my body and moved between my thighs, breathing hard against my wet pussy. "Do you want me to taste you, Cherry?"

I shook my head. "No."

"You sure about that?" Bastian inched my shorts and panties over my hips. "Because I think you're a liar."

He pulled my panties down a few more inches, exposing my waxed skin to the chill in the air. It was always colder in Devil's Creek because of the breeze blowing off the bay. I shivered when his lips brushed the skin right above my waistband.

Bastian glanced up at me and wet his lips. "Do you want me to keep going?"

"Since when do you ask for permission? We both know you'll do it no matter what I say."

He lifted my leg over his shoulder, leaving a trail of hot kisses on my inner thigh. I trembled with each carefully placed peck and moaned when his teeth grazed my skin.

"Take off your shirt," he ordered before dropping my leg back on the bed. He sat up between my thighs, his eyes like lasers burning my skin. "Let me get a good look at this gorgeous body."

My hand shook as I slid my finger beneath the strap on my right shoulder. Bastian's lips parted, and his eyes filled with hunger as my breast popped out from the fabric. He was patient, though, his chest rising and falling.

I stripped off my shirt. A moment passed between us where we stared at each other, letting the tension build. My skin crackled with electricity, all the way down my fingertips. Bastian leaned forward, and I thought he might crawl up my body and kiss me. But instead, he ripped off my shorts and panties.

He glanced down and shook his head. "Look at you, Cherry. So wet for me." Then he rolled his thumb over my clit in slow, circular motions, ripping a scream from my throat. His finger eventually slipped between my folds, working in unison with his thumb. "You're so tight. I can't wait to be inside you."

Throwing my legs over his shoulders, he leaned forward and licked me straight down the middle.

"Oh, my God," I whimpered.

Bastian studied my face as he tasted me. His eyes never left mine, not even for a second. It was so hot my insides felt like they were going to explode. I cried out his name with each flick of his tongue, overwhelmed by pleasure. Finally, I came on his tongue, and he held me down, sucking my clit into his mouth.

His teeth grazed my sensitive skin. Then he went back to licking between my folds, eventually swapping his fingers for his tongue. Screaming his name, I fisted his thick, dark hair in my hands, yanking harder as I came again.

Bastian sat up and blew out a few deep breaths. He wiped his mouth with the back of his hand. "Jesus, woman. Are you trying to kill me?"

"I thought you like it rough," I quipped.

"When the time comes," he said, licking my cum from his lips, "I will destroy you. You'll have an imprint of my cock in your pretty pussy."

"What happened to Damian fucking me first?"

"You don't know what awaits you," he said with a creepy grin. "All in due time, Cherry." He squeezed my breast and rolled onto his side of the mattress. "It's time for bed."

He reached for the light on the bedside table. I was about

to ask him to wait because I hated the dark. And then, I noticed our resident creep hiding in the room's corner.

Hand over my racing heart, I gasped. "What are you doing in here?"

Bastian chuckled as his eyes lifted to meet Damian's. "He's been here the entire time."

Damian stood in the entryway with his hand down the front of his boxer briefs. His cock was hard. A moment of panic ensued until I realized he wouldn't touch me. He didn't like to sleep with people, so at least he wouldn't climb into bed with us.

I shook my head in disbelief. "Are you kidding me? You let him watch us?"

Bastian flicked off the light and laid back on the pillows beside me. "Go to sleep, Cherry. You'll hurt yourself thinking about it."

Chapter Twenty-Seven

LUCA

I sat in the armchair across from the Knights. We gathered in my office instead of the temple to stay closer to Alex. With the Volkovs lurking outside our walls, I wasn't letting her pretty ass out of my sight.

I raised a snifter of scotch to my mouth, surveying the room's mood. The Knights looked on edge. The attack at the marina had rattled each of us in different ways.

Sonny Cormac didn't look as put together as usual. Drake Battle had dark circles under his eyes from searching the Dark Web for the past three days. Bastian, Damian, and Cole were out late last night looking for the Russians with Marcello and Alpha Command. They slumped in their chairs as if they were seconds from falling asleep.

Sonny steepled his hands on his lap and glanced over at me. "Is Marcello coming?"

I shook my head. "He's dealing with Alex."

"It should be you," Sonny countered with hate dripping from his tone. "Marcello isn't marrying her. So you should protect our queen."

"Thanks for the reminder, Dad, but I have more important shit to worry about—like saving her fucking life."

"Alex is in danger," Drake interjected. "We don't have time to argue. If we're not united, we'll lose her. Our enemies will sniff out our weaknesses and pick us off one by one." His gaze drifted to me. "Let's focus on keeping Alex alive."

"Which is why we're here today," I reminded them. "The point of this meeting is to discuss Alex, not me." I sipped from my glass, then set it on the table and grabbed a cigar from the box. "Drake got a hit on the Russians using his AI software. But they disappeared off the map before he could chase down the lead. They will list Alex for sale at the next Il Circo auction."

"Not gonna happen," Drake said with an intense expression. He scratched the dark stubble along the corner of his jaw. "I'm working around the clock to find them."

It was nearly impossible to track Il Circo's owners. The name meant the circus in Italian, and the elite club for the world's deviants sure as fuck lived up to its name. It was like a traveling circus where you could bid on anyone and anything.

Anything went at Il Circo.

But they had one rule you couldn't break. If you listed someone for sale at the auction, you had to produce them. Men would search for Alex, and not just the Russians.

I nodded at Drake. "Shut down the website when it pops up. We can't afford to have Alex listed."

"I'll do my best."

"Your best isn't good enough when it concerns our queen."

"Whoever runs their site is untraceable," Drake shot back. "A fucking ghost. I can't track their IP address. Every time I get close, they crash my fucking servers."

"You're the tech genius, Battle. Find a way. I don't care who we have to bribe or kill to make it happen. We're not letting predators bid on her on the Dark Web."

"I can help with tactical planning," Cole Marshall offered.

Cole was the youngest of the local Knights and the son of a Founder. He was only twenty-one and in his final year at

York Military Academy. His family owned the school that Cole and his younger brothers had attended since they were children. Like Marcello, he had a mind for war. He could see different angles and assess the threat.

"I want you to coordinate with Marcello," I told Cole. "He may have other ideas about how to approach this situation."

My brother was the muscle, and I was the brains. So I relied on him to view my plans from a different lens, to find any flaws.

"The Founders Society Elders issued a kill order for every member of the Volkov Bratva," I informed the group. "They have everyone under their scope out looking for them. It's only a matter of time before they resurface."

"What about The Serpents?" Drake asked. "Have they made any progress?"

I nodded. "They found someone connected to Konstantin Volkov and are working a new angle."

"Such as?" Drake inquired.

"A close American friend of Konstantin Volkov has a taste for young girls," I said as I blew out a puff of cigar smoke. "He also has a raging drug addiction. The Serpents are working with our Sicilian friends to exploit that weakness. So far, it seems promising. They got a lead on a safe house the Volkovs use in Brooklyn. We'll see how that pans out."

"What are we going to do?" Finn Cormac asked. "I'm not sitting on my ass, twiddling my thumbs until they bring the fight to us again."

"I have notifications set up," Drake said. "If anyone lists Alex on the Dark Web, I will know immediately."

"And if that happens," Bastian said, "we will have a bloodbath on our hands."

"Maybe we should temporarily move to a safe house," Damian suggested. "We don't need them bringing a war to Devil's Creek."

"Let them," I shot back. "We're prepared."

"This is our home," Drake cut in. "I don't want that shit brought to my doorstep."

"It's the smart play." Sonny took a puff of his cigar, blowing rings in front of his face. "We don't want blood all over the streets of Devil's Creek. Drake is right. This is where we live. Gunfire will draw a lot of attention from the surrounding towns."

"Who fucking cares?" I rested my wingtip on my knee and leaned back in the chair, my eyes on Sonny. "We own the police, the mayor, the goddamn governor."

"Without a queen, we can't admit new Knights," Drake said, annoyed. "One of you needs to lock down this marriage with Alex."

"I have it under control," I assured him.

Drake's phone dinged. He shot up from the couch and held out his cell phone. "Volkov is on the move again."

The Knights jumped to their feet, looking to me for instructions.

"I'll tell Marcello to add a few more guards on Alex's floor," Bastian announced. "Just in case this is a trap."

I nodded. "Text Marcello, tell him to be discrete. He's too forthcoming with Alex."

Bastian shoved a hand through his dark hair, sweeping it off his forehead, and removed his cell phone from his pocket.

I grabbed the guns from the side table and shoved them into the holster strapped to my chest. "Let's go hunt monsters."

The Knights grinned in satisfaction.

Chapter Twenty-Eight

MARCELLO

A lex was dead to the world, lost in her art. She laid on her stomach on a drop cloth in front of a canvas. We'd been in my mother's studio for over two hours, and she showed no signs of finishing her painting.

When I was a child, I was a lot like Alex. A free spirit without a care in the world. I wanted to be like my mother and spent most of my time painting and studying art in her studio.

My mother lit up every room with her smile. She was the only good thing I had in my life. Hell, she was the good in all of our lives.

My father was always cruel and cold, but he hardened with each year since her passing. Luca was like him and had adapted quickly to the changes in our house. I retreated into myself, spending more time painting and sketching in my mother's studio. Until one day, my father was in a foul mood and ended my dreams of becoming an artist.

It was the fifth anniversary of my mother's death, and my dad was a complete disaster. I was in her studio, kneeling in front of a canvas with a rigger brush cradled between my fingers. My father swayed into the room with a bottle of Macallan in his hand. He muttered curses in Italian as his eyes traveled across the room, shifting between her paintings and me.

When I was younger, he saved his punishments for Luca, taking out his anger on him. Luca didn't mind learning his lessons and took them in stride. But to hell with that shit. I wasn't a psychopath like my brother. I wanted to get out of this house and as far away from the violence as possible.

But I never had a choice.

Dad stopped in front of my mother's self-portrait and pressed his hand to the wall beside the framed oil painting as he sipped from the bottle. I could hear him speak to my mother in Italian, his words muffled.

She was the glue that held our family together. Without her, we were falling apart.

My father dived headfirst into work while Luca learned the family business. A genius, my older brother, spent most of his time with his nose in a book, devouring its contents. Luca would take over for my father and run Salvatore Global one day. He was more suited for the role, and I was glad I didn't have to take on the responsibility.

I preferred to be left alone.

After Dad finished staring at my mother's portrait, he strolled across the room, downing the rest of the scotch. His eyes were red-rimmed and glassy. I wondered if it was from the alcohol or if he'd cried over my mother.

Luca found our mother on the floor of her studio, with her head turned to the side, her lips as blue as the ocean. That was the only day my father shed a tear.

Just one.

Dad glared at me, his mouth twisted into a scowl. "What do you think you're doing, Marcello?"

Confused by his question, I looked up at him. "I'm painting."

He shook his head. "I told you not to come into this room."

"Sorry, Dad. I just wanted to be closer to her."

My hands trembled when he bent down in front of me.

"She's dead! You hear me, Marcello, dead. Nothing can bring her *back. So when I tell you to stop with this nonsense, I mean it. No more painting. It's time for you to act like a man and learn the business."*

He swatted the paintbrush from my hand. Paint splattered on his black Brioni suit, on my T-shirt, and across the floor. His eyes glazed over as he took in the sight of the red acrylic paint.

I tried to recreate one of my mom's paintings and failed miserably. My talent didn't even compare to hers.

The empty bottle in his hand crashed to the floor, shattering into pieces. He reached down and gripped the collar of my shirt, choking me with the fabric as he pulled me up from the floor. I was almost as tall as him and gaining more muscle from playing football.

Even at his age, he was still as strong as an ox. He blew out a deep breath while I held mine, terrified of what he would do this time.

"Look at what you did," he snapped.

It was his fault, but I knew better than to talk back. I wasn't Luca. I would never challenge my father the way my older brother did.

He tightened his hold on my throat, and I gasped for air.

"Dad," Luca said from behind him.

I had never been more thankful to hear my brother's voice.

"Stay out of this, Luca," he boomed. "This is between Marcello and me."

Luca hated me when we were kids and even tried to kill me once. He treated me like I was another responsibility for most of my life. But after our mom died, he often stepped in front of me and defended me against my father's attacks. I had assumed he'd made a deal with my mother that was unbreakable in his mind.

My brother moved toward us with a purpose, dressed in a navy blue suit and brown wingtips. For someone in high school, Luca already looked like a man, the future leader of our family's company.

"What did Marcello do?"

My dad waved his hand at the mess on the floor. "Marcello was about to accept his punishment."

"Dad," Luca groaned. "Not today. Can't this wait until tomorrow?"

"Don't challenge me, son." He gritted his teeth. "Your brother disobeyed my orders, and he will deal with the consequences of his actions."

Luca stripped off his suit jacket and handed it to me. He held my father's gaze as he unbuttoned his white oxford. "Then let me take it. Let this be an example for Marcello not to do it again."

He was right.

Whenever Luca accepted the punishments on my behalf, I never repeated the same mistake. I didn't want him to suffer for my actions.

"Leave, Marcello," Luca ordered as he unbuttoned his shirt.

His chest and back were scarred beyond repair, much worse than mine.

"No," my father said with a bite to his tone. "He has to watch. That's his punishment."

I took Luca's shirt from his hand and sighed. We should have been celebrating the life of the most incredible woman who ever lived. Instead, my father only proved how much he was fucking up our lives.

He'd adopted Bastian and Damian, who were probably snapping the necks of rabbits in the backyard. They were fucked up like my father and Luca. The four of them were like peas in a pod. I was the one who didn't fit into the equation.

Luca sank to his knees as my father gripped the Fendi belt in his hand. I wished I could be as fearless as him. Luca looked up at me, his eyes never leaving mine as the belt cracked open his skin. He balled his hands into fists and clenched his jaw. Not even a single sound escaped his mouth as if he had trained himself not to feel the lashes.

My stomach ached as he tore open old scars, creating new ones, and by the time my father finished, I wanted to punch him.

If he weren't so powerful, I would have run from him. I would have stolen enough cash to leave this stupid town and never returned.

But I would never leave Luca.

I owed him for enduring most of my punishments. So I vowed to never step out of line after that day. For Luca, I promised never to cross my father. It was the least I owed him for coming to my rescue.

My father rubbed his hand over his face, and then he stormed away *from us as if the room were on fire. I handed Luca his shirt. He winced as the fabric molded to his back, clinging to his open cuts.*

"I'll do whatever he wants," I said. "You won't have to take another punishment for me."

Luca yanked his suit jacket out of my hand and slipped it on without a word. He stared at me for a moment. "There will come a day when I need something from you," Luca said in a hushed tone. "Something you won't want to give me, but you will do it, anyway."

"Like what?"

He shrugged. "You'll know when the day comes."

After that day, my father had the staff cover the furniture and easels with tarps. Alex was the first person to step foot inside the room in years.

I thought about Luca and what he'd done for me so many times. So when Carl Wellington offered Alex a choice between us, that was the day.

And I owed him.

My mother would have loved Alex. When I watched my mom paint, she would tell me to sit in the chair in the corner. No matter how sad she looked, she always fucking smiled. She always looked happy when her eyes landed on me.

I thought about the last time I saw her in the same spot as Alex. With her fingers wrapped around a paintbrush and two more stuffed into her hair like chopsticks. She always did that to push the hair off her face. Dad would kiss her and laugh, promising to buy diamond clips to tie up her hair.

He was a different man back then. My parents were lucky. They married for love. When Alex's mom ran from Devil's Creek and broke off the engagement with my father, it allowed him to marry outside of the Founding Families.

Some days, I wished for freedom—a free pass to do what I wanted without recourse. But I'd grown up knowing my father would choose my bride.

I lifted one of my mother's paintbrushes from a wooden

table, rolling it between my fingers. Alex's brush moved across the canvas, her movements fluid and graceful.

She startled as I sat in the armchair next to the easel, holding her hand over her heart. "Marcello, you scared me."

I leaned forward and rested my elbows on my thighs. "What are you working on?"

She tucked her feet under her butt, twirling the brush in her hand. "Something for my showcase."

Her long, blonde curls spilled over her sun-kissed shoulders, stopping at the tops of her breasts. I licked my lips, my cock jerking at the sight of her perfection. Pale skin, delicious curves, pouty pink lips, high cheekbones, and sparkling blue eyes.

"Wanna help me?" Alex asked.

I swiped the palate from the floor. "Which colors do you need?"

Her face brightened. "More red, orange, black, and white." She pointed at the exact bottles on the floor beside my foot.

"How come you're using acrylic paint?" I filled the circles in the palette with paint as she grabbed three more synthetic brushes.

Alex groaned. "Don't get all snobby with me about oil versus acrylic. Andy Warhol used acrylic."

"He also painted pop art," I shot back.

It was a hotly debated topic in the art world. Some artists believed oil was the only way to go, but prominent artists were getting into acrylics.

"I'm not," I assured her. "Just wondering why you're deviating from your usual."

"I've been getting headaches from the oil fumes." She sighed. "I thought I'd try something new since this is a new series."

My mother preferred oil and also complained about the

headaches from the chemicals. Toward the end, she dabbled with acrylics but never used them for her showcase pieces.

Alex's smile touched her eyes. My God, I loved when she looked at me this way, like for once, she didn't want to claw out my eyes.

Dipping a rigger brush into the black paint, Alex made a slow, steady line across the canvas. Each line was ten inches apart, rounding out the uneven square at the center of the canvas.

I watched in awe for what felt like hours. The rough slats on the top, bottom, and sides looked like shards of glass, mirrors that revealed pieces of the overall aesthetic.

She looked at me with her palms on the floor and her tits falling out of her lacy bra. She'd taken off her coveralls after accidentally spilling paint on her clothes. Alex studied my face as if she were trying to commit every curve to memory.

"What are you doing?"

She gave me a sexy smile and pressed her finger to her lips. "You're my muse. Be quiet, so I can think."

I opened my mouth to protest.

"No, you can't stop me," she said defiantly. "Don't even try."

"I can drag you out of this studio by your hair and lock you in your room."

"Marcello, please. Stop killing my vibe," she whined.

Alex grabbed an angled brush and dipped it into orange paint that reminded me of a sunset. She leaned forward, oblivious to her tits spilling out from her bra. The lace did nothing to hide her nipples.

Fuck.

Why did I have to feel something for her? Even if that feeling was a mixture of hatred and lust. There were times, like this one, when something unfamiliar stirred in my belly. A foreign emotion I hadn't experienced since my mother was alive.

Neither of us had a choice.

We had to marry, produce heirs, and make our families happy. I hated having that obligation. But when Alex looked at me, like she was gazing deep into my soul, a sense of calm washed over me. It was intimate, emotional, and so damn heartbreaking. Because I knew I could never give her what she deserved.

I studied the canvas on the floor in front of her. "Is that me or Luca?"

She had my mother's gift, the ability to see what people were hiding.

"Do you like it?"

"It's brilliant," I whispered in disbelief. "How do you do that?"

My voice sounded distant, unsure of my question, even though I wanted an answer.

"Do what?"

"Make me feel like she's still here."

"It's an artist's job to make you feel something."

I cupped the side of her face, my fingers brushing her skin. "That's the problem with you."

She cocked an eyebrow at me. "Are we still talking about art?"

Our eyes met, and I tucked her blonde curls behind her ear, breathing against her lips. A trail of heat rushed down my arms and spread throughout my body like fire. How did she make me feel so many emotions at once?

I grabbed the back of her head and pulled her mouth to mine. She felt the same way about me as I did her. We hated how much we wanted each other. But once our lips collided and our tongues tangled, we were fucking made for each other.

She was everything I wanted.

Everything I craved.

The balance to my madness, the angel on my shoulder

when I wanted to do nothing but sin. My inner demons were screaming, begging to come out and play. I slipped my fingers through her hair as she climbed onto my lap, wrapping her thighs around me.

"Marcello," she moaned as I kissed her neck.

I licked and sucked on her skin, nibbling her hot flesh with each moan I stole from her. Throwing her arms around my neck, she rocked her hips to meet mine, desperate to create friction. My cock pressed against my zipper as she rubbed her pussy on me.

"Slow down, princess." I bit her lip, and she moaned. "Keep grinding on my cock like this, and I won't be responsible for what comes next."

"You're not taking my virginity on this floor."

Alex's virginity had remained intact because it was part of the deal. None of us could fuck her until we were all together. Until she was ready and we all agreed there was no turning back.

Throughout her high school and college years, we had ensured no man touched her. But, like a piece of fine art, we wanted to preserve Alex.

Make her ours.

"Who said anything about fucking?" I gripped her shoulder, pushing her onto her back. "I'd rather you ride my face and let me taste your sweet cunt."

She giggled, shoving her fingers through my hair. "You're such a bad boy, Marcello."

My tongue swept into her mouth as I slid my hand up her bare stomach and pinched her nipples over top of the bra.

"Marcello," she whispered. "Please."

I sucked her lip into my mouth. "Patience, my queen."

"Touch me," she whined. "I can't stand it anymore."

I twisted her nipple between my fingers, and she squealed. "I am touching you. My queen needs to learn some self-control."

She whimpered when I sucked her nipple into my mouth over the fabric. Then, giving equal love to each of her tits, I licked, sucked, and bit the tiny buds until they were sore and sensitive, and she was screaming my name.

Pressing my palm to the tarp, I left a trail of kisses down her stomach. I was the patient one, so I took my time, wanting to savor every second. But she was desperate for release.

She grabbed my hand and shoved it into her panties. "Stop torturing me, Marcello. I've waited too long for you to touch me."

I winked. "A little torture and pain will improve your orgasm. By the time I'm done with you, princess, you'll be glad you waited."

I pulled her panties down a few inches, exposing her smooth, waxed skin. She smelled so fucking good I almost lost control.

Almost.

I never lost control.

She shivered when my lips brushed the skin above her waistband. Slow and steady, I took my sweet ass time tasting every bit of her flesh.

"Marcello," she screamed. "I'm going to die if you don't make me come."

I laughed, and she trembled from my breath on her skin. Alex was a drug I could never kick, a high I would chase until the day I died. And this woman would be the death of me.

She was like sin, rolled in chocolate and dipped in a shot of whiskey. One taste, and I was fucking high.

I tore her panties clean off her body, and she squealed as I thrust my fingers into her. She was tight and wet, and I wanted to be inside her, but this wasn't about me.

Throwing her leg over my shoulder, I fucked her with my fingers, ripping a series of moans from her beautiful lips. "How's this, princess?" I licked her straight down the middle, and she cried out in pleasure. "Feel good?"

"Yes."

She arched her back, lifting her hips off the floor, letting me devour her like a starved animal. Her eyes slammed shut when I sucked her clit into my mouth and tugged on it with my teeth. I swapped my fingers for my tongue, licking her between her slick folds as I rubbed her clit with my thumb. She screamed my name, fisting my hair in her hands. With each moan, she yanked harder, ready to rip my hair from my scalp.

Not like I cared.

I got off from the pain.

Forcing my tongue to go deeper and deeper, I tasted every inch of her. She writhed beneath me, panting and swearing. I slung her other leg over my shoulder and grabbed her ass cheeks.

As her body trembled, I flipped onto my back, pulling her on top of me. She rocked her hips, riding my face so goddamn hard I couldn't breathe as I licked her pussy. My name poured out of her mouth, my cock growing harder, straining against my dress pants.

Her legs shook, and one after another, her orgasms spilled out of her in violent waves. She rolled off me after she came on my tongue, attempting to catch her breath.

"Fuck, princess." I held my hand over my racing heart and stared at the ceiling. "You almost suffocated me with your pussy. But it would have been worth it to die with your taste on my lips."

She laughed. "You're crazy."

I sat up and licked my lips to get every drop of her. She rolled onto her side and pulled on my belt.

I pushed her hand away, and she gave me a surprised look. "Get dressed. I'm taking you to Beacon Bay for dinner."

Alex's pretty face illuminated from the smile that touched her eyes. "Like a date?"

"Sure." I shrugged. "It's a date."

My beautiful girl practically skipped out of the room. But before we left the studio, I studied the canvas. She signed the corner with the name *Queen D*—Luca's nickname for her.

Chapter Twenty-Nine

ALEX

We sat on the patio at Café Lacroix, sipping espresso as people walked past us. A few middle-aged women stopped at our table to say hello. They flashed smiles and blushed as Marcello spoke to them.

Beacon Bay was even smaller than Devil's Creek, a seaside town that only had access to the bay from one side. So we were close to the water, sitting outside on a paved veranda, eating gourmet sandwiches that cost too much.

Even after years of being exposed to this kind of wealth, I still hadn't adjusted to it. I couldn't fathom the idea of paying twenty-five dollars for a sandwich. But since Marcello was paying, I figured, why not.

Several men tipped their heads in acknowledgment. One of them was Sonny Cormac's dad. He congratulated me on my new role at the Franco Foundation and wished me future success.

After he walked away, I turned to look at Marcello. "For a mute, you sure have a lot of friends."

"They're not my friends," he shot back, his eyes on the water fountain at the center of the space. "And I'm not mute."

I took a bite of my turkey sandwich, smiling at him with

my eyes as I chewed my food. "Why are you so grumpy, Marcello? When was the last time you had fun?"

"Depends on your idea of fun."

I wiped my mouth with the napkin on my lap. "What do you consider fun?"

"I like to sail," he offered, which surprised the hell out of me. "I would live on a boat if I could."

"I was expecting something more... illegal." I laughed. "I mean, I don't know. You seem like the shy, quiet type who would spend his weekends at strip clubs."

He scoffed at my accusation. "I don't need to pay for pussy."

"I'm pretty sure women would pay you." I turned my head away from him. "I didn't mean that."

"Yes, you did." He smirked. "How many times did I make you cum?" Marcello leaned forward, resting his elbows on the table, his voice a whisper. "Three the last time I checked." He placed his hand on the table and opened his palm. "Pay up, princess."

My nipples hardened into peaks at the sound of his deep voice. Heat coiled in my belly and spread down my thighs. I slapped my legs together and stuffed the last bite of my sandwich into my mouth, avoiding his gaze.

Marcello and his brothers liked to watch me. They were obsessive and possessive, and those psychos were all mine.

"How come you work security while your dad and brother handle the business?" I asked to change the subject.

He drank from his cup and rolled his broad shoulders. "I prefer to work alone."

"Yeah, I can see that." I gave him a cheeky grin. "That's what I love about my art. I can spend hours in silence with nothing more than my charcoals or my paintbrush."

Marcelo glanced down at his watch. "We have to leave soon."

I downed the last of my drink and dropped the cloth

napkin onto the table. "Where is Luca? He's been avoiding me."

"In New York."

"Is he planning to come home?"

His phone dinged with a new text message. He typed back a quick reply and tucked the phone into the inner pocket of his suit jacket. "He'll be home tomorrow night."

Red-hot anger swirled inside me, heating my skin. "He hasn't spoken to me since the night of the gala. Why?"

"Luca is in charge of a multi-billion dollar company. He can't be at your beck and call at all times, princess."

"The way we left things…" I stared down at my hands folded on my lap and sighed. "Luca makes my head spin."

Marcello scratched the corner of his jaw, eyeing me up. "Are you mad he wouldn't fuck you?"

"No," I snapped. "I just thought… Whatever, it doesn't matter." I shot up from the chair, the legs scraping across the pavers. "He always does this. Anytime we get close, he pushes me away."

"My brother hates intimacy," he said in a cold tone. "I wouldn't expect much from him. He's incapable of giving you what you want."

"Then why should I marry him?" I moved between his spread thighs and bent down until our lips almost touched. "Why should I marry any of you? All of you treat me like shit. Like a pawn in some sick and twisted game."

He pushed me onto his lap. "You're not a pawn, Alex." His long fingers brushed my cheek, a soft touch that seemed unnatural for someone like Marcello. "You are our end game."

I swatted his hand away from my face. "Because you need me. Not because you care about me."

"That's not true," he challenged, and his words sounded sincere. "I've spent years watching over you, ensuring you have everything you need. So have my brothers. Our methods may be unconventional, but we would do anything for you." He rose from the chair, holding me in his arms as he set my feet on the ground. "And we're not letting you go."

Maybe the Salvatore boys weren't so bad after all. If Marcello's confession even closely mirrored his brothers' feelings, it was worth getting to know them better. I was a long way from choosing one of them as my husband. But I would let each of them convince me.

"I need to use the ladies' room before we go," I told him.

He grabbed my ass as I walked away from our table and headed inside. I strolled through a crowded dining room packed with dozens of people. At the end of a long hallway, I stepped into the women's restroom and went about my business.

I washed my hands, then fixed my hair in the mirror. Of course, my curls were all over the place and frizzing. That was the problem with being this close to the bay. Running my fingers through my curls, I did my best to untangle them and tucked the long strands behind my ears.

I spotted a tall man with dark hair propped up against the wall when I exited the bathroom. He wore a leather jacket with the collar raised and smelled of cigarettes. I turned to the left, and he grabbed hold of my arm. His fingers dug into my skin and yanked me backward.

"Let go of me!" I screamed, elbowing him in the chest.

His grip loosened just enough for me to kick him in the balls and bolt down the hallway. I was going in the opposite direction from where Marcello waited for me. But with this jerk on my tail, I didn't have many options.

I ran through the kitchen's double doors, hoping one of them would hit him in the face on the backswing. His pace didn't falter. A man I'd never seen in my life dodged the kitchen staff, yelling for them to move.

"Get out of my kitchen," a man wearing a chef's hat shouted.

That earned him an elbow to the face. He fell to the slippery tiled floor like a sack of bricks. I apologized to the people I passed and pushed my way out of the side entrance.

Outside, men lifted boxes from the back of a food truck.

"Help me," I screamed and pointed over my shoulder at the man who was seconds from reaching me. "He's trying to kill me."

One man narrowed his eyes at me, confused.

No one bothered to help me. With Marcello on the opposite side of the restaurant, I had no way to reach him. No purse. No phone. I didn't think I would need it.

"Marcello," I yelled as my feet pounded the pavement. "Marcello, help me!"

For my sake, I hoped he could hear me.

The small town had a lot of narrow streets and alleyways that would make it easier to lose this asshole. At the very least, I could ditch him at Finnegan's Rock. A spot at the edge of the woods connected to the beach right below the Salvatore Estate.

They had guards that manned the edge of the cliff. If I could get back to the estate, I could get some fucking help. So I hauled ass toward the woods, running as fast as my heels would allow. Adrenaline coursed through my veins, propelling me to keep going, even though my lungs felt as if they were ready to give out.

Tires screeched behind me.

I didn't bother to look over my shoulder.

Once in the woods, I bolted down a walking path that veered to the right and followed it until I reached a dead end. A chill from the bay rolled over the land. Fallen branches snapped beneath my shoes. I did my best to follow the marked path, which led to the beach.

To lose this asshole, I turned off the main hiking trail. He only had to follow the posted signs to figure out where I was going. So I hid behind a tree and hunched low to the ground, using the tall grass to shield my body.

What felt like ten minutes passed. My heart raced as a twig snap snapped beneath his feet. With my hand over my mouth, I poked my head out from the tree, doing my best to steady my rapid breathing.

A man stood about a hundred feet in front of me. He had medium-length dark hair and pale skin. "Alexandrea," he said in a thick Russian accent. "Don't make me chase you."

He passed by my hiding spot, the mud beneath his shoes crunching as he walked. I slipped out from behind the tree.

What did he want?

When my stalker was at a safe distance, I flew down the dirt path. Dirt stuck to my bare feet—leaves and sticks and who knows what dug into my skin.

"Hey," he yelled. "Get back here."

He barreled toward me, snaking his arm around my middle, lifting my feet off the ground. "Where do you think you're going?"

"Please," I whimpered as he tightened his grip. "Just let me go. You don't want to do this."

"Oh, but I do." I could feel the smirk gracing his lips as he pressed them to my cheek. "I hate the Salvatores. They have taken everything from my family. And now, I'm going to take the one thing they want most."

"They don't want me," I screamed. "I have money. I'll give you whatever you want. Just let me go."

He dragged me over to a tree and pinned me against it. I kicked him and yelled for help, but it was no use. His strong arms held me down as he reached between us to push up my dress.

"Stop it! Please." I raised my knee to kick him in the balls, but he was too fast and caught it midair.

"There's no point in fighting me." He bunched my dress around my hips and then worked on unbuttoning his pants.

"Your virgin pussy is worth more than money to the Salvatores. By the time I'm done, they won't even recognize you. No one will want you."

I yelled for help, tears streaming down my cheeks. He pushed down his boxers, and I raked my fingernails across his cheek.

Cursing at me under his breath, he fisted his cock. Tears leaked from my eyes and coated my cheeks. I couldn't scream with his hand over my nose and mouth. His skin smelled like cigarettes and aftershave, a mixture that made my stomach churn.

"Payback is a bitch," he grunted.

I closed my eyes and waited for him to push inside me, knowing I couldn't do a damn thing about it.

But nothing happened.

Something warm splashed across my face and into my hair. The man fell forward, caging me against the tree with his heavy body. I opened my eyes and screamed.

Chapter Thirty

BASTIAN

I drove with Damian to our safe house in Beacon Bay. My brother had fucked up again. And as usual, I had to deal with the consequences of his sickness. Damian wasn't like other people. He was never right in the head, an uncontrolled psychopath who needed my help to satiate his dark desires.

I parked in front of my family's abandoned apartment building and hopped out of my Porsche. Damian slid out of the passenger seat, licking his lips as he glanced up at the top floor. The wheels were already turning in his sick mind. We all had our vices, so I didn't have room to judge him. But I was getting annoyed with his urges.

"Make it fast," I said in a level but firm tone. "I'm not spending all day here. Alex and Marcello will be home soon."

He smirked. "Eager to chase after our pet?"

We all wanted Alex Wellington. What man wouldn't want the blonde bombshell? But I mainly wanted to beat Luca to her virginity.

Her cherry was mine.

"D, I'm tired of this shit." I slammed the car door and pulled the keys to the apartment building out of my pocket.

"We shouldn't even be here right now. You promised the last time would be the last."

"I got carried away." He rolled his shoulders. "What do you want me to say? He was lurking outside of Wellington Manor. I did it to protect Alex."

"Yeah, fine. You did good." I turned the key in the lock and pushed the door open. "But murder isn't a sport."

He followed me into the building, breathing down my neck. "Dad doesn't have a problem with it."

I walked upstairs beside him. Damian wasn't my brother by blood, but we had been brothers long before Arlo Salvatore adopted us. We were only three months apart and had been inseparable since we were babies. Our parents were best friends and had co-founded Atlantic Airlines. After we graduated from Harvard University, we resumed control of the company.

"Dad doesn't know about all of your victims."

"Don't call them that," Damian snapped.

"I don't have a problem with you killing our enemies. But seeking new victims for fun is sick. I know what you did last week, D."

"They're not victims!" Damian's arms flew above his head as he shouted, "I choose people who deserve to die."

When we reached the second-floor landing, I gripped his shoulder and slammed his back into the wall. "Who are you to decide? Are you God?"

He smirked, then shoved my hand off his shoulder. "Where was our god when we were kids?"

Then he stormed off, rushing down the hallway, humming a tune under his breath. I loved him to death, but my brother was a legit fucking psycho.

"D," I called after him. "I'm serious. You need to chill with this shit. We have enough issues with the Volkov Bratva. We don't need to be on opposing sides."

We'd been fighting the Bratva for months. Then last week,

this sick fuck decided it was a good idea to kidnap and torture one of the highest-ranking men in their organization. All because the man fit the profile for Damian's illness. We were already paying the price for his mistake. Alex was now in danger, a side effect of our illegitimate business.

Halfway down the corridor, Damian halted in place. "We will never be on opposing sides." He glanced over his shoulder at me. "You're my brother. Nothing will ever change that."

"I'm not okay with what you're doing."

"I don't need your approval."

I placed my hand on his shoulder. "Do you want me to walk away like everyone else?"

His face dropped in horror. "You're not leaving me."

"I want to keep her. Alex is good for us," I insisted. "I think she might even like our fucked up games. But you can never show her this side of yourself, or the game is over." I ran my hand up and down his back in a soothing motion, something I'd done since we were children. It always calmed him down when he was out of his mind. "Don't fuck this up. You need to stay in control around her."

"I haven't lost control." He raised his head until our eyes met. "Why do you think I've stayed away from her?"

"This is the last time until after we deal with the Bratva. Understood?"

He nodded.

Without another word, we headed into the last apartment on the left. Damian rubbed his hands together, drooling over the piece of shit he had tied to the table in the living room. Well, it wasn't much of a living space anymore. The place looked like Dexter's kill room, with the walls, floor, and ceiling covered in plastic.

My brother busied himself by organizing a collection of weapons on the kitchen island. I looked at the poor bastard who got on Damian's radar.

At least he wasn't innocent.

He was a piece of shit, another dirtball off the streets. Damian was doing the world a service by getting rid of men like him. Still, I hated his obsessions.

We'd had the same fight more times than I could count. He was grating on my last nerves with his mental illness that only my father and I could control.

After Damian revealed his true nature, our dad let Damian explore this side of himself. He needed an outlet, and our adoptive father was more than happy to oblige. At first, he indulged Damian by letting him dispose of our enemies. The world was better off without those assholes.

But then Damian started going off on his own. Like a cat bringing home a dead bird for its owner, my brother started doing the same thing with people. Our dad would never allow him to bring them home. So Damian used one of the torture rooms at the safe house.

Even when we were children, we shared toys. We had a bond that went deeper than family.

You couldn't keep us apart.

So when my father made a deal with Carl Wellington, I knew I would have to share Alex, even though I wanted to keep her to myself. The beautiful blonde was mine from the moment I laid eyes on her.

But it was too late.

Damian had already touched her, tasted her. Despite her fear, she liked him but was smart enough to realize he was a predator.

"He keeps moving. Bash, I need your help." Damian opened his palm and held out a clamp. "Get his right side for me."

I didn't want to be here.

I hated watching him turn into a monster. It was easier to forget his issues when we were acting like ordinary men, getting high and fucking women. But when my brother veered off the deep end, I had to pull him back before he drowned.

I shook my head, disgusted by this method of torture, but I took the clamp from his hand. Why could I never tell him no? I could have walked away from him years ago. Yet, I could never find the strength to do it.

No one wanted Damian after The Lucaya Group murdered our parents. The newspapers called it an accident, but I knew the truth. Everyone tried to break us up, and I wouldn't let them. My parents' friends and some of my degenerate family members offered to take me.

They all wanted the money. And none of them wanted Damian, which was a deal-breaker. So when Arlo Salvatore showed up, we became a family for real. Arlo adopted both of us, gave us his name, and showed us how to adapt.

"This is the last time," I said through gritted teeth, the clamp clutched in my hand.

Blood and violence consumed our world, but even I had my limits. I stared at the man on the table beneath me and took a deep breath. Then I pulled my attention back to Damian, who had gone to another place.

My brother was no longer in the room with me. Damian's eyes turned a deep shade of green that appeared black in this light. He was a fucking demon.

"You hear me, D. This is it. No more."

A sly grin stretched the corners of his mouth as he leaned over the table. "Yeah, brother. This is the last time."

An hour later, we left the building in silence, covered in another man's blood. I peeled out of the empty parking lot and drove through the streets of Beacon Bay. The small coastal town was only five minutes from Devil's Creek, but the significant difference in wealth separated the haves from the have-nots.

I drove past the woods that led to the beach, serving as a divider between Devil's Creek and Beacon Bay. Out of the corner of my eye, I saw a woman with long blonde curls slapping her back, running in a dress and heels for her life. A man with dark hair chased after her.

"Fuck."

I slammed on the brakes as Alex ran into the woods. We got out of the car, guns at our sides.

"Was that Alex?"

"Yeah, D." I took off down the hiking trail beside Damian, hoping we would get to Alex in time. "And that's one of Volkov's men."

Chapter Thirty-One

ALEX

Damian gripped a hunting knife in his hand, blood dripping down his wrist. He had an even more sadistic look than my almost rapist. Bastian clutched the man's shoulder and threw him onto the ground as if he weighed nothing.

He was still alive.

My eyes widened at the Russian man gasping for air, clutching the gash on his throat. Blood poured out from his mouth, trailing down his cheek. Damian studied him with a satisfied smile on his face.

He was proud of his work.

As the man slowly bled out, I held Damian's gaze for a moment, and the dead look in his eyes terrified me. He just killed a man to save me.

And he liked it.

Bastian pulled me into his arms, stroking my cheek with his long fingers, hugging me so hard it helped to quell the tremors shaking through me. "Did he hurt you, Cherry?"

I was so in shock it took a few seconds before I could speak. "No. But he would have if you hadn't shown up." I closed my eyes and breathed through my nose before I could look at him again. "How did you find me?"

"We were on our way home and saw you running into the woods."

Bastian and Damian had blood on their suits and faces. Yet, neither of them seemed all that phased. It wasn't the first time I'd seen the Salvatore brothers with another man's blood on them.

Glancing over Bastian's arm, I couldn't take my eyes off Damian. He stared through me like a true hunter. Until tonight, I had been the hunted, his prey. He still scared the fucking shit out of me, but at least I knew he would protect me.

I knew he was on my side.

He smiled as the man took his last breath. Damian seemed way too pleased with himself. Like he enjoyed the sight of blood.

Bastian's lips pressed into a thin line as he scanned my face for bruises, gliding his fingers over the blood on my cheek. "You're lucky we were on our way home from Beacon Bay."

"I guess I should thank my captors for killing my almost rapist."

"Don't give me that attitude," Bastian snapped. "You are one of us now. And that means people will hurt you to get to us."

"He said your family took everything from his."

He grinned. "They got what they deserved."

"He also said no one will want to bid on me. Do you know what he meant?"

Bastian shook his head, but he refused to meet my gaze like he was lying to me. "Nah. Don't worry yourself with unnecessary details."

I was still too out of it to carry on a decent conversation.

"We're taking you home," Bastian said.

"What about the body?"

He traced his fingers down my bare arms. "We'll deal with him later."

Damian rose to his feet and wiped the knife on his shirt, staring at me strangely.

"What?" I asked him.

No response.

"Why do you keep looking at me like that?"

Bastian wrapped me in his warm embrace. "Don't poke the dragon, Cherry."

Damian sliced open a man's throat as if it were nothing like he wasn't even a person. I was thankful he saved me, but at what cost? He just fucking murdered someone in cold blood.

Did he even hesitate?

Did he enjoy killing people?

Bastian's cell phone rang, and he raised it to his ear. "Yeah, we got Alex. One of Volkov's men almost raped her. How the fuck did you let this happen? Luca is going to kill you."

It must have been Marcello on the phone, frantic when I didn't return to our table.

After Bastian hung up, he placed his big palm on my back. "Let's go home. We need to clean you up."

I let Bastian guide me through the woods and back to his Porsche without another word. I sat on Damian's lap in the two-seater, disgusted by the feel of blood on our clothes and skin. I tried not to think about it too much as we drove in silence.

Bastian floored the gas pedal into The Hills, up the steep incline toward the guarded gate that separated Founders Way from the rest of Devil's Creek. We blew through the front gate at the Salvatore Estate manned by armed soldiers. The tires screeched as we stopped in front of a garage that housed dozens of exotic cars.

There wasn't a single car worth less than a hundred thousand dollars. Not like that was much of a surprise. The Salvatores owned global companies worth billions of dollars. And Bastian and Damian were the youngest billionaires in Forbes' history.

Damian hadn't spoken a single word. He looked somewhat excited.

Did murder turn him on?

Knowing that psycho, it would not have shocked me. There wasn't much that would have surprised me about either of them.

Once we were on the second floor, Bastian slipped his fingers between mine and led me into my bedroom. We went straight into the bathroom that adjoined Damian's room with mine. His door was open, but I couldn't see much other than black walls.

It looked fucking depressing.

Like a coffin or a dungeon.

Bastian stripped off his bloody shirt before turning the shower knobs. Blood streaked his chiseled chest. It seemed odd that he'd gotten so much blood on his body from one cut.

"Why do you have so much blood on you?" I asked.

Bastian shrugged. "It's from earlier."

"Earlier?" I raised my eyebrows in confusion. "What did you do earlier?"

"We had to take care of some business."

He wasn't forthcoming, so I didn't push him for answers. As he worked on the button of his pants, his steel-gray eyes met mine.

My throat just about closed up as he unzipped his pants. He slid them over his hips with his boxers, and his big cock sprang free. I licked my lips at the sight of him.

Damian peeled off his bloody clothes beside me without a word, dropping his belt onto the floor with a clang. I stood between them, still fully dressed, my eyes shifting between them. My heart sped up as I took in every detail of their naked, muscular bodies.

I licked my lips, and Bastian smirked.

Cocky bastard.

"It's your turn, Cherry." He stepped forward and tugged on the straps of my dress. I covered myself with my hands, and he chuckled. "You don't have to be shy with us."

Even though I didn't slit his throat, I still felt guilty for what we'd done. All of us were implicit in a crime.

But he deserved it.

Damian moved behind me and yanked down my dress. The fabric fell to the tiled floor, exposing my bare breasts. Bastian rolled his thumb across his bottom lip, staring at my painfully erect nipples. My heart crashed into my rib cage as their heated gazes seared my skin.

Bastian stripped off my panties, and we got into the shower, blood tinting our skin. Damian squeezed my ass and pushed me under the water.

In complete silence, they scrubbed the blood from my body. A moan escaped from my throat as hands slid down my arms, stomach, and thighs.

It was wrong to want them.

Stupid to act on my feelings.

It was nothing but attraction with Damian, but I still desired him. I traced my fingers down Bastian's chest, staring up at my beautiful nightmare. He was so gorgeous my heart ached.

Bastian's hand moved to the back of my head, then his lips collided with mine. Pinning me against the wall, he raised my arms above my head, claiming my mouth with rough possession. Damian moved to my side and dipped his head down to suck my nipple into his mouth. I kissed Bash, hard and greedy, needing more of his tongue.

They worked in unison, torturing me. It felt too good to have their hands and mouths on me. For once, they acted as if they cared about me. Bastian's kisses were still rough, but he wasn't as aggressive as usual. I saw the hesitation in his eyes. I noted the way something had changed between us.

Damian's hand slipped between my thighs, his fingers seeking my wetness. Hooking my arms around Bastian's neck, I bit his lip and rocked my hips into Damian's hand. A wicked smirk pulled at Bash's lips. He raised my thigh and wrapped it around his back to change the angle. His long, hard cock rubbed my stomach as Damian fucked me with his fingers, ripping screams of pleasure from me.

I slid my hand up and down Bash's shaft, reaching over to grab Damian. My hands were too small, all the Salvatores so damn big. People said it hurt the first time.

Blood pooled on the floor, the evidence of our crime disappearing down the drain. My body trembled as I came on Damian's fingers, squeezing them with my pussy. I fell back against the wall, still jerking their shifts, watching their faces as they coated my hands with their cum.

Breathless, I dropped my hands to my side, attempting to collect myself. What had I just done? It was the first time I'd ever willingly touched either of them.

I wanted them.

Damian's big cock was hard again, and he stroked himself as he reached out and twisted my nipple. He didn't look anywhere done with me.

Bastian kissed my forehead, then tapped Damian on the shoulder. "Take care of our girl."

He left me alone with Damian, who stared at me like a predator eyeing up his next meal. My beautiful monster. They were all sick and twisted, deranged psychos.

Could I ever love them?

I grabbed a towel from the hook on the wall and climbed out of the shower. Smoke fogged the mirror. So I wiped off the condensation away with my hand. As I stared into the mirror, I ran my fingers through my hair to get rid of the knots. My curls were so unruly and hard to tame—like the men in my life.

When I looked up again, Damian was behind me. I gasped at his sudden appearance. He was so damn quiet I didn't hear him.

We exchanged a look before he bent down to grab his clothes from the floor. I worked my fingers through my hair one more time, getting rid of the last kink.

Lost in my thoughts, I didn't even notice Damian with a belt in his hand. Not until it was too late to run. Still wet and naked, he lowered it over my head and bent me forward, pressing my palms to the counter.

He tugged hard on the leather.

I slapped his hand, gasping for air. "Damian, stop it!"

And then everything went black.

Chapter Thirty-Two

ALEX

D amian tightened the belt around my neck, staring at me in the mirror with a vacant expression.

Where the fuck did he go?

I thrashed and screamed and begged for someone to help me. But as he pulled on the buckle, I struggled to maintain my bearings, losing my grip on the counter. My eyes slammed shut. And before I passed out from the lack of oxygen, Bastian pulled Damian off me.

"Are you fucking crazy?" Bastian slapped Damian on the side of the head. "You could have killed her!"

Damian inched toward him, a sour look on his face.

Bastian raised his hand. "No. Go to your room. Don't even look at Alex. Don't come near her. You're not using this bathroom anymore." He slammed his palms into Damian's chest and knocked him into the wall. "Get the fuck out! Now!"

Damian gave his brother one last pouty look before leaving the room and locking the door behind him.

Tears streamed down my cheeks, flowing like a dam breaking. My throat burned as I cried on Bastian's chest, squeezing his muscular arms for support. Why hadn't I cried after almost being raped? Not even after Damian killed that man. Nearly dying at Damian's hands was the final straw.

"It's okay, Cherry." Bastian palmed the back of my head, slipping his fingers through my curls. "I'm sorry, baby. I thought he would be okay by himself."

Marcello entered the bathroom, chest heaving, his dark hair a fucking mess. He looked like he had run from the café. His eyes widened as he studied my naked body, his intense gaze moving up to the red ring around my neck.

"What the fuck happened?" Marcello touched the bruise. Then his eyes shifted to Bastian. "Please tell me Damian didn't do this."

Bastian nodded. "He almost killed her."

Marcello scooped me up and carried me out of the bathroom. The three of us left my room, passing Damian's locked door in the hallway. Cradling me in his arms, Marcello sat on Bastian's bed and ran his hands up and down my arms and thighs. There was nothing sexual about it. Just him trying to make me feel loved and protected.

"Alex is not staying in that room alone," he told Bastian. "For now on, we'll rotate shifts. You have her tonight. She'll sleep with me tomorrow after I return from my mission."

"Agreed." Bastian nodded. "But I don't think Damian will go near her again. He knows he fucked up."

Marcello held the back of my head and breathed in my scent as he kissed my forehead. "I'm sorry, princess. I shouldn't have left you alone. I'm so sorry. I don't know what else to say."

I peered into his sad blue eyes. "Say you won't let anyone hurt me ever again."

His lips brushed mine. "I promise."

He held me for a long time as Bastian sat on the bed beside us, quiet for once. His hand rested on my knee, and on occasion, he tapped his fingers and hummed a tune. None of us knew what to say. Marcello felt horrible for not keeping his eye on me at all times. But it was just the bathroom. He couldn't have anticipated that man trying to attack me in a restaurant.

When I grabbed his hand, Marcello shifted his weight, about to rise from the bed. "Wait. Don't leave me. Not yet."

"I can't stay, princess." He leaned over and kissed the top of my head. "Duty calls. I'll be back in the morning. If you need me, I won't be far, okay?"

I kissed him, a soft peck that barely grazed his lips. "Okay. I'll see you tomorrow."

After Marcello left the room, Bastian dropped to his knees in front of me. He tilted my head to each side and inspected my neck. "I should have known better. I wouldn't have left you with him if I didn't think he could handle it."

"Handle what?"

"Damian loves blood and death." Bastian wiped away my tears with the swipe of his thumb. "He has a mental illness. What just happened in the bathroom, the doctors call it erotophonophilia. Sexual arousal from murder. You got him off, so I thought he would be okay alone with you."

I narrowed my eyes at him, startled by the news. How did I hitch my wagon to a legit fucking psychopath?

"His kinks are like a serial killer?"

Bastian slipped his fingers between mine. "I know how it sounds, but…" Eyes downcast, he sighed. "He developed the condition after our parents' murders. At least, that's what the doctors believe. But I think he was this way long before they died."

"Murdered? The newspapers said they crashed because of a mechanical failure."

He shook his head. "It's easy to spin lies when you have enough money. A terrorist organization killed our parents. It wasn't an accident." He blew out a deep breath and ran his hand through his dark, wet hair. "We should have been on the flight with our parents."

"Where were you?"

"I had a last-minute piano recital." Bastian sat on my right, still holding my hand, the mattress dipping beneath his weight. "One pianist dropped out. They asked me to fill in. Damian was only there because he begged his parents to come with me. After that, we went everywhere together."

Since he was sharing, I figured this was an excellent time to learn more about the mysterious Salvatores. "How did you end up here?"

"Arlo was good friends with our parents. So he offered to adopt us."

"I bet the money had a lot to do with it."

He glanced over at the grand piano by the window and shook his head. "No, he wanted something more powerful than money. Like you, I'm from a Founding Family. So is Damian."

My lineage traced back to Alexander Hamilton. The Wellingtons were considered American royalty, but I'd never felt like a princess, not even for a second.

"I'm related to John Adams," Bastian told me. "My grandfather is Fitzgerald Archibald Adams IV. He's the current Grand Master of The Founders Society and owns the largest bank in the world. That old bastard is meaner than a pit bull on steroids. But we lucked out with Arlo. He gave us a home and welcomed us into his family. I have nothing but respect for him."

"I hate being a Wellington," I confessed. "My life sucked before my grandfather saved us. Pops made it sound like I could have this Cinderella story life if I moved to Devil's Creek. I didn't know the dream came with strings attached. Being related to a Founder has only made my life worse."

"I know how you feel, Cherry." He stroked my cheek with his long fingers. "The money, the company, all of this shit I would give back just for another second with my parents. I never cared about any of it." He lowered his gaze and bit the inside of his cheek. "At least I have Damian. As much as he gets under my skin, I doubt I would have survived this long without him."

"That's how I feel about Aiden. He's my rock." I leaned forward, elbows on my thighs, and glanced over at him. "You're not related to Damian. So why did Arlo adopt both of you?"

Bastian's eyes held mine. "He only wanted me, but I wouldn't go without Damian."

"Why so much loyalty to him?"

He shrugged, unaffected by my question. "Because he's my brother. Damian needed me."

"Why did Arlo want you and not him?"

"Damian has always had problems. His parents tried to get him help, but… I don't know. He was never right in the head."

"Yeah, but he listens to you. He was so subservient when you yelled at him."

"We have a special bond." He tapped his fingers on his thigh, drawing my attention to the fact he was still shirtless and only wearing tight black boxer briefs. "I don't know how else to explain it."

"Is that why you two always tag team me? You like sharing with him?"

He bobbed his head. "Damian will never have a normal relationship. He can't feel like other people. He doesn't know how to process emotions." Bastian brushed a strand of hair behind my ear. "He likes you. I know it's hard to believe after what he did. But he's never acted the way he does around anyone else."

I laughed. "Are you kidding me? He acts like I'm a possession instead of a person. He calls me Pet. That's not a term of endearment. It's him claiming his ownership of me."

"He gets aroused by death," he said in his brother's defense. "All the blood on you… It probably flipped the switch in his brain. He didn't mean what he did. Sometimes, he gets carried away."

"I'm not the first woman that's happened with, am I?"

He rolled his shoulders, indifferent. "Some women like that rough kinky shit."

I slid my fingers beneath his chin, bringing his eyes to mine. "Promise me you'll never leave me alone with Damian."

His fingers traced down my thigh in a soothing motion. "Don't worry your pretty little head about it. He won't touch you without my permission." Bastian pushed himself up from the mattress and extended his hand to me. "I was in the middle of composing a song. Wanna help me finish it?"

"I don't know how to play the piano," I said as he helped me up from the bed.

He led me across the room to the grand piano that overlooked the bay. I sat beside him and stared out the windows, smiling at the beauty of the light reflecting off the water. This place was peaceful. If only the men who inhabited the estate were more like their surroundings.

Bastian lifted me onto his lap and laid my hands on the keys. Sparks of electricity raced up my arms from his delicate touch. In these moments, I could see myself with Bastian. He was nothing like I had imagined and everything I craved.

He put his hands over mine and glided my fingers across the keys. An unfamiliar, haunting tune filled the air.

"I'm playing the piano," I said in awe that we were creating music together.

He laughed. "How does it feel to play?"

"The keys are softer than I thought they would be."

Another chuckle. "I've been working on this song for a while now. What do you think?"

"It's beautiful." I glanced over my shoulder and smiled at him. "I love it. What's it called?"

"Not sure yet. I have to let it come to me."

He moved my fingers across the keys, and by the time the song ended, I had tears in my eyes.

"Wow," I whispered. "You're incredible, Bash."

He pressed his lips to my bare shoulder and kissed my skin. Until now, I'd completely forgotten I was still naked.

Snaking his arm around me, he rested his hand right below my breast. "You're my muse. This song is about you."

I turned so I was sideways on his lap and draped my arm across the back of his neck. "You're kidding."

He drew a breath from between his teeth as our eyes met. And without warning, his mouth descended upon mine. This time, he took things slowly, a sensual kiss that made my insides ignite from the shock waves of pleasure spreading throughout my body.

He wrote a song for me.

In his way, Bastian made a romantic declaration. I was so thrilled that I kissed him until our lips bruised, aching for more after our lips separated. Bastian gripped my hips and set me on top of the piano. He kissed my inner thigh and lifted my leg over his shoulder. I shoved my hand through his short, dark hair and encouraged him to come closer.

With his mouth near my sensitive flesh, I needed to feel him. He stuck out his tongue and rolled it over my clit like a good boy.

"Bash," I moaned. "Mmm… That feels so good."

He licked between my folds, his tongue darting in and out of my wetness. My fingers wove through his hair. I thought I saw a smirk when I tugged harder, and he drove into my pussy with a greedy look in his eyes, sucking on my clit. Bastian shoved two fingers inside me and made me scream his name.

My eyes slammed shut from the powerful sensation that commanded control of my body. A wave of heat rushed over me as I came on his tongue, tugging at the ends of his hair.

He growled against my pussy.

"You like that, Bash?"

He nodded and continued licking and sucking until another orgasm wrecked me. "Cherry, you don't know what you do to me, woman. I made a pact with my brothers, but I don't know if I can keep it."

"What pact?"

"Nothing." He looked up from between my legs and licked my juices from his lips. "Doesn't matter."

"It matters to me." I slid my fingers beneath his chin and forced him to look at me. "Tell me."

He blew out a deep breath, eyes on the piano keys. "Years ago, when you first moved to Devil's Creek, Luca made us swear not to fuck you."

I narrowed my eyes at him. "Why?"

"Because he wants your cherry." He wiped his mouth with the back of his hand. "But I'd already claimed it for myself."

"What did Luca make you swear?"

"That none of us could fuck you alone. We have to do it together."

My eyes widened at his confession. "All four of you can't take my virginity."

"Yeah, I know." His laughter filled the air. "But all of us have to be there when it happens."

I shook my head at their ridiculous agreement. "Who said I'm having sex with any of you?"

He smirked. "Cherry, we both know you've been holding out for me." Bastian kissed my inner thigh, so close to my core I thought he would kiss me down there again. "You're mine, always have been."

"Luca seems to think I belong to him."

"Where is he now?" He cocked an eyebrow. "Last I checked, I saved you from that Russian pig. Luca only cares about satisfying our father's deal with The Founders Society."

"What kind of deal?"

"Marriage. An heir. The Salvatores are not Founders.

They have no right to ascend to the next level, not without a marriage to a Founder."

"My grandfather told me. But why is it so important? The Salvatores are billionaires. Do they need to be part of some stupid secret society?"

He tipped his head back and laughed. "Oh, Cherry, you're so naive. You don't know how the world works."

"I guess I have a lot to learn, then."

He gripped my hips, helping me off the piano so I could straddle him. "I have a lot to teach you."

Shirtless and only wearing black boxer briefs, his big cock poked through the slit in his boxers. I wrapped my hand around his shaft, giving him a few tentative strokes.

His gaze dropped to my mouth.

When he looked into my eyes, I whispered against his lips, "I want to learn how to please you. So teach me, Bash."

"I've waited a long time to hear you say that." He licked his lips and covered my hand with his, helping me stroke his shaft. "This is what you do to me, baby. You want to learn how to please a man?"

I slid off his lap and got on my knees in front of him. I glanced up at him with my hand on his thigh, ignoring the nerves shaking my limbs. "I want to please you, Bash."

He groaned as if he were in pain. "Fuck, baby. Give me your mouth. Wrap your pretty lips around my cock." He slipped his fingers through my hair and gave it a light tug. "Roll your tongue along the tip."

I stuck out my tongue, and he hissed as I sucked the head of his cock into my mouth. "That's it, Cherry." His eyes closed as if he were trying to focus on the feeling of my mouth on him. "Goddamn, baby. Keep going."

I did as he commanded, but it was a real challenge to fit him. He was long and so thick my cheeks puffed out with each inch I forced into my mouth. He grunted when he hit the back of my throat. "You're so good at this," he said, his chest rising and falling. "That's it, Cherry. Keep doing that. I'm so close, baby."

Once I got a good rhythm going, his eyes opened, lips parted. He pushed my hair off my forehead and watched me swallow his enormous cock.

"Fuck." He reached between us to pinch my nipples between his fingers. "Your mouth feels so damn good, baby." His grip tightened on my hair, his eyes wide as his legs trembled.

When I felt his cock pulse, I knew he was about to come. Seconds later, his warmth filled my mouth. I wasn't sure what to do, so I swallowed all of him. It was a lot more than I had expected and tasted salty.

He slid his thumb across my lips, and then he grabbed me under my arms, lifting me onto his lap. We were both out of breath when he kissed my lips.

"Are you ready for bed, Cherry?"

I rested my forehead against his and breathed him in. "I could use another shower."

He hooked my legs around his back and then rose from the bench. "One more shower and then bed."

Bastian had a prescribed bedtime and planned his life down to the minute.

Control-freak.

He carried me into the ensuite bathroom and set my feet on the cold tiled floor.

"What about the body?" I asked. "We left him in the woods."

Bastian shrugged off my concern. "Damian has dealt with it. He probably left the house after I yelled at him. That Russian fuck is in pieces by now."

Steam filled the bathroom as we waited for the shower to warm up. Bastian kissed me once more, a quick peck that left me begging for more.

"Get in, Cherry." He tapped my ass. "We don't have all

night."

He tipped his head toward the glass shower and followed me inside. This time, we didn't kiss or make out. Bastian helped me wash my hair and lathered my skin with body wash.

As if racing against an invisible clock, he had us washed and dressed in record time. I changed into one of Bastian's T-shirts, which stopped past my knees, and I got into bed with him. He flicked off the light before I got comfortable.

"Hey, I'm not ready."

"You are now." The bed shifted beneath his weight, and he rolled onto his side to face me. His warm breath fanned across my lips. "Time to conquer your fear, Cherry. No one will hurt you in this room. I'll protect you."

"I don't like the dark."

"I don't have a nightlight, baby. Kinda grew out of those after I was two."

"I'm not a child. I just don't like the dark."

He rolled off the bed, lit a candle, and placed it on my bedside table. The glow gave me a partial view of his handsome face. "How's that?"

"Better. Thank you."

He got back in bed, then draped his arm across my stomach. "Consider yourself lucky. You're the only woman I've ever let in my bed."

"I'm honored," I quipped.

He turned on his side and kissed my forehead. "You should feel very honored. This room is my sanctuary."

"Did you tell Luca about what happened tonight?"

"With the Russian?"

"And Damian."

"Yeah, Marcello told him." He ran his fingers through my wet hair. "Go to sleep, Cherry. We have a big day ahead of us."

"But I need music to sleep."

"Jesus, woman." He laughed before rolling onto his side to grab his cell phone from the nightstand. "You're so high maintenance."

Act I of Tchaikovsky's Swan Lake played through his speaker a few seconds later. The sound instantly calmed me. It was one of the many coping mechanisms the doctor had suggested after my grandfather had brought me to Devil's Creek.

I'd had non-stop nightmares for most of my life. Therapy helped. The pills also came in handy when I needed them. So did my art.

But I wanted to learn mechanisms to control my PTSD and the awful flashbacks of the past. So the doctor had suggested music therapy. I fell in love with the ballet after Pops took us to see Swan Lake, and from that moment, the soundtrack became the one thing that soothed me other than my twin.

I needed it to sleep.

Bastian curled my body into his muscular chest, his big hand cradling my breast. "Sweet dreams, Cherry."

As if his words put me under a spell, I was asleep within minutes, drifting to thoughts of my dark prince.

The following day, I woke up screaming, the sound of my shrill voice snapping me right out of my nightmare. I held my hand over my heart, unable to catch my breath.

"Aiden," I whispered.

Someone clutched my shoulder. "Wake up, Cherry."
Bash.

Letting out a deep breath, I opened my eyes. The candle

flickered on the table beside me, casting a glow on the dark room.

I rolled onto my side so I could see him. "Where is my brother? Tell me the truth, Bash."

"I don't know," he said, though it sounded like a lie. "What were you dreaming about, pretty girl?"

With my head on the pillow, I glanced over at him, seeking his beautiful gray eyes for a sign of malice. "Everything that happened last night. That guy... Damian. I need Aiden. You need to help me find him."

He sat up, bringing me with him, his back propped up against a stack of pillows. "I'll keep you safe from Damian. As for the other asshole, he's six feet under."

Of course, he ignored the most critical question.

"My brother, Bash. Where is he? I need to talk to him."

"Okay, okay." He clutched my shoulder and kissed the top of my head. "I'll talk to Marcello. See if he can track down Aiden."

"Promise me."

"Yeah, I promise." His fingers slipped through my hair in a soothing motion that helped to slow down my racing heart. "I got you, babe. Don't worry." He cradled my head against his chest. "Just go back to sleep."

It was five o'clock in the morning, but I wasn't ready to sleep, not after dreaming about my brother lying dead in a ditch. I couldn't think straight without Aiden. He'd been missing for weeks, probably since I left Brooklyn.

"I'm not tired anymore."

Bastian stretched out his long legs and moved me between them. I laid my head back on his chest, soaking up this moment. Over the past few weeks, Bastian had surprised the hell out of me. Someone I craved so much I couldn't wait to ditch my virginity.

His fingers trailed up and down my arms, a soft massage that gave me goosebumps. As he leaned forward to suck on my earlobe, the scent of bergamot filled my nostrils. I loved the way he smelled. His usual cologne mixed with the saltiness of the sea. Whenever I was around the Salvatores, I could smell it on them.

Another trigger for my PTSD.

It was a scent that set off a series of flashbacks and panic attacks. But now, it comforted me.

"Who was that man?" I glanced up at Bastian, who looked so damn peaceful. "What did your family do to his? I need to understand why I almost got raped. Why did killing turn Damian into a psycho."

"Ever hear of the Volkov Bratva?"

I slipped out of his grasp, tucking one leg under the other, and gripped my knees. "He was Russian Mafia?"

"He was one of Volkov's men."

"But, why me?"

"Because you belong to us." He gripped my hips and lifted me on top of him. "You'll never be safe. We will always have enemies knocking at our door. But we won't let anything happen to you."

"You say I belong to you like I'm a possession. If you want this to work, you need to treat me like your equal."

"You are more than my equal." His fingers wove through my hair, his lips inches from mine. "You're a queen."

Chapter Thirty-Three

ALEX

Marcello was back from his short mission for Salvatore Global the next night. He didn't offer any details, and I didn't bother to ask. I was too excited about seeing his bedroom, which sounded so childish.

But according to Bastian, Marcello didn't even let them on the fourth floor, not unless they were going to his father's office.

My eyes swept over Marcello's bedroom, taking in every inch of the space. The room had a high ceiling, tall windows with dark curtains, and a balcony overlooking the bay. He had the same room as Luca but one floor above him.

I stood at the center of the room and noted the detail in the mural, which spanned two walls.

Marcello can paint.

A smile stretched across my face, and a strange feeling stirred in my belly. His mom would have been so proud of him. I thought about the fresco in Evangeline's studio. She saw her sons as stars with their perfect golden crowns, the light illuminating their handsome faces.

Smooth brushstrokes created a world that belonged to Marcello, his bedroom a testament to his raw talent. Black, red, orange, and a hint of white paint swirled across his walls. Back in Brooklyn, I had painted the Greek Underworld version of Devil's Creek on my bedroom walls. All the devils were there. But Marcello's mural was the underworld.

A man stood at the center of the skull and fire landscape, his head down, dark waves atop his head. He had snakes wrapped around his legs, slithering up his arms. What looked like a king cobra sat on his shoulder, its tongue hanging out.

"Marcello," I stammered. "This is…" I turned to look at him, my mouth hanging open. "You're so talented."

He winked. "We have a lot more in common than you think."

"You could pursue an art career. We could…"

"No," he said before I could finish. "I don't want anyone to know." He shook his head, dark hair falling onto his forehead. "My art is the only thing not corrupted by evil. And my father would never allow it. So that's why I don't let anyone near this room."

I smiled so wide my cheeks hurt. "It's our little secret."

Marcello's eyes flicked back to the mural.

I studied the man with the snake wrapped around his body. "Aiden painted something like this years ago."

Marcello nodded. "You know the mural behind the bakery? We did it together."

I lifted my brows. "The one in Beacon Bay?"

"Yeah. It was Aiden's idea."

I wrapped my fingers around his wrist and looked up at him. Now it all made sense. Artists were natural introverts, content with cutting themselves off from the world.

The loneliness suited him.

"You were friends with Aiden? But he always acted as if he hated you."

"It was better that way." He rolled his broad shoulders. "Luca would have harassed Aiden more if he knew we were friends."

"How did that even happen?"

"Back in high school, I shared a lunch period with Aiden. And one day, I found him out back of the school spray painting a scene from The Iliad. It's my favorite book, so I asked if I could join him."

"Which scene did you paint?"

"Achilles striking the final blow at Hector."

I smiled. "Aiden loves Greek mythology."

"Me too." He pressed his finger to my lips to silence me. "Before you ask about Aiden, I don't have any answers for you. Aiden is a big boy. He can handle himself."

"But I need him."

"You have us now, princess." He swiped the pad of his thumb across my bottom lip, and his intense blue eyes laser-focused on me. "We're all you will ever need."

"Just answer one question about Aiden."

He groaned. "Depends on the question."

"Did he accept my grandfather's offer?"

He nodded.

We both knew one day they would come for me. And when they did, Aiden wouldn't be able to fight my grandfather for much longer.

"Is he safe?"

Another nod.

"Do your brothers know you paint?"

He led me by the hand toward his king-size bed. "We only talk about work, the Knights, and you. They haven't been in my room since we were teenagers. Not since my dad forbid me to paint."

"I wouldn't have survived growing up without my brother." I moved my hand to his thigh, seeking his warmth. "Aiden made everything better. The night terrors. All the shit with our parents. That's why he was so protective of me. Why he never wanted Luca near me. I miss him," I whispered, doing my best to hold back the tears. "Every day. It's only been a month, but it feels like years without him."

An awkward silence passed between us.

He looked down at my hand on his thigh. His fingers grazed mine, my skin on fire from his touch. "You deserve better."

"Than you?"

"All of us." His voice was deep and smooth. "You're too good for this place. For this life. So much like her."

"Your mom?" I guessed.

He nodded, lips pressed together, deep in thought. "You remind me of her." He traced a circle on the top of my hand with his finger. "At least what I remember."

"What was it like losing your mom so young?"

He stared over my shoulder at the wall. "After our mom died, the house was silent. No laughter. No music. Nothing. Just fucking silence. She was the only good in our lives. The light in the darkness. Then came the violence. I adapted to my environment."

"My house was a nightmare," I told him. "I hated it."

He cupped my face. "Your mom will pay for what she did to you."

I felt a spark between us, an instant connection that made my skin sizzle with heat. "What's happening between us, Marcello?"

His eyes held mine. "I don't know."

"I know this marriage is important to your family... but I don't want to marry Luca."

He gripped my shirt collar and pulled me to him. His breath ghosted my lips. He smelled like scotch and cigars mixed with the scent of his citrus aftershave and clean linen.

"I want you, princess. I want you to be my wife." His thumb brushed my nipple over the top of my shirt, and then he tugged on it. "But I made a promise..."

I cried out, a whimper on my lips. "Marcello."

"Fuck, I love when you moan my name."

"Marcello," I whispered as he pinched the tiny bud again.

He smirked. "If you were mine, I would never treat you like he does." The pad of his thumb swiped over my painfully sore nipple. "What do you want, Alex?"

He looked at me with those wide blue eyes. So beautiful. We breathed hard, lips parted. I attempted to speak, but nothing came out.

What did I want?

No one had ever asked me that.

"Right now, I want you to keep playing with my nipples." I bit his bottom lip and sucked it into my mouth. "I want you to make me come, Marcello."

An excited groan escaped his throat. "You never paid up for the last three orgasms I gave you," he said in a taunting tone, laughter in his voice. "Do you think you deserve more?"

"Bash has been teaching me," I confessed. "I've learned a few things."

"Oh?" Marcello smiled. "What did Bash teach you?"

"How to suck cock." I wet my lips. "Make me come, and I'll show you everything I've learned."

He pinned my back to the mattress, his lips caressing mine. "Open your legs, princess." His hand dipped between my thighs, prying them apart. "Be a good girl and scream for me."

Chapter Thirty-Four

DAMIAN

I fucked up more than usual. Bastian and Marcello wouldn't even look at me, let alone talk to me. Luca wasn't speaking to any of us. After people threatened to list Alex for auction, he spent late nights in his office, making deals with shady people from the criminal underworld.

No one could disturb him.

Despite his attempts to hate Alex, he didn't, not really. Luca wanted her just as much as the rest of us.

My father was in Italy on business, halfway around the world. Apart from Bash, he was the only one who knew how to quell my urges. So I left a message with Dr. Lansing, demanding a callback. Unfortunately, I didn't know how to fix what I did. That part of my brain didn't work.

Alex hated me, and it was ruining my bond with Bash. So I left for the New York office the following day. I figured we all needed some space and that it would give Bastian time to explain the situation to Alex. She had issues, so I hoped she would understand.

I told myself she wasn't like Evangeline, even though I wasn't sure. Alex was a lot like my adoptive mother. Beautiful, intelligent, full of passion and intensity. A little crazy, too. Eva never accepted me, called me the devil. She saw the dark side of my personality and wanted me out of her life and her family.

What if Alex feels that way?

If Evangeline hadn't died, she would have convinced Arlo to get rid of Bastian and me. Because of Arlo, we weren't orphans. Our father welcomed us into his home and family and called us his sons. I never felt like an outsider with Arlo. He embraced my darkness and showed me how to control it and use it to my advantage.

Arlo was my father in every way that counted. My bio-dad never even bothered with me. When he wasn't cheating on my mom, he was usually at the office trying to expand Atlantic Airlines with Bash's dad. Now, he was nothing more than a faint memory, just a man who donated his sperm and fortune.

I sat behind my desk and rested my shoe on my knee. The headquarters for Atlantic Airlines were in Manhattan and overlooked Central Park. So I had the perfect view from the seventieth floor. But this place felt cold and empty without Bastian across the room from me. We shared a three thousand square foot office with a bar, kitchen, full bathroom, and a bedroom for when we worked late nights.

I was keeping a low profile until Bastian stopped acting like a dick. So I stuck with my usual stalking, something I had perfected over the years. The computer screen in front of me had dozens of camera angles of the Salvatore Estate.

I missed my family.

They hated me now, but they would get over their anger. Bash would eventually come around.

He always did.

Alex was in Eva's studio with Marcello. He hovered over her, leaning forward in the chair to look at her painting. She laid on her stomach on the floor on top of a tarp with a paintbrush in her hand.

She was so fucking talented. A natural like Bastian, with a

real gift for bringing out our strengths and weaknesses. She was painting one of us, but I couldn't tell who. Her paintings often resembled Luca or Marcello, but lately, when I checked on her, she was painting Bash with a golden crown and horns. I was a little disappointed she hadn't painted me yet.

Maybe someday.

Flipping between the screens, I scanned the feeds for Bastian. He was in our shared office on the second floor. It was large enough to accommodate two large oak desks, a boardroom table, and a big fireplace.

He stood between the French doors that overlooked the bay, dressed in a suit with his hands on his hips. He looked deep in thought, and I wondered if he thought about me.

Does he miss me, too?

It was only a few days, but I needed him. I would probably always need him to help me translate the world around me. He was the one who handled clients and business associates, while I usually dealt with foreign customers since I spoke seven languages fluently. Bash never wanted to learn more than Spanish and Italian, a necessity in the Salvatore home.

A loud beep snapped me back to reality, and my secretary's flowery voice floated through the speaker. "Mr. Salvatore, I have Dr. Lansing on the phone."

I hit the intercom button. "Put him through."

The phone rang, and I raised the receiver to my ear. "Dr. Lansing, thanks for calling me back."

"You sounded upset, Damian," the older man said, his voice trembling. "Is everything okay?"

I scared him.

So I paid him thousands of dollars to let me divulge the truth about my addiction without him running to the cops. But if he did that, I'd have to kill him, too, which would have been a shame because I liked him. He'd helped me a lot over the years.

"No," I admitted to the doctor. "I lost control a few days ago."

"What happened?"

I explained how I choked Alex without mentioning the man I killed or why I got so carried away.

He breathed deeply into the phone. "Damian, you can control your urges. It would help if you wanted this for yourself. Alex is too important to you to chase her away over a misunderstanding."

Dr. Lansing didn't know I killed people. That I lived for the moment when I drained the last breath from a person. He thought I had compulsions and that I could control myself. I had self-control with most things, especially in the bedroom, but not with my cravings.

After years of fighting the urges, I gave into them when I was in high school. A man tried to kill my father. It wasn't the first or last attempt on his life. So I slit his throat, splashing blood all over me, staining my clothes.

I went home afterward and stared in the mirror. At all the blood on me. Thinking about what I did, I whipped out my cock and stroked it so fucking hard I rubbed it raw by the time I'd finished. I had never been so fucking turned on. And after seeing Alex covered in another man's blood—the man I killed to protect her—I wanted to do it again.

I wanted to kill someone.

I wanted to wrap my hands around their throat and squeeze. But I was too out of my mind to realize it was Alex. I didn't mean to hurt her. It was as if my body was physically in the bathroom with her while my mind was elsewhere.

"I'm fine now," I assured Dr. Lansing. "But Bastian won't talk to me. Same with Alex and Marcello."

"Alex is important to you," he said firmly. "You talk about her a lot."

I stared out the windows at Central Park, watching all the

ordinary people live their fucking lives. "She's the most important woman in my life."

I couldn't give Alex a normal life. None of us could. We didn't know how to conform to societal norms. All of us were lucky to grow up with money and have everything come easy. We had too much darkness inside us to survive with everyone else.

"Then you need to apologize," Dr. Lansing insisted. "Explain to her what happened. Tell her about your urges so she understands you lost control."

My gaze flicked back to the computer screen, where Alex kissed Marcello. She rubbed her pussy on his cock, and I got hard thinking of how I wanted to wreck her tight virgin pussy.

"Bash has probably already done that by now."

"She needs to hear it from you, Damian." His voice reached a higher octave as if he were sick of my stubbornness. "You didn't mean to hurt Alex. If you talk to her, she will understand that and possibly forgive you."

I bit the inside of my cheek, contemplating his suggestion. "What do I say?"

I wasn't being difficult. It was a legitimate question. Bastian was usually around to help me deal with shit like this. He was the most normal one of us, apart from Marcello, who was quiet and kept to himself most of the time.

"Start with the apology. Maybe try a romantic gesture."

My nose wrinkled in disgust at the idea. "Romance?" I laughed. "Doc, I'm not capable of romance. I'm lucky if I can get through the day without having to fight off my desires."

"You're capable of more than you realize, Damian. The limitations placed upon you are all in your head. If Alex likes you as much as you like her, she will at least hear you out."

Like was too basic of a word for Alex. I didn't just fucking like her. That woman possessed me, consumed my thoughts and dreams. I obsessed over her. For years, I'd watched her, studied everything about her. There wasn't a single thing I didn't know about her.

All hunters stalked their prey.

We had watched her from afar and made sure she was safe. The heir to the Wellington fortune had a lot of attempts on her life. She was lucky enough not to know about any of them. We had agreed to share and protect her.

Alex was *ours*.

I went and fucked up the group vibe because of my cravings. But she looked so good, too tempting. I could still see the blood on her face and neck when I looked into the mirror and wrapped my belt around her throat.

Fuck.

My cock got hard thinking about it.

"How do I get Bash to stop hating me?" I asked the doctor.

Dr. Lansing shifted the phone in his hand, and I heard a chair creak in the background. "Bastian is your brother. Family. Give him some time to cool down. He will forgive you if you apologize."

"I tried a dozen times already. He won't even answer my calls, and we run a fucking company together!"

I couldn't make Bastian forgive me. Nothing worked on him.

He would ice me out until I returned to normal, or he got sick of ignoring me. This was part of our process. I hated it. I hated waiting for him to calm down.

"Try calling Bastian," he suggested. "If you get him on your side, it will make it easier to speak to Alex."

"A romantic gesture?" I said as I considered his advice. "What exactly would that entail?"

He cleared his throat to cover his laughter. "Women like flowers. That would be a nice start."

Flowers seemed too cheap and simple. But what kind of

present says, Sorry for almost choking you to death? If only Google had an answer for that question.

"Damian, I'm sorry, but I have to cut this conversation short. Call my office and schedule an appointment if you want to discuss this further."

I could never tell him the truth. He would have to break doctor-patient confidentiality if he knew how many people I killed. That was a long fucking list. I could never be myself around anyone, only my family. And now Alex was screwing with our flow, so I needed to get her on board.

After I hung up with the doctor, I called Bastian. The line rang a few times, then went to voicemail. I left what felt like the hundredth message in the past few days. I could see him on the video feed in the office, ignoring my call.

Asshole.

A few minutes later, I received a text message from Bash.

Bastian: Do the right thing, D.
Damian: I'm trying.
Bastian: Not hard enough. Get your ass home. Now.

Chapter Thirty-Five

ALEX

After Bastian finished work on Friday, he walked into his bedroom dressed in a black suit, his dark hair slicked back. He usually let his wavy hair fall all over the place, the chaos to his disorder.

I dropped the book on the bed, letting my eyes wander the length of his body. "Why are you so dressed up?"

"We're leaving the house," he said as he entered the room. "Get ready."

"What should I wear?"

Bastian closed the distance between us with a mischievous smile in place. "Before you ask, it's a surprise. Wear something short and tight."

His two favorite words.

I smiled so wide my cheeks hurt. "Are you taking me to dinner, Bastian Salvatore?"

"Maybe." He slid his arm behind my back, his fingers digging into my hip. "Get dressed before I change my mind."

Excited about leaving the house, I squealed as I ran out of his room and down the hall. I entered my room and rushed into the walk-in closet with Bastian on my tail. The bergamot in his cologne burned into my nostrils after several nights of sleeping in his bed.

I let my clothes drop to the floor. He stood in the entryway, hanging onto the doorframe with a crazed look. His charm and good looks often made it easier to see past the devil behind the mask.

It was all a game with him, smoke and mirrors. He would show his true colors at some point, and the facade would crumble. I was waiting for that moment. Everyone in my life had disappointed me, so it was only a matter of time before he revealed himself.

Scanning the never-ending racks of dresses, I plucked a black one from the hanger and slipped it over my head. As Bastian requested, it was tight as fuck, clinging to my body like plastic wrap, and stopped midway up my thighs.

He licked his lips and whistled. "Damn, girl. I can't wait to rip that dress off you."

"Good luck getting it off." I pushed it the rest of the way down my thighs. "I can barely move in this thing."

Bastian dipped his head down and licked my cheek. "I want to taste every inch of you, Cherry."

"Have you spoken to Damian?" I leaned back to rest my head on his shoulder.

He hooked his arm around me. "Just a few text messages. He's home from New York, but I haven't seen him around the house."

"You were okay with Damian holding me down and spanking me."

"That was different." He tucked one of my curls behind my ear, his face expressionless. "It was in a controlled environment with my supervision. I knew he wouldn't hurt you."

"Is he that bad?"

"He almost killed you." His nostrils flared. "I'm not talking to him, so he can fully understand the consequences of his actions. It's the only way he learns."

"Is this something you have to do with him regularly?"

His hand dropped from my chin and to his side. "Often enough. Damian has lost control too many times. I can't take any chances with you."

"How are you able to control him? Does he answer to Luca and Marcello the way he does you?"

He shook his head. "Damian doesn't need much in life, but he needs me. Without me, he's off-balance."

"Will he lose control if you're not around to stop him?"

He shrugged. "It's possible. At least I know where you are and that he can't hurt you."

I liked the idea of Bastian being my protector, my white knight. He showed me all the possibilities of what I could have with him.

But I was waiting for him to pull the rug out from under me.

After I inspected my appearance, Bastian led me downstairs. Much like its occupants, the Salvatore Estate was cold and haunting. It looked like a seaside palace, but on the inside, it was about as warm and inviting as Dracula's castle.

Damian descended the staircase at the front of the house as we neared the entrance doors. My heart nearly stopped as his shoes hit the marble floor. Tall and gorgeous, I salivated as he ran a hand through his jet-black hair. He was beautiful. But like hemlock or wolf's-bane, he was also deadly.

"Bash," Damian said with a sad look. "Can we talk?"

Bastian shook his head. "Not now."

"It's okay," I told him. "Go ahead. I can wait outside."

My handsome protector stiffened beside me, clutching my hip with possession.

Damian's eyes dropped to his brother's hand on my waist, and then his eyes met mine. "I didn't mean to hurt you, Alex. I'm sorry."

Alex?

Not Pet?

Pressing my lips together, I stared up at him, wanting to repair his relationship with Bastian. I shouldn't have given a damn, but I didn't want to cause a rift between them. Isolating Damian from Bastian would only backfire on me.

He killed a man for me. So I nodded to acknowledge his apology, even though I wasn't ready to forgive him.

"Don't wait up for us." Bastian patted Damian on the shoulder, grinning. "We can talk in the morning."

I didn't look back as we left the house, though I could feel his intense green eyes on my back. We hopped into Bastian's Porsche parked in front of a garage that housed a fleet of luxury cars. The Salvatores had everything at their disposal, yet they had nothing but problems.

Bastian drove off the estate, blowing through the front gates like we were on a freeway. He raced down Founders Way and took a hard right turn.

"Can you slow down?" I asked him on our way down the steep hill.

He tapped his fingers on the steering wheel and glanced over at me. "Are you scared, Cherry?"

I glanced out the window, too aware of how fast we were going through a residential neighborhood. When I didn't answer Bastian, he shifted gears and moved his hand to my inner thigh. I snapped my attention back to him, but his eyes were on the road.

His fingers inched closer to my core. "Do you want me to stop?"

I clutched the door handle, heart racing. Then his hand slipped beneath my dress, and I pressed my lips together as he traced the seam of my panties.

"Bash," I choked out. "You should slow down."

"It's the thrill you love." His long finger slid down my wet slit, and I closed my eyes, breathing through my nose. "Am I right, Cherry? That's why you never fight me. You want this."

"No," I lied.

"Yes, you do." He teased my folds, stroking them with care, his pace never faltering. "You want Damian, too. Don't you? You want all of us."

With that, my eyes snapped open. I turned my head to the side to meet his gaze. My gorgeous captor grinned with satisfaction, pumping his finger into me, working my inner walls.

"Admit it," he growled. "You hate us. But you want us. I saw the look on your face when we ran into Damian. Even after he choked you, there's still a part of you that desires him."

"I want you more," I moaned as he added another finger.

With one hand on the wheel, he fucked me with his fingers. "Hurry, Cherry. If you don't come before I have to shift gears, you're not coming."

"Bastian," I whimpered, rocking my hips into his hand, greedy for release. "You're such an asshole."

His wicked laughter filled the car. "Time to come, baby."

As we neared the bottom of the hill, a wave of heat rolled down my arms. My orgasm shook through me hard and fast as I dug my nails into his forearm and screamed his name.

"On command," he said with an evil glint to his gray eyes. "Luca was wrong about you."

His quick thrusts drove me to the finish line with just enough time. Bastian sucked my cum from his fingers, then placed his hand back on the shifter and switched gears.

I tugged my dress over my thighs and sighed. "What are you talking about?"

"Luca said we couldn't train you. He was wrong."

"I'm not a dog," I snapped. "You can't train me to come."

He tapped his fingers on the shifter and smirked. The bastard didn't even bother to respond because he was right.

"Where are you taking me?"

He pointed his finger. "To the marina."

I looked out the window at the yachts floating in the bay. Devil's Creek was picturesque. A cool breeze wafted through the open window, blowing my hair as we drove toward our destination.

He parked in the front space that said Reserved for the Salvatores.

"Over there." Bastian pointed at the building to my right. "That's the Devil's Creek Belles clubhouse. Your grandmother is the president. One day, you will take over for her."

I snickered. "I hate Blair. My grandmonster can keep her crown. I don't want the job."

"We don't get to choose our fate, Cherry. Men like me marry women from powerful families to secure our legacy. We all have roles to play."

"You don't need me the way Luca and Marcello do."

"No, but I want you." He turned in his seat, studying my face with care. "I'd be a fool not to want a woman as smart, talented, and beautiful as you for my wife."

Be still, heart.

"Does Arlo expect you to marry someone you don't love?"

He rested his hand on the center console as his eyes held mine. "For someone who pretends to hate me, you're concerned with my heart."

"I only wanted to know about your scar."

He smirked. "Just admit you're curious about me."

I blew off his comment by changing the subject. "You don't need Arlo anymore. How come you're still here?"

He shook his head. "That's where you're wrong. I owe everything to him. I have no intention of ever leaving Devil's Creek. This is my home. The Salvatores are my family."

"Your parents left you an airline and billions of dollars. It's not like you need Arlo."

"He promised us the one thing we don't know how to get on our own." I raised an eyebrow, and he continued, "Revenge for our parents' deaths."

I gasped at his confession. "He knows who killed them?"

Bastian bobbed his head. "The man who attacked you worked for the Volkovs, who works for The Lucaya Group."

"So why haven't you gotten revenge yet?"

"Because it's a global organization and impossible to track down. We've been looking for them for years. There are too many layers between the foot soldiers and the bosses. Revenge is a long game. So we have to bide our time and wait until we find the men responsible for their deaths."

"I'm sorry," I whispered. "I can't imagine what that must have been like for you and Damian."

He blew out a deep breath and leaned back against the leather seat. "What can I say? Life sucks. Nothing we do will bring our parents back. But killing the assholes responsible will help me feel better."

He slid out from the driver's seat and was at my side within seconds, yanking me out of the car. Instead of heading toward the Belles clubhouse, we descended a flight of stairs.

"Where are you taking me? I thought we were going to dinner."

Bastian led me down a narrow stone hallway that tunneled deep below ground. He stopped in front of an iron door and knocked three times in a strange succession. It sounded like a passcode, each tap different from the last.

A few seconds passed before I heard metal sliding across a hard surface. Then the top half of a man's face came into focus through a small window.

"What the fuck is this place?"

"Don't worry, Cherry." Bastian winked. "You'll like it here."

The heavy door groaned as the tall man on the other side appeared in the entryway. He had broad shoulders and thick arms corded with muscle.

"Mr. Salvatore." He stepped to the side so we could pass him. "Welcome back to the Founders Club."

My throat nearly closed up as Bastian guided me into the

dark space. It reminded me of a casino and brothel rolled into one. Men played poker and craps at tables to our right. There were dozens of tables with men who were getting lap.

A group of women danced on a stage, grinding their naked bodies against the poles. Even the women carrying trays of drinks were topless. I was the only woman fully clothed.

When men looked at Bastian and me, I felt as if they were undressing me with their eyes. Club members acknowledged Bastian with the tip of their heads. Several security guards walked toward us with a gray-haired man between them, wearing a black suit and a dark blue tie.

"Mr. Salvatore." He stopped in front of us and extended his hand to Bastian. "Welcome back. Are your brothers joining us for the auction?"

What auction?

My heart hammered, forcing me to place my free hand on my chest to calm my nerves. I knew it was too good to be true. He was only being nice to get whatever he wanted from me.

"Luca and Marcello are on their way. Damian is sitting out tonight." Bastian offered my hand to the man. "This is Alexandrea Wellington."

"It's a pleasure to meet you, Miss Wellington." His gaze swept back to Bastian. "Follow me. Your usual table is ready."

The club manager turned on his heels, and Bastian slid his arm behind my back. We walked down a long, dimly lit hallway with red carpets and black walls and then entered a set of double doors at the end of the corridor.

It surprised me to find a dining room with circular booths with high walls that gave the patrons privacy. Women's moans filled the air. Sure, some people ate dinner. But mostly, it looked like one big orgy.

"Thank you, Michael." Bastian shoved a few hundred-dollar bills into his hand. "We'll take it from here." After he walked away, Bastian pointed at the booth. "Sit."

I ignored his demand, too busy staring around the room. Not in a creepy way. More out of curiosity. I'd never been to a place like this before.

Bastian dipped his head down and brushed his lips against my earlobe. "Sit before I bend you over this table in front of everyone and spank you for defying me."

I stood on my tippy toes and got in his face. "Are you going to sell me at the auction if I don't?"

His palm came down hard on my ass. "Test me and find out."

Chapter Thirty-Six

ALEX

Despite all the moaning and debauchery surrounding us, The Founders Club served food. And here I was expecting a romantic dinner with Bastian.

Though, I should have known better. This was the equivalent of eating at a strip club. But, instead of bar food, we ate a five-course meal.

After our server removed the last of our plates, Bastian slid his arm across the back of my neck, resting his hand on my bare shoulder. I hated how normal this felt for us.

Like we were dating.

The overhead lights dimmed, and then someone tapped a microphone. A man announced the auction would start in five minutes. People scrambled across the room. Half of the people in the dining area were naked or missing some clothing. We were the only people still dressed.

"I thought Marcello and Luca were coming."

Bastian turned his head to the side, a sly grin on his lips. "They're parking now. Should be here any second."

"So what kind of auction is this?"

"Are you afraid I listed your virgin pussy for sale, Cherry?"

A shiver rolled down my arms. "No. But I'm wondering

why you brought me here. This isn't a place you take a woman on a date."

"I already told you. We came here to eat and watch the auction."

"Since when is your family in the business of buying women at auctions?"

"We're not. My dad has a hard rule about anything that involves women and children. These women come here because they need money. The Founders Club has clients who will pay millions to fuck a virgin."

"Lucky you," I remarked. "The four of you are getting me for free."

"Not quite, Cherry." He clicked his tongue. "Nothing in this world is free."

Before I could get in another word, Marcello slid into the booth beside me. Luca sat on Bastian's right with an evil look aimed at me. I hadn't seen the bastard since the day I overheard their conversation with Arlo. His brothers claimed he was working, that he wasn't avoiding me. But it sure as hell felt like it.

Marcello stole me from Bastian's grip, moving me across the bench so that he could lift my left thigh over his. "Miss me, princess?"

I looked up at my handsome prince and smiled. "Yes."

He dipped his head down to kiss me, claiming my mouth with violent possession. His kisses were hungry and angry like he wanted to tear me apart. Liquid heat pooled between my thighs, my pussy so wet from his sinful touch that I almost couldn't control myself. I wanted to climb onto his lap and mount him. Show him exactly how much I had missed him.

Marcello and Bastian were the lesser of two evils, and they were slowly becoming my obsession.

"That's enough." Luca cleared his throat. "Get your shit together, Marcello. You're not a teenage boy."

As our lips parted, I instantly missed the feel of his soft lips on mine. Every nerve ending in my body was on fire, hyper-aware of the gorgeous men surrounding me… and how they all made me feel out of control.

"Fuck off," Marcello said to Luca. "I can kiss our girl whenever the fuck I want."

Not like Luca wanted to kiss me. The few times he did, it almost seemed painful for him. Like at the beginning of Twilight, when Edward couldn't kiss Bella without looking like he would be sick. Maybe Luca was a vampire. He was cold and heartless, a royal bastard who enjoyed making my life miserable.

"Where have you been?" I asked Luca.

He glared at me as if I was insignificant, like nothing I said mattered to him. "Working."

"All week?"

"Yes, Drea. All fucking week. I don't answer to you."

"I hate you," I said under my breath.

"Good," Luca shot back.

Needing his warmth, I leaned into Marcello, who snaked his arm around my middle. "If I have to choose between you and Luca, it's you."

"Don't act like a spoiled brat," Luca hissed.

"You could at least act like you give a shit about me." I glanced over at him, teeth clenched. "It wouldn't kill you to treat me with an ounce of respect."

He rolled his broad shoulders against the leather bench. "It might."

Why did he hate me so much?

Something had happened in the past between our families. He'd alluded to that many times over the years, and yet, I still didn't know what had made Luca so hateful. The past few weeks had softened Marcello's hard exterior. But his older brother was a lost cause.

A moment later, the auction began. The house lights dimmed as the announcer took the stage and moved behind a podium. Three girls who looked not much younger than me lined up beside him in skimpy lingerie.

Bastian's fingers trailed down my arm, his delicate motion whipping me out of my Luca-induced fit of anger. Sometimes I forgot Bastian was the enemy. And in these moments, I wondered if I was falling for him.

A woman's screams of pleasure pierced the air like gunfire. The announcer hadn't even introduced the auction girls before the woman two booths over was riding out an orgasm. Skin slapped and men grunted. It was like being trapped in a porno.

Marcello's hand dropped to my thigh, his fingers inching up to my aching core. My breath hitched as Marcello peeled my panties to the side, baring my wet pussy to the cold air.

It was freezing in the club.

And with Marcello exposing me to everyone at our table, a shiver rushed down my arms. Bastian noticed my chest heaving, the soft moans escaping my throat. His eyes flared with desire, the irises changing to a lighter gray that almost appeared blue.

Jealous of Marcello's hand between my thighs, Bastian yanked on my leg and pulled me closer. They both took a knee on the bench, leaning over me like hungry savages. Their hands slipped between my thighs, spreading me wide enough for Luca to see.

Luca's eyes shifted between the stage and me. His brothers held me down, but I wasn't fighting them. Nope, not this time.

I wanted them.

Luca sipped scotch from the snifter in his hand, his eyes on me. The announcer's voice blared through the speakers. He introduced more girls, but the men at my table were too busy focusing on me to care. Even Luca gave me his undivided attention. His gaze lowered to my pussy, then he licked his lips like he wanted a taste.

Marcello reached into his pocket with his other hand and produced a knife.

My eyes widened. "What are you doing?"

He slid the blade beneath my panties and cut them off my body. Bastian yanked the ripped lace and threw it on the table, right in front of Luca's glass.

"Lighten up, brother," Bash said with laughter in his tone. "Our girl has the prettiest pussy in this club. So sit back and enjoy the show."

"That she does," Marcello said against the shell of my ear, sucking the lobe into his mouth. He took the blade's pommel and rubbed it up and down my slick folds. "Are you scared, princess?"

He inched the cold metal inside me just enough for my pulse to pound in my ears. It was so loud I wondered if they could hear it. I couldn't believe I let him touch me like this in public. My bully boys had pushed me so far out of my comfort zone that there was no going back.

"I swear to God, Marcello, if you accidentally cut me, I will kill you."

He smirked. "I know what I'm doing, princess."

Luca slid closer to Bastian, his fist on the table, jaw clenched. What the fuck was wrong with him? Even when I was practically naked and dripping for them, he didn't even crack a smile. His brothers held my legs and teased me with their long fingers.

Both of them.

At the same time.

Oh. My. God.

My eyes slammed shut as Marcello slid his finger inside me, taking his time at first before he slammed into me.

"Fuck, princess. You're so tight." He massaged my inner walls, in and out, so damn slowly my skin pebbled with tiny bumps. "Open up for us. Make room for Bash."

My eyes widened in surprise.

Bastian lifted my leg while Marcello fingered my pussy. No matter what they did to me, Luca made no move to join them. The bastard stared at me, lips squeezed tight, his body rigid.

He tapped the platinum serpent ring on the table, watching as his brothers fucked me with their fingers, working in unison. My body tensed, chills spreading down my arms. I'd never felt so full, not until I had both of their fingers working their magic on me.

"Bash," I moaned, grabbing his dress shirt, my back pressed against Marcello's chest. "Oh, fuck. Mmm… Marcello." I licked my lips and looked up at him. "Harder. I want more."

Marcello and Bastian had the perfect rhythm going, both of their fingers thrusting into me simultaneously. A whimper slipped past my lips.

Maybe I shouldn't have said more. But it felt so damn good.

"You like this, Cherry?" Bastian pulled down the front of my dress, taking my nipple between his teeth. He stared up at me as he nibbled on the tiny bud. "Huh, baby? Tell us what you want."

"I want to get fucked."

Marcello groaned into my ear. "Princess, you're gonna get fucked."

For the first time since Luca sat down, his face illuminated with one of his sexy smirks. He looked pleased by my confession. So did my other handsome princes.

Bastian's pace didn't falter, pumping into me along with Marcello, stretching me out. "My sweet Cherry wants to get fucked?"

"Yes," I whimpered, on the verge of another orgasm. "I'm ready."

"Not without Damian here," Bastian said, his voice strained.

They had a pact, an unbreakable bond. None of them would act without all of them here.

"Then let's go home."

Luca shook his head. "Not happening, baby girl. It's not time."

The announcer's voice blended into the background. Women screamed around me, begging for more. Everyone in the room was having sex or watching it. Just hearing other people's pleasure intensified my own.

My cheeks flushed, heat spreading down my body. I arched my back, milking both of their fingers and rocking my hips into their hands. Luca scooted closer and raised his drink to his lips. He watched me with those beautiful but predatory eyes, sipping from his glass.

I held his gaze, wondering what he was thinking. Wishing his fingers were inside me, too. He always knew how to torture me and make me want him even more.

Marcello's hand closed over my throat. "Come for us, princess."

My orgasm tore through me, stealing my last breath. I came on their fingers, moaning each of their names—even Luca, who studied me with fascination.

"Fuck. Me." Bastian groaned. "I can't wait to pop your cherry, baby."

"You're not popping shit," Luca spit back with fire behind his words. "Her pussy is mine."

"Go to hell, Luca." I leaned forward, my top lip quivering. "I don't belong to you."

He glared at me, and his dark blue eyes narrowed into slits. "Yes. You. Do."

"She's right, bro," Bastian tossed out with an attitude. "You don't own her. Alex is ours. Or did you forget?"

"No, I didn't forget. But we have rules."

"Ah, well, I've never been all that good with following

rules." Bastian laughed. "You should try living a little. Stop being so uptight."

"I'm not in the mood for your bullshit, Bash." He chugged the amber liquid and set the glass on the table. "I've had a long week. We're in over our heads. Alex's pussy is the least of our worries."

"It's the only thing I'm worried about," Bastian quipped.

"She won't be around for long if you don't take your head out of your ass." Luca reached into the pocket of his suit jacket, scrolled through a few screens, and then threw the phone at Bastian. "See if this changes your mind."

I tried to steal a peek at the screen as Bastian read whatever was so important, but he hid it under the table, out of my reach.

"What's going on?"

Bastian ignored me and continued reading, shaking his head with a sigh. Of course, Luca gave nothing away. His face was like marble, perfect and lifeless. He looked at Bastian, who passed the phone to Marcello. After they both finished reading, Luca took his phone and stuffed it back into his pocket.

"What are you guys keeping from me?"

No answer.

The tension in the booth reached an all-time high now that none of them would speak to me. I should have known better than to trust any of the Salvatores.

Bastian squeezed my knee. "You should watch the auction, Cherry."

Marcello sat painfully still, his eyes on the front of the room.

"Never know when you'll find yourself on a stage like that one," Luca said with a sick grin. "Men like us will pay a lot of money for virgin pussy."

Chapter Thirty-Seven

ALEX

The following day, I woke up to my wrists and ankles burning, red-hot pain searing throughout my body.

I figured it had to be a dream.

Except it was far from one.

I gasped at my arms and legs tied to the bedposts as I opened my eyes. I tried to sit up, but the knots were too tight.

Did Damian sneak into Bash's room? Where the fuck is Bastian?

"Bash!" I yelled, struggling against the restraints. "Bash, help me!"

I kicked and screamed, panic settling deep into my bones. Five minutes passed before the bathroom door opened. Bastian walked into his bedroom with a towel wrapped around his narrow waist, and his dark brown hair was freshly wet from a shower.

"You're awake," he commented as if it were a normal day, and I wasn't fucking shackled to his bed. "I thought you were going to sleep all day."

"Untie me. Damian." I struggled to get the words out. "He's fucking crazy. You said you wouldn't let him near me."

Laughing, Bastian approached the bed, stripping off his

towel. I could hardly think straight with his muscled chest on display, his big cock that was semi-hard and aimed at me.

"I did this to you, Cherry. Damian hasn't come near you."

My cheeks flushed with anger, tears ready to spill down my cheeks. "What is wrong with you?"

He snorted with laughter and turned his back to me, searching for boxer briefs in the chest of drawers across from the bed. "How about we start with good morning?"

"I'm going to kill you," I screamed. "Let me go, Bash."

"Last night, you said you wanted to learn more about me. Are you reconsidering?"

I kicked my feet again, but it only made the ropes dig into my skin more. "I meant for you to open up and tell me personal things, not chain me to your fucking bed."

After pulling on a pair of boxer briefs, he strutted over to the bed, looking like a gilded god. Bastian sat on the mattress beside me and tapped my thigh with his fingers. "Look at you, Cherry." He licked his lips as he appraised my naked body. "I've wanted to show you what I like since the first night you slept in my bed."

"Let me go," I whimpered. "My wrists and ankles are killing me. You tied the ropes too tight."

"I was hoping you'd be into this," he said with a frown, carefully studying his handiwork. "So far, you haven't disappointed me."

"Well, I'm not into this shit." I couldn't even move my hand to reach over and tug on the knot. "It hurts. And not the good pain like when you spank me."

He lay on his side and ran his long fingers down my stomach. "You're no fun, Cherry." Then he reached over and started working on the first knot.

When he freed my left wrist, I slapped his thigh. "Asshole. Don't ever do this to me again."

"Must I remind you who owns your gorgeous body?"

Bastian straddled me as he pulled on the next rope. "I will do whatever I want with you."

"I thought we were finally getting somewhere. Why bother showing me the other side to you if you're going to turn back into a monster?"

He dropped the rope onto the bed and sighed. "I never claimed to be anything else."

I sat up, shaking out my wrists and rubbing them softly to remove the sting. Bastian moved to the foot of the bed to free my legs, taking his sweet ass time.

"You could have shown this to me last night. When I was awake!"

"Noted." He glanced over his shoulder and winked. "So you're cool with bondage when you're awake?"

"No, absolutely not."

"Wait until we fuck." Bastian untied the last rope, and I fought the urge to kick him in the face. He crawled up to me and dropped onto his side. "You'll enjoy having your wrists bound behind your back. Your ankles tied together. Oh, the things I'm going to do to you, my queen."

"No, you won't."

"Try it before you knock it, Cherry." He nibbled on my earlobe. "Pain heightens the pleasure."

"I'm not ready for hardcore, Bash."

He brushed his lips against mine. "I'm going to blow your mind, baby. Wait until you see what I have planned for you."

"If it's anything like this, you can keep it."

"Damian wants to talk to you." He tucked my hair behind my ear. "I know you're still pissed at him and have every right to be. But you can't hold a grudge forever."

"Your brother scares me."

The truth.

"Just hear him out."

Bastian slid off the mattress and disappeared into the walk-in closet. He hummed a tune that sounded like the song he'd been writing. I smiled as I listened to him, wondering if there was hope for Bastian. Was it possible for someone like him to love a woman?

I was an idiot for wanting him, for giving in to him so quickly. But after seeing his softer side, I was desperate to learn more about him.

Bastian emerged from his closet, dressed in a black suit with a red tie and black wingtips. He always looked like a billion dollars.

I let my legs dangle off the side of the bed and waited for him to close the distance between us. "I'll talk to Damian. But you better promise not to let him near me when you're not around."

He nodded. "I'll do my best."

"Fine. Give me a minute to get dressed."

He grabbed my ass as I bent over to collect my clothing from the floor. After I changed into my pajamas and fixed my hair, Bastian opened his bedroom door.

"D, get your ass in here!"

Damian strolled into the room, dressed in a black suit and tie, his entire wardrobe devoid of color. Clasping a bundle of flowers in his hand, he walked past Bastian, who patted him on the shoulder. He dropped to his knees in front of me and offered me the dark burgundy flowers.

"Black dahlias?" I took them from his hand and looked over at Bastian. "Interesting choice."

A flower that signifies betrayal.

"I'm sorry," he muttered, unable to meet my gaze. "I didn't mean to hurt you."

Bastian tipped his head, gesturing for me to touch his brother. After how he treated me, I wasn't so sure he deserved any form of comfort from me. But since this was important to Bash, I placed my hand on Damian's shoulder.

"Don't do it again."

He lifted his head until our eyes met and nodded.

Damian was doing this for his brother. They needed each other too much to stay apart for this long. And even though he would never admit it, Bastian needed him, too.

I sniffed the flowers, which had a powdery smell, and then handed them to Damian. "Find a vase for these and put them beside my bed."

After Damian walked out of the room, Bastian clutched my wrist. I squealed from the pain the ropes left behind and pulled away from him.

He grabbed my hand, softly rubbing the marks on my wrist, then raised it to his mouth. "Come here, Cherry. Let me kiss all of your bruises better."

An uncontainable smile touched my lips. I let him kiss up and down my arm and glide his warm tongue over the red mark around my wrist. He looked so tempting I wanted to kiss him.

"What happened to Damian after that night? He seems different. Where's the psycho?"

Bastian lifted his head and grinned, holding my wrist inches from his mouth. "You like that side of him, don't you?"

"I like that side of you, too."

He kissed my wrist, leaving a trail of kisses up my arm. "Good. Because I wouldn't get used to this. And as for Damian, he'll be back to normal soon."

Chapter Thirty-Eight

LUCA

I stared at the security cameras on the wall. Alex painted in my mother's studio with Marcello sitting beside her. He was so fucking pussy whipped. Bastian and Marcello feared for her life, so they took turns letting her sleep in their beds, even though Damian hadn't been home all week.

"Put aside your differences with Alexandrea." My father placed his hand on my shoulder. "The Founders Society is breathing down my neck. They won't wait much longer, Luca."

"I hate her," I bit out between sips of scotch, glaring at her image on the screen. The words stung as they left my mouth. "Her family is responsible for mom's death. She would still be here if it weren't for them. So how do you expect me to go through with a marriage to a Wellington?"

My anger surged inside me like a tornado. When I thought about the Wellingtons, I had more than my usual amount of rage. It bubbled up in my chest, spilling over at the sight of the Wellington whore. Just hearing that last name incited dozens of emotions, most of which made me want to squeeze the life from Alex.

"There's no room for feelings in business," Dad snapped,

venom dripping from his tone. "Act like a man and do the right thing. The future of our family depends on you."

"Marcello can marry Alex."

"Not if you want to lead The Devil's Knights."

I sat in the leather armchair by the fireplace, considering his statement. Since childhood, I knew I would lead the Knights. It was my birthright as the oldest Salvatore. And then The Founders Society demanded my family produce an heir from a Founding Family, throwing an ax into my plans.

My father took his place across from me, resting his black dress shoe on his knee. "Marcello isn't strong enough to lead this family. It has to be you, Luca."

He was right about my brother. Marcello was physically strong and an asset to our security team but incapable of leading the Salvatores. My younger brother hadn't bothered to gain the skills and knowledge required to command a global company.

I tapped the ash falling from the tip of my cigar into the tray on the table beside me. "What do you suggest I do?"

"Get your mother's ring from the vault." He surveyed me with a stern expression, a highball glass raised to his mouth. "Propose to Alexandrea. Make this official."

"She'll say no," I said with certainty.

"Welcome her into our home." He breathed deeply and blew it out, leaning back in his chair. "You can charm everyone on the board of directors, even get the Knights to follow your orders. If you can do that, you can get a silly girl to marry you."

"I gave her the job at the Franco Foundation," I pointed out. "Even let her work in mom's studio. That should have been enough to win her over."

My father laughed. The fucker tipped his head back and laughed. Mocking me.

"What's so funny, Father?" I said, not the least bit amused.

"You have much to learn about women, Luca. When I

met your mother, she didn't care how much money I had. She wanted nothing from me. Your mother was the biggest challenge I'd ever faced."

"Mom wasn't like other women. She was special."

My mother had that extra something, a certain magnetism that drew everyone to her. No one was like her. No one would ever be like her. Not even my future wife would ever compare.

"I saw potential in your mother," my dad said with a rare smile. "She was so talented but misguided. Alexandrea has a lot in common with your mother."

That was the problem with Alex. She reminded me too much of my mother. Every time I touched her, I felt like I was doing something wrong. Like I was disgracing my mother's memory by wanting her.

"A woman who doesn't want or need anything is not an easy woman to please." He set the glass in his hand on the table, eyes on me. "It took me six months to get your mother to agree to one date. But I never gave up on her. Every week, I drove to Brooklyn to ask her one question until she finally said yes."

Alex moved to Brooklyn after art school so that she could be closer to my mother's roots. She idolized her. But I'd always wondered how she would feel about her idol once she discovered the truth about her family's dirty past.

"I already know this story," I shot back. "You want me to do the same with Alex."

My mother's side of the family was from Calabria. Sicilian Mafia. Dad sought her out because of her ties to the family in the old country, and he ended up falling in love with her. The Basiles blamed my father for her death.

For the past fifteen years, they held it over our heads. They forced us into shady deals with criminals because they wanted revenge. But we didn't hurt her. Lorenzo Basile and his thugs looked in the wrong direction for my mother's killer.

He tapped his serpent ring on the arm of the chair, his

scary brown eyes aimed at me. Marcello and I had inherited his looks, everything except for our mother's dark blue eyes. I loved my father, but I hated when he tried to manipulate me. It was hard to outsmart a man with a 165 IQ, but he tried anyway.

"We have plans for Alex," I assured him. "We're taking her to The Mansion tomorrow night."

"Good." He grinned with delight and tipped his head toward the door. "Now go get your mother's ring. You'll need it."

I stopped on the second floor to see if Alex was still in my mother's studio, popping my head into the room. She laid on the floor on her stomach, stripped down to her bra and panties. Marcello sat in the chair beside the easel, his eyes on our beautiful queen.

My younger brother was warming up to her. All the anger and resentment he'd once felt toward her was slowly dissipating. Marcello was the right choice for her to marry. He would have loved her, given what she'd always wanted from me.

But I could never love a Wellington. To do so would disgrace the memory of my mother. She deserved so much better than what she'd gotten. All because of the fucking Wellingtons and their need to control everything.

I looked at Alex one last time before heading downstairs to the catacombs. The tunnels that ran beneath Devil's Creek led to each of the Founders' mansions. We had secret passageways throughout the house and dozens of ways to escape. A safeguard my ancestors had built to ensure they could evade the cops back in their bootlegging days.

I rounded the corner, following the lit pathway to the vault. Pressing my hand to the screen on the wall, I leaned forward for the device to scan my eyes. The metal door slid to the side, the lights turning on one at a time to illuminate the Salvatore treasures.

My family had made their money primarily from illegal

activities. Stolen paintings. Precious jewels. Anything to make a quick buck. My great grandfather, Angelo Salvatore, had the vision that propelled us into the future.

By the time my father had taken over the family, he had turned our millions into billions. Salvatore Global was my father's doing. He had secured our legacy and made deals to create an alliance with The Founders Society.

I would not let him down.

I entered the vault and stood at the center of the room. We had everything from unrecovered works of art to jewelry worn by royals. But I was here for one specific piece.

The Salvatore diamond—my mother's engagement ring.

I cracked open the dark blue box and studied the thirty-carat round brilliant cut diamond. It had been fifteen years since I'd seen this ring on my mother's finger.

As I stuffed the box into my pocket, my cell phone dinged with a new message. A group chat from Drake Battle and The Devil's Knights.

Drake Battle: Our queen is on the Il Circo auction page.

I knew The Lucaya Group would eventually succeed, despite our best attempts to keep her off that fucking site. Even with intervention from The Serpents and our cartel friends, we couldn't stop it.

Drake included a link that contained images of Alex naked. That was my fault. I'd saved a few pictures of her on my phone.

Luca Salvatore: Then get her the fuck off it, Battle!

Drake Battle: Easier said than done. I'm working on it.

Sonny Cormac: Our queen looks fuck-hot.

Cole Marshall: Bet all those sleazy motherfuckers will pay up to get a look at her.

Marcello Salvatore: This isn't the time for jokes.

Luca Salvatore: Call my girl fuck-hot again, and I'll slit your throat.

Bastian Salvatore: She's ours.

Sonny Cormac: Calm down, psychos.

Damian Salvatore: Who are you calling a psycho? **crossed swords emoji**

Cole Marshall: 6 years. How have none of you fucked her yet?

Sonny Cormac: I'd give my left nut to fuck her.

Cole Marshall: So will the men bidding on her.

Bastian Salvatore: This isn't funny, dickheads!

Luca Salvatore: I'm glad all of you are taking this seriously. I'll find another way to get her off that site.

I tapped the three dots in the app's corner, clenching my jaw so hard it felt like it would crack in half. *Luca Salvatore has left the chat* flashed on the screen.

My cell phone rang. I expected it to be Marcello or even Drake, but it was my father.

I raised the phone to my ear. "I assume you've heard about Alex."

"This complicates matters," he said in a firm tone. "We need to rush the wedding. It's the only way to keep her safe."

The criminal underworld had rules about wives. Girl-friends and children were fair game, especially heirs, but wives were off-limits.

I stuffed the jewelry box into my pocket. "I have mom's ring. By the time we get back from The Mansion, Alex will be my fiancé."

Chapter Thirty-Nine

ALEX

A mysterious box appeared on my bed, black with a pink ribbon. I slid my finger beneath the pink ribbon, and my heart raced with anticipation. A black, silky gown and a gold-and-black carnival mask were inside. Beneath the mask, I found a gold envelope with black writing.

You are cordially invited to The Mansion.
Wear your mask, follow the rules, and enjoy your peek into the forbidden.

I dropped the card on the bed, staring in awe at the words, the dress, this mask they expected me to wear. Nerves stirred in my belly, twisting up my insides. I removed the dress from the box and held it in front of me. It was beautiful, expensive, and sexy.

"Do you like it?"

Luca's deep voice sent my heart racing into overdrive. He had a habit of appearing out of thin air.

I laid the dress on the bed and spun around to face him. "Yes, it's beautiful."

"I chose it for you."

I pressed my lips together, unable to take my eyes off him. "I figured as much."

Luca had impeccable taste. Only the best for the heir to the Salvatore billions.

He approached me, dressed in a three-piece black Brioni suit with a gold tie. As usual, he looked like a billion dollars, armed with his cocky but sexy smirk. Of all the Salvatores, he infuriated me the most. He never let me close, never got personal with me.

Aside from what my grandfather had told me, I knew almost nothing about Luca.

Mysterious.

Elusive.

Gorgeous.

He was everything I craved, yet I never felt like I could have him. Luca was always out of my reach, untouchable in every way.

He tugged on my towel, and the fabric fell to the floor at my feet. His eyes traveled up and down several times before his eyes met mine. I stood there in silence, my skin humming with an electrical current as he inspected every inch of my naked body.

Luca terrified me, but not in the same way as Damian. I feared Luca because I knew I would lose my heart if he ever let me into his closely guarded world. I would have given him everything.

We were both so fucking damaged, and I felt a connection to him. Like he understood all the shit I'd gone through as a child. Like he could read my thoughts without even speaking to me.

His brothers had endured their share of cruelty, but Luca took the brunt of it. In some ways, we were kindred spirits. I wondered if he stayed away for the same reason.

As his long fingers glided down my bare arms, he looked as if he had stopped breathing. Was this painful for him?

He cupped my right breast and rolled his thumb over the swollen bud. "Turn around."

I did as he asked, breathing hard with my back to him.

He pressed his hand to my lower back and bent me over the bed. My skin sizzled with heat, igniting a fire wherever he touched. I hoped he would continue his slow exploration, but instead, he grabbed the dress. Draping it over his forearm, he leaned forward to brush my curls off my shoulder so he could kiss my neck. I nearly melted into the bed, biting my lip to stop moaning.

Luca kissed my shoulder. "Time to get dressed, baby girl."

I turned around to face him, and he lowered the gown for me to step into it. It hugged my curves like a glove. Luca moved behind me, staring at me in the mirror as he zipped my dress.

The silky black fabric had thin straps and barely covered my breasts. Not like it mattered. You could see my nipples through the material. A slit ran up the length of my thigh, the cut so high I couldn't wear panties.

My body trembled when Luca pressed his warm body against my back, snaking his arm around me. "Don't be afraid, my queen," he whispered.

"What is The Mansion?"

I felt him smile as he pressed his lips to my cheek. "It's whatever you want it to be, Drea."

After I finished fixing my hair and makeup, he led me downstairs. His brothers waited in the sitting room, drinking from highball glasses. All three of them stopped talking when we walked into the room.

Bastian raised his fingers to his mouth and whistled. "Cherry, I'm going to devour you, baby." He swiped his dark hair off his forehead and groaned. "Fuck, you're killing me."

Damian licked his lips.

Marcello leaned forward, elbows on his thighs as he drank me in. "I second that, princess. You look good enough to eat."

"Let's go," Luca ordered. "We don't have time to waste."

He placed his hand on my back and led me out of the sitting room, headed toward the front door. His brothers trailed behind in silence. I could hear my heart pounding as we approached the limousine that waited for us out front.

Once we drove off the estate, Marcello grabbed a bottle of champagne and poured each of us glasses. Damian hit a button on the wall, and a rap beat floated through the air, ridding us of the awkward silence.

Bastian slid across the bench and clutched my thigh, pulling me away from Luca. He lifted my leg onto his lap and spread my legs wider. "Already making my cock hard," he groaned. "Mmm, this dress... I can't wait to tear it off your gorgeous body."

Luca must have been jealous. He dug his fingers into my hips and moved me to his lap, one hand on my breast and the other between my legs.

He sucked on my earlobe. "Tonight, you're mine, baby girl."

I rocked my hips, rubbing my ass on his hard cock. "You gonna be nice for a change?"

He teased my wet slit, gliding his long finger between my folds. "I'm always nice."

I laughed at his ridiculous statement. "You're never nice, Luca."

Marcello and Damian sat across from us. They looked like they were ready to pounce on me. Bastian adjusted the massive bulge in his pants, licking his lips.

Tonight was the night. One of them would take my virginity.

Luca was acting more possessive than usual. I wondered if it would be him or Bastian. They had both expressed their intention over the years. The other two didn't care as long as they got to have me. But for Bastian and Luca, it was all a game.

Who would win my cherry?
Who would marry me?
Bunch of sick motherfuckers.

Luca moved his hand back to my thigh, and I instantly missed the overwhelming sensation.

I glanced over my shoulder at him. "Why did you stop?"

He tipped his head at his brothers. "Look at them. They won't make it to The Mansion."

"Speak for yourself," Bastian cut in. "I'm not the one with self-control issues."

They looked at Damian.

"It was one time." Damian threw up his hands in defense. "And I fucking apologized." He pointed his finger at Bastian. "So don't look at me like that."

"I hope you're not wearing a belt tonight," I said.

Damian shook his head. "I won't hurt you, not unless you beg for it."

Beg for it? I couldn't think of a time when I would ever beg a man to hurt me, but whatever.

"He'll behave," Bastian said to reassure me. "No more incidents."

"Sure, talk about me like I'm not even here," Damian snapped at his brother.

"You almost killed her. We don't trust you alone with Alex."

When Damian glanced around the limo, his brothers nodded. He crossed his arms over his chest and stared at the glass divider at the front of the car, blowing out a breath of air.

"Where is this place?" I asked.

"About an hour away." Marcello downed the rest of his champagne and poured another glass. "It's pretty remote. You need the coordinates to find it."

"Why is it called The Mansion?"

"For obvious reasons, Cherry." Bastian laughed. "It's what you would expect."

"It's a sex club, right?"

He bobbed his head. "One of the best in the world."

"And it's in Connecticut? Convenient that it's so close to home."

Bastian smirked. "Who do you think owns it, Cherry?"

"Then why leave me an invitation? And why do I need to wear a mask?"

"You'll see," Damian said with a crazy smile that illuminated his emerald eyes.

"You could have just told me where we're going instead of being so secretive."

Luca snickered, then bit my earlobe, creating tiny bumps along my skin. "Now, where is the fun in that?" He removed a silk scarf from his pocket and put it over my eyes. "There's one more rule about The Mansion."

My throat closed up as he tied the fabric to the back of my head. I hated the dark, hated not being able to see.

It's just a scarf.

You're safe.

You're okay.

"No one knows the location of The Mansion." Luca slid his hand up my throat, tapping his fingers right over my windpipe. "Only us and our drivers."

"You can tell me."

"No." Luca secured the scarf behind my head. "Not until you become a Salvatore."

A n hour later, our limo slowed to a stop. I couldn't see a damn thing with Luca's scarf over my eyes, but I assumed we had arrived at The Mansion.

"Can I take this thing off yet?"

Bastian leaned over and tugged on the fabric, dropping it onto the leather bench. He swiped the pad of his thumb across my bottom lip with a smile. "You did good, Cherry. You're overcoming your fear of the dark."

"Not quite." I bit the inside of my cheek and attempted a glance out the tinted windows. "I don't think I'll ever like the dark."

"You better get used to it, baby girl." Luca tapped my ass, encouraging me to sit up when the driver opened the door for us. "Because we live in the darkness."

I climbed out of the limo with Luca's big hand on my ass. He hadn't stopped touching me all night. It was weird to have so much of his attention. For years, I'd practically begged for a second of his time. And now, he was giving me exactly what I wanted, which meant he wanted something.

My men put on their carnival masks, so I took that as my cue to follow their lead. Our masks were black-and-gold, except mine had a black feather sticking up over my left eyebrow.

Luca slid his arm behind my back, warming me up as he led the way to the front door. The coastal mansion reminded me of the Salvatore Estate, only more isolated. I couldn't see lights for miles, the sky an inky black.

My dress swept across the ground as we walked closer to the ocean. I felt like a Roman goddess in this dress, elegant and ethereal. In every way, I finally felt like a queen.

Their queen.

We stopped in front of tall wooden doors, which had tons of intricate markings on them. The symbols reminded me of

The Devil's Knights temple. Two men opened the doors, greeting us with the slight tip of their heads.

"No names," Bastian whispered into my ear. "That's another rule."

Rubbing my lips together, I nodded as we strolled into the foyer.

Two cascading staircases led to the second floor, where a man in a suit bent a naked blonde woman over the railing. People passed by them as if they'd seen it all before, not even distracted by her screams.

On the main floor, dozens of naked women walked around with various colors of masks on their faces. Some had huge tits and tons of curves. Others were thin and toned. Girls of every shape, color, and size let men lead them to different rooms.

I stood under the monstrous chandelier that had strings of pearls and panties dangling from it. The ceiling was high, the walls decorated with interesting art. Naked people were fucking. Women were sucking big cocks. Not exactly the art you would find at the Salvatore Estate.

Luca stood behind me, his hands on my shoulders. "What do you want to see first?"

"I don't know," I muttered. "What is there to see?"

"Live sex shows," Luca said.

"Spanking, whipping, bondage." Bastian waggled his eyebrows at the last one. "I'd love to tie your pretty ass up again."

"Not tonight. Break me in first."

He twisted my nipple over the fabric of my silky dress. Damian grabbed my ass from behind.

Luca nudged both of them with his elbows, asserting his dominance. "There's one more rule, baby girl." He slid the thin straps down my shoulders. "You need to ditch the dress."

Chapter Forty

ALEX

W e watched an orgy. A real-life fucking orgy with at least a dozen people. I went from zero to sixty in one night.

There were so many people on the stage, naked and moaning, that I couldn't keep track. I sat in the front row on Luca's lap, my pussy so wet I soaked his pants. If he noticed, he didn't seem to care. Luca held me tight, his fingers digging into my hip, his other hand massaging my breast.

After staring at so many naked people, I couldn't stand to watch them get off when I wanted my men to fuck me. I'd waited years to lose my virginity. All because my gorgeous princes never let people get too close to me.

People avoided me in high school. Some boys looked but never spoke to me. College was my fresh start, four years of freedom from these psychos. Guys would ask me out. But they would always disappear afterward or make excuses. After the tenth time, I knew it was because of the Salvatores. Somehow, they had gotten to them.

Tonight, I was losing my fucking virginity. So I grabbed Luca's hand and shoved it between my thighs, forcing his fingers inside me.

He pumped his fingers into me, breathing hard against my cheek. "Are you ready for my cock, baby girl?"

"Yes," I moaned, riding his hand as I watched the people fucking in front of me.

With the mask obscuring my face, I didn't feel self-conscious. No one knew me here. No one gave a damn about my nakedness. Being with my men, knowing they would take care of me, helped me lower my guard. The walls I'd constructed to keep them out had come crashing down over the last few weeks.

Bastian rolled his thumb over my clit in slow circular motions. Then his lips descended upon mine with his usual rough possession. "Come for us, Cherry," he growled against my lips before tugging on my bottom lip with his teeth.

Marcello leaned over Luca's left leg and took turns with Bastian, rubbing my clit until my entire body trembled. Damian moved to the row behind us and grabbed my breast, pinching my nipple between his fingers. He pulled harder, and I moaned, careful not to say their names.

"It's time." Luca knocked his brother's hands away and got up from the chair, taking me with him. "Let's go."

I'd barely come down from my high before he led me out of the crowded theater with his brothers in tow. Luca didn't speak a word, his sole focus on navigating the dark hallways. We'd gone right from the entrance to the sex theater, so I hadn't gotten to see much of the house.

The place was massive. Men and women fucked against walls. Women went down on each other while men watched. Several men dominated the same woman in a private room at the back of the house.

We climbed the back stairwell to the third floor, dodging people running down the stairs. Loud music blared through speakers on the wall, a sexy beat that didn't have words. I moved to the song's rhythm, and Bastian slapped my ass.

"Stop teasing me, Cherry."

On the top floor, we stopped at a set of double doors. This was it. I was finally going to lose my virginity to one of these heartless monsters.

Luca turned a key in the lock and pushed open the door. I inched my way into the apartment with expensive paintings on the walls and leather furniture. This room felt more like their home than a private room in a sex club.

My heels clicked on the white marble floor. I stripped off my mask and set it on the table in the living room, staring at the space. We had a full-size kitchen with a marble island and ceiling height cabinets. Half a dozen windows covered with black drapes spanned the exterior wall. A leather sectional couch sat at the center of the room with plush decorative pillows.

Bastian moved behind me and gathered my hair in his hands. The anticipation of what would come next was killing me. He dipped his head down to pepper kisses along my neck. Damian moved in front of us, watching as he shrugged his suit jacket over his broad shoulders.

He loosened his tie, and then his long fingers trailed down my hot skin, his touch leaving fire in his wake. I recalled Bash's words, promising that Damian would be on his best behavior. So I let him touch me and enjoyed myself. My skin pebbled with tiny bumps from his slow exploration of my body. His big hands moved up to my breasts, and I moaned when his thumbs rolled over my nipples.

I leaned back against Bastian's chest and closed my eyes, consumed by the pleasure of his lips on my neck and Damian's hands on my body. He clutched my chin and tilted my head until our eyes met. When Bash looked at me, every nerve ending in my body ignited. We had a powerful connection, one I could not shake.

No matter how much I told myself that he was a monster, an asshole who only wanted to use and abuse me, I still searched for him. My heart beat faster whenever he walked into a room. His smell, touch, and everything about him set my soul on fire.

Damian's eyes raked over every inch of my naked body. I whimpered in Bastian's mouth, desperate for more of them.

As Damian pinched and flicked my nipples, Bastian slid his hand between my thighs. He rolled his thumb over my clit and kissed my neck. A flush of heat rushed through my body, my eyes slamming shut with each moan he stole from my lips.

Luca stood beside me and fisted my curls in his hand, tilting my head to the side. He cradled the back of my head, his eyes flickering with heat, wild and intense. He licked his lips, knowing full well what I wanted from him.

A second of hesitation ensued before he moved Damian out of the way. Luca yanked on my hair, parting my lips with his tongue. His tongue swept into my mouth with fury, his pain clear in each kiss. I never understood why he hated intimacy, why he hated kissing me.

The kiss didn't last long.

He stole his lips from mine, and our moment of desire only made me crave him more. I reached out, but of course, he stepped back. I searched his eyes, desperate to know what I'd done to make him so disgusted by my touch.

Bastian's fingers burrowed into my hips, his rough touch branding my skin. I needed to feel something from someone who wanted me. So I turned to face Bastian. I wasn't handing over my virginity to a man who couldn't even kiss me.

I hated Luca Salvatore.

So why did I want him?

Why did he make me so mad?

Bastian controlled the moment, kissing me with a savage hunger that helped me forget about Luca. He nibbled on my lip until I moaned in his mouth.

I smiled at my gorgeous prince. He was so damn sexy he took my breath away. "I want you, Bash," I said against his lips. "I'm ready."

Bastian liked to plan everything. I knew he would make tonight a night I would never forget.

Bastian smirked, then he looked at Damian. "Do you hear that, brother? Cherry wants us to mark her." His lips brushed my cheek. "To claim her virgin pussy."

Damian was gorgeous but also terrifying. With everything I knew about him and his desires, I feared him hurting me.

But I trusted Bash.

At least I wanted to believe I could trust him with my life. He'd saved me from Damian once. And he wouldn't let Damian go too far.

"Do you want that, Cherry?" Bastian stroked the length of my arm with his fingers, creating tiny bumps along my skin. "You want both of us?"

They were a packaged deal. Despite my fear of Damian, my pulse pounded in my ears each time he looked at me with those hunter's eyes.

I rolled my head back on his shoulder and whispered, "I want all of you." My eyes flicked between the four of them. "But I want you to take my virginity."

He bent down to my height and smirked. "Why do you think I call you Cherry? You were always mine."

I'd fallen in love with my captor. How stupid and pathetic did that make me? But it didn't detract from the truth. I had slowly and painfully slipped under the spell of the devil incarnate.

"No," Luca snapped. "Not like this. You're not ruining that fucking couch." He tipped his head toward the back of the apartment. "In the bedroom."

Bastian lifted me over his shoulder as if I weighed nothing and hurried down the hall to another set of double doors. He kicked them open and set my feet on the floor in front of the bed. All four stood before me, partially dressed, eyeing me up.

After Bastian moved behind me, Damian caged me against Bastian's muscular chest. For a split second, I thought he would kiss me. But he surprised me by dropping to his knees as Bastian wove his fingers through my hair. His teeth grazed my neck when his brother clutched my thighs, burying his head between them.

I moaned when his lips brushed my sensitive flesh. Luca and Marcello watched Damian's tongue slide between my slick folds. They studied every flick of his tongue, each scream he ripped from my throat. Then they slowly stripped off their suits. But they were so meticulous they couldn't just throw their clothes on the floor.

Taking their sweet ass time, they hung their jackets on the hook behind the door. Then, they slowly unbuttoned their white oxfords. It was killing me not to see them naked and on their knees.

Bastian bent down to suck on my nipple, taking it between his teeth. "Are you going to come for us?"

"Yes," I whispered.

"Good girl."

Intense waves of pleasure rolled off my skin like flames. While Damian worked his magic on my clit, sucking so hard my legs trembled, I tugged on the ends of his hair. The harder I pulled, the more this seemed to encourage him, and he devoured me like he was desperate for a taste.

They took turns kissing me in every place imaginable. I fisted Damian's hair as I moaned into his brother's mouth. The thought of fucking two hot men did sinful things to my body. It was wrong to want them, dangerous to crave them.

Damian made me come twice before he sat back and looked at me, his lips glistening with my cum. Then he stood to his full height, wiping his mouth with the back of his hand. He stripped off his tie and hooked it around my neck. Another creepy ass grin stretched the corners of his mouth. He was the devil. Or, at the very least, Dexter's hotter and more vicious twin.

"Damian," I warned.

"He's fine," Bastian told me. "Don't worry, baby. You're in good hands."

I studied my cruel, beautiful monster, biting my bottom lip as Damian unbuttoned his dress shirt. Needing to touch him, I slid my hands up his chest, feeling the ridges of his muscles. He worked quickly to peel off his shirt and strip down to his boxer briefs. Without hesitation, I had my hands on him again, leaning forward to kiss my way down his ripped stomach.

His cock poked through the slit in his black boxer briefs. So I took his long length in my hand, giving him a few strokes. Bastian pulled me backward onto the bed with him. I sat between his open legs as Damian climbed between my thighs, jerking his shaft as he bent down to lick me again.

Luca got into the bed on my right side, Marcello on my left. With the four of them touching me, studying every inch of my body, I felt out of my element. I'd never even been with one man. So how could I handle all of them?

I grabbed hold of Luca's big cock and sat up so I could take him into my mouth. A sinister groan ripped from his throat when I sucked harder, practicing what Bastian had taught me.

As Damian plunged his tongue inside me, he gripped my thighs. I moaned with Luca's cock in my mouth, his hand on the back of my head. Luca yanked on my hair, forcing me to choke on his dick. Bastian sucked on my nipple as Damian spread me open with his tongue while Marcello rolled his thumb over my clit.

I gagged on Luca's cock, tears streaming down my cheeks as he held the back of my head in a vise. It should have bothered me. I should have been mad at him for being so rough.

I came hard on Damian's tongue, my arms and legs shaking uncontrollably. Waves of heat, then cold, rushed throughout my body. Luca tightened his grip on my hair, his legs shaking, riding waves of pleasure as he filled my mouth with his cum.

He popped his cock out of my mouth, a crazed hunger in his eyes. Then he slid his thumb across my bottom lip and smirked. "Which one of my brothers taught you how to suck cock?"

"Bash."

Out of breath, I laid back on Bastian's chest to regain my bearings. His long fingers slid beneath my chin, and then he shoved them into my mouth for me to suck. Marcello was naked beside me. Damian hadn't moved from between my thighs. Luca stroked his cock. He was hard again, licking his lips as he stared at my pussy.

The Salvatore brothers were hunters. And I loved this side of them.

Bastian raised his hands and clapped. Then the room plunged into darkness. It was so black I couldn't even make out their faces.

"Don't be afraid," Bastian whispered in my ear. "Without sight, you'll have to use your other senses. Trust me, baby. This will feel good."

"I won't know which one of you I'm with."

I felt him smile as his lips brushed my cheek. "That's part of the fun, Cherry."

Chapter Forty-One

ALEX

I breathed through my nose, trying to find my center, and reached out to feel their skin. Then, I ran my fingers over each of their muscled chests one at a time.

Marcello was much thicker in the arms, so I spotted him first. Luca was the tallest but the leanest, with zero body fat. Damian had a patch of hair on his chest that trailed down to his cock. And Bastian had an X over his heart, an unmistakable scar I felt with the pad of my finger.

"That's enough of that, Cherry."

Kneeling on the bed between them, I whispered, "Are you ever going to tell me how you got that one?"

"Not now." Bastian moved my hand to his cock and helped me stroke him, growing harder in my hand. "Yeah, baby. Like this."

Someone on my left grabbed my free hand and wrapped my fingers around his length. Closing my eyes made it easier to adjust to the darkness. Without sight, I needed to use my other senses. So I tipped my nose up, consumed by their delicious scents, stroking two enormous dicks.

I noted the bergamot in Bastian's cologne and the sandalwood in Luca's. Marcello's aftershave had a hint of citrus.

Damian's cologne had a woodsy scent. But with all of them this close, I had a hard time concentrating. For the life of me, I couldn't tell them apart.

I quickened my pace, jerking their shafts in a rhythmic motion. Groans of pleasure filled the air, and then someone moved behind me. I felt him shift his weight, then grabbed my ass cheeks with both hands. A tongue split me down the middle, slipping between my folds, lapping up my juices.

I screamed from the intense sensations shooting down my arms. "Oh, my God."

Who was licking me? Luca? Marcello? I honestly didn't know. I allowed myself to let go, reveling in the feeling of their hands, tongues, and mouths on my body.

After warmth filled both of my hands, I felt two of them change positions on the bed. Now I wasn't sure who rolled their tongue over my nipple. Or who had their finger in my ass, working in unison with the man sucking on my clit.

Strong hands gripped my thighs, holding me in place as an earth-shattering orgasm swept over me. Someone massaged my breast and bit my nipple. Another hand moved between my legs. A long finger slid inside me, then another.

Without seeing their faces, I knew two of them had their fingers inside me, spreading me open. They were preparing me for what was about to come. Sharing this part of myself with them removed all the barriers between us. I'd never felt so liberated in my entire life.

For many years, I had felt as if I couldn't be myself, that I had to play a role. But the Salvatore brothers didn't judge me. They didn't give a damn what anyone thought about us or our unusual relationship.

After I came on their fingers, the one licking my pussy moved out of the way. A hand clamped down on my shoulder, pushing my back to the mattress. One of them climbed on top of me, and nerves coursed through my body.

None of them were ever sweet with me. And from what

I'd heard from other girls, the first time always hurt. So I expected the sharp pinch as his cock breached my folds. Holding my breath, I waited for him to keep moving. He was so big, stretching me out, rocking his hips in a slow-motion that surprised me.

He inched into me slowly, making room for himself with each thrust. Even with him being gentle, it still fucking hurt like hell. I ignored the pain as my body adapted to his size.

"I'm okay," I whispered. "Don't stop."

No answer.

Of course, they wanted me to guess which one of them fucked me. Maybe it was better this way. If I didn't know, I couldn't form a special attachment to one over the other. It was as if I had lost my virginity to all of them.

He must have felt my body relax because he picked up his pace. He groaned in my ear with his palms on the mattress beside my head, then stuck out his tongue to suck on my earlobe. And then, without warning, he pulled out of me.

I wasn't very experienced, but I knew he hadn't come yet. He slid off me, and then hands pried open my thighs. A warm tongue licked my pussy. Another tongue rolled over my nipple. Then a different tongue on the other. I fisted his hair in my hand, encouraging him to drive his tongue deeper and deeper inside me.

"Remember what I told you about Damian?" Bastian whispered the words against the shell of my ear.

I attempted to recall one of the many horrible things he'd told me about his brother. But, at the moment, I didn't care.

"He likes blood," Bastian said with a cruel smile I felt on my cheek. "We all wanted different things from you, Cherry."

I didn't know who had taken my virginity.

"He's been dying to taste you, Cherry." He kissed my lips, and I melted into him for a second. "Me? I want to fuck every bit of innocence from your beautiful body."

"Fuck me," I whispered, arching my hips to get more of Damian's tongue. "Please. I want more."

Bastian tapped his brother on the shoulder. "That's enough, D."

Damian sat back with a groan, and I instantly missed the loss of his mouth on my sensitive skin. Bastian gripped my hips and flipped onto his back, moving me on top of him. He reached between us, fisting his cock, teasing my wetness with the tip. And then he pumped into me, fucking me without mercy.

"I think you're broken in now." He groaned. "But fuck, baby. You're so tight."

Even with me on top, Bastian was in control. My pussy ached from all the pounding he did between my thighs. And by the time he lifted me off him, turning me around with help from his brothers, I squeezed his thighs between mine and rode him into the mattress.

Now facing another Salvatore, this one yanked my hair, pulling me forward. Bastian gripped my hips from behind, satisfying the ache in my core. It was easy for me to suck one of their cocks into my mouth in this position.

My sense of smell was so off I couldn't trust it. I'd sworn Bastian was the one who popped my cherry, but now I wasn't so sure. I should have touched the scar over his heart. But it felt so good I got lost in the moment, forgetting about the minor details.

One of them grunted as I swirled my tongue around the tip. Impatient and greedy for more, he placed his hand on the back of my head and fucked my mouth while Bastian fucked me hard, gripping my hips as I rode him in reverse cowgirl.

A hand came down hard on my ass. I squealed with a mixture of pain and delight. Bastian didn't give his brother a chance to cum in my mouth before rolling me onto my back without breaking stride. He threw my legs over his shoulders, possessed with his need to make me come as many times as possible.

Overwhelmed by a mixture of pain and pleasure, I lost myself to the next orgasm that swept over me like a hurricane. One of my guys kneeled on the bed with his legs on each side of my head. He stroked his cock, brushing the tip across my lips.

Bastian's legs trembled, and his entire body shook as he came inside me. Then his brother was right behind him, coating my tongue with his warmth.

After we came, Bastian pulled me onto the mattress beside him. He curled me into his sweaty body and laid my head on his chest so that he could kiss my forehead. "You were worth the wait, Cherry."

My eyes fluttered from the exhaustion commanding control of me. Every inch of my body hummed. I would need to sleep off this night for days. There wasn't a single muscle or bone that didn't hurt, but I was okay with that. One night with them was worth it.

"Can you handle more, Cherry?" Bastian licked my earlobe, and even with his delicate touch, I could hardly keep my eyes open.

"Uh-huh," I muttered.

My words said one thing, while my body said another. Seconds after my head hit Bastian's chest, my eyelids fluttered.

"Bash," I whispered, drunk with pleasure. "I hope it was you... because I think I love you."

Surprised gasps echoed between them.

Exhausted beyond belief, I didn't care if he didn't love me back. It didn't matter if none of them ever could find it in their black hearts to love me. And before he could answer, my eyes shut, no longer able to fight sleep.

Chapter Forty-Two

LUCA

I woke up in a room filled with white smoke. A vinegar-like scent floated through the air, and when I opened my mouth, an acidic taste hit my tongue. I covered my nose and mouth with my hand and rolled onto my side.

My throat went dry, and my tongue started burning as if it were on fire. Then my lungs spasmed as I breathed in the nasty smell, nearly collapsing my chest.

"What the fuck?" I struggled to speak, the words stinging my tongue. "Wake up, Bash." I tapped my brothers on their backs, shaking each of them. "Marcello. Damian. Get up!"

Where the fuck is Alex?

My brothers were still naked and unconscious on the bed beside me. I shook each of them again, the toxic fumes in the air making my head spin.

None of them ever slept this soundly. Under normal circumstances, Damian would have already been awake since that crazy motherfucker rarely slept. He snored with his arm covering the side of his face, naked and on his back beside Bastian.

Alex did a number on them.

Bastian and Marcello were like me, light sleepers with

strict schedules. They never slept for more than a few hours at a time. And yet, they both lay on their stomachs, breathing hard against the mattress. They must have inhaled too much of the fumes.

Through the cloud of white smoke, I searched for Alex and called out to her. A few hours ago, she'd passed out between Bastian and me. I yelled her name a few more times.

No answer.

After we came, she confessed her love for Bastian, then fell asleep on his chest. None of us said a word after that. Even Bastian didn't know what to do with that information.

Our queen had worn us out, so we curled up beside her. We hated sleeping with anyone in their beds, and for her, we did it. We would have done anything for Alex.

I blinked a few times to clear my blurred vision, feeling around the bed. "Where the fuck is Alex?" I shouted, sliding off the mattress, barely able to hold up my weight.

I heard a muffled sound coming from the living room. Was she still here? Several sets of footsteps tapped the tiled floor. Then the front door slammed shut behind them.

Fuck.

Someone was here.

They'd taken her.

The fucking auction!

I dragged my tired ass off the bed, and I had zero energy when I tried to stand. My brain and body were completely out of sync. Clutching the mattress, I pulled myself up from the carpet.

We thought she would be safer away from Devil's Creek. The Mansion was off the grid, and few people knew the coordinates. But it wouldn't be the first time the Lucaya Group had outsmarted us.

I had planned to stay the weekend, or at the very least long enough to ask Alex to marry me. But unfortunately, my family couldn't wait much longer to seal the deal with the Wellingtons.

As I staggered out of the bedroom, I fell into the wall in the dining room. I tried to stand on my own, but it was pointless. My legs trembled, forcing me to grip the table for support. A sharp pain penetrated my skull, the throbbing so intense I couldn't move. Slowly, my mind and body succumbed to the fumes as the toxins worked their dark magic on me.

Alex was gone.

I had seconds to make a decision that could save Alex's life. They couldn't have gotten very far. Using every ounce of my energy, I tapped the button on the side of my watch. The emergency signal would alert The Devil's Knights we were in danger.

Drake Battle would track our location. It wouldn't be long before the Knights found us. And as I slowly lost consciousness, I hoped they would find Alex in time.

The Frost Society

Welcome to The Frost Society!

You have been chosen to join an elite secret society for readers who love dark romance books.

When you join The Frost Society, you will get instant access to all of my novels, bonus scenes, and digital content like new-release eBooks and serialized stories. You can also get discounts for my book and merch shop, exclusive book boxes, and so much more.

Learn more at JillianFrost.com

Also by Jillian Frost

Princes of Devil's Creek

Cruel Princes

Vicious Queen

Savage Knights

Battle King

Boardwalk Mafia

Boardwalk Kings

Boardwalk Queen

Boardwalk Reign

Devil's Creek Standalone Novels

The Darkest Prince

Wicked Union

For a complete list of books, visit JillianFrost.com.

Get to know Jillian Frost

Watch Jillian's latest videos on TikTok
@jillianfrostbooks

Become part of a reader community when you join Jillian's
private Facebook group called Frost's Fangirls

Check out the latest teasers and updates on Jillian's Instagram
@jillianfrostbooks

About the Author

Jillian Frost is a dark romance author who believes even the villain deserves a happily ever after. When she's not plotting all the ways to disrupt the lives of her characters, you can usually find Jillian by the pool, soaking up the Florida sunshine.

Learn more about Jillian's books at JillianFrost.com